SUNSET on MONARCH BAY

PATRICIA YAGER DELAGRANGE

Alameda, California

Printed in the U.S.A.

Digital ISBN: 978-1-954395-12-1
Print ISBN: 978-1-954395-13-8

Chapter One

Stella stood in her kitchen, hands balled up at her sides, staring out the window above the sink, happy she wasn't seeing her reflection staring back at her, knowing what she looked like today. She bent her head and rubbed her temples with her fingertips. Her temples. One of the few places that didn't hurt when she touched the skin.

When she saw herself in the bathroom mirror that morning, the truth hit her in the gut, almost as hard as Robert's fist last night. The awful reality glared at her in a spectacularly colorful display of proof: a swollen left eye, rimmed in a light-purple bruise, blood caked under her nostrils, left cheek puffy and discolored. Reminded her of when she had the mumps as a kid. She noticed a ringing in her left ear that was not tinnitus. Perhaps a busted ear drum?

She didn't know. Might never know, since she wasn't allowed to visit the doctor's office. Robert said Corvallis, a town of 58,000 people in central western Oregon, was too small, everyone knew everyone else's business. Plus he always insisted she'd be fine. Give it a couple of days, and she could resume her normal duties—cleaning house, going to the local super market, watering the front lawn, preparing meals—all tasks Robert expected an obedient wife to perform in exchange for the good life she and the twins were privileged to live. Thanks to Robert's position as head of the Spanish Department at Oregon State University.

After washing her face with cool water and applying gobs of make-up, Stella looked reasonably okay, as long as no one came too close. The waves of her long, dark hair hid the sides of her face and neck. So there was that. She hobbled downstairs and limped to the kitchen table, left leg hitching at every step. Pain shot from her knee to her thigh and she gently lowered herself onto the chair.

The burner phone she'd bought lay next to the bowl of fruit in the center of the table, and she reached for it with her left arm. Ouch! Her left arm only stretched out half-way before another zinger flew from her wrist to her elbow. She gently laid that arm on the table and grasped the phone with her right hand.

She'd memorized the number the private investigator found yesterday when she called him from the only phone booth still in existence in this town. Everyone nowadays owned a cell phone, but why get rid of a functioning telephone? Thank goodness someone in the city government was old-fashioned enough to stick with a good thing.

Robert checked all her incoming and outgoing calls each night after work. She couldn't take the chance he'd see a number he didn't recognize. He'd think Stella was having an affair with Phillip Milton. Which she wasn't and never would, of course. She'd honored her marriage vows for eighteen years. She wasn't about to take any chances at this point anyway. Not when she finally saw a teensy glimmer of hope on the horizon.

If the phone number Phillip Milton gave her was correct, all she had to do was punch it in and hope to God her sister Katrina answered. Stella's options for changing her and her seventeen year old twins' lives hung in the balance. What if Katrina answered but didn't want to talk to Stella? Stella had not spoken to Kat in ten years. Robert wouldn't allow it. But Katrina didn't know that.

"What is wrong with me?" she whispered to no one. But she knew the answer. This was her last hope, and she was so sick and tired of disappointment being her constant companion. Just one more ounce of it and she knew she'd just give up. Give up and succumb to her fate. Live the remainder of her days with a man who wouldn't let her go. Continue to be married to an abusive bastard for another eighteen years. She was forty years old —that would make her fifty-eight then! Holy tomoly! The only way she'd ever leave Corvallis would be in a coffin. Even then, Robert would bury her in the Corvallis cemetery, so she'd never be able to escape this place.

"Please answer, Katrina." Tears dribbled down Stella's cheeks. She swiped them with her functioning right hand. "Suck it up, Stella."

She straightened her sore back, shook her head like a wet dog, pressed the eleven numbers, then listened to the ringing.

Chapter Two

"Monarch Manes. This is Katrina Swanson. Can I help you?"

Stella's lips parted. She held her breath. The P.I. had found Katrina. He'd really found her sister. My God! Stella hadn't one-hundred percent believed it when Phillip Milton gave her a number for her sister. Stella found Milton in the yellow pages of an old phone book months ago, never believing he'd track down her sister. After all these years, Katrina had married and thus, had a different last name. No longer Katrina Montgomery, she was now Katrina Swanson.

"This is Monarch Manes. Is anyone there? Can I help you?"

Stella opened her mouth to speak, and nothing came out, her surprise so great, speaking seemed unimaginable. "Katrina," she whispered.

"Excuse me. I can hardly hear you. Hey, turn off the blow dryer for a second, will you Hello? Whoever this is, could you speak up a bit, please?"

Stella cleared her throat. "Katrina, it's Stella."

"Could I have a little quiet around here?" Kat shouted.

Stella heard voices in the background, then silence.

"Stella? Is that really you?"

More tears slid down Stella's cheeks, and she sighed. Then she smiled. Katrina hadn't hung up on her. Maybe everything was going to be all right. "Yes, it's me. Please tell me you don't hate me, Kat. He wouldn't let me look for you. I had to hire a private investigator to find you. But it's really you. I can't believe it."

"Stella, where the hell are you? Jesus Christ. What the fuck happened to you? I called you a hundred times. You never answered. And there was no answering machine. You weren't listed anywhere when I did a Google search for you and Robert. I can't believe I'm talking to you right now. Goddamn."

Stella heard the distinct click of the key in the front door and immediately glimpsed at the clock on the wall—10:45 in the morning. What was Robert doing home? He taught a Spanish class five days a week at 10 a.m.

"Stella!" Robert called out.

Stella cupped her hand to the side of her mouth, covering the edge of the burner phone. "I'll call you back, Kat. Don't call me. Please. If I ever want to see you again. Do. Not. Call. Me. Back." She pressed the red key to end the call, then stuffed the phone in the front pocket of her jeans, stood, pulled down her shirt past her waistline to cover the bulge in her pocket, then did her best to walk without hobbling toward the front room.

"There you are, honey." Robert pulled Stella toward his chest and kissed the top of her head.

"What are you doing home so early?" Stella's words came out muffled, her mouth squished against Robert's starched, white button-down shirt.

He grasped her upper arms and leaned back.

Stella's eyes widened when she noticed a smudge of pink lipstick smeared around a button of his pure-white shirt.

Robert glanced down, then raised his eyes slowly to meet hers. "You do know how to get that out, right?" he said, his voice low and threatening.

Stella nodded, tears imminent. She hurt all over and couldn't take any more today. Please, not again today. "I'm sorry, Robert. I can get a freshly ironed one for you right now."

"That's good to hear. So… you happy to see me? I had to cancel class. There was a fire in the first floor of the building. They evacuated us, and by then class was half over, so I decided to come home for a quickie." He smiled and rubbed his groin against her stomach.

She felt his arousal, and at the same time her mouth began to water. She knew she was close to throwing up. But she hadn't eaten anything yet today. She had a hard time keeping anything down after he beat her, the anxiety and stress so intense, her stomach constantly clenched as if someone were holding that organ in their hands and squeezing—all… day… long. Sometimes it took weeks before she could eat a complete meal. She'd lost ten pounds and at one-hundred and fifteen, she wasn't the picture of health she had been "back in the day."

Robert tipped her head with his finger and she had no choice but to look in his eyes.

"I'm not feeling too good today, Robert."

He rubbed up against her again, leaned down and skimmed her lips with his tongue. "Having sex is good for relaxing, Stell. Let me make love to you. Show you how sorry I am about last night. It was all a misunderstanding."

Stella drew her eyebrows down and tilted her head. "What did I misunderstand, Robert?"

"I thought you and that guy you were talking to in the front yard were acting… I don't know. Squirrely. Like you were having a little you-know-what with him while I was at the university."

Stella drew in a breath, backed up two steps until Robert's hands dropped from her shoulders. "He's the gardener *you* told me to hire to put in the sprinkler system for the new sod you planted. If you didn't want a man coming around the house, you shouldn't have told me to hire him."

Robert edged slowly toward her, his face void of expression, eyes locked on hers. "Oh, you have quite a mouth on you today, Stella, my love. Don't you get sassy with me, though it is a bit of a turn-on." He rubbed against her again and again, his erection growing. "I saw the way you two were looking at each other. I know I hired him. Sod and a sprinkler system will make your life much easier. I did it for you, my darling. No more hand-watering, no wasted time in the front yard for everyone to see you in your—" He took in her jean shorts and ribbed T-shirt with a slow glance. "Your clingy top with your… your private parts practically falling out of those too-short shorts."

Stella's insides squeezed together, from her throat to her intestines. She was wearing a pair of baggy jean shorts to almost her knees and her "stretchy" cotton top was at least two sizes too big. Robert was delusional on top of everything else. But she knew if she answered him in any way that remotely inched toward sticking up for herself, his anger would escalate.

She couldn't take another round like last night. The exhaustion, pain, and anger, the disappointment and fear balled up in her stomach like a python. She had to become the actress she'd dreamed of becoming when she was a teenager. This was her opportunity to prove to herself she could shine under the imaginary lights of a movie camera.

She pressed her palms on Robert's chest and stared in his eyes with a subtle smile on her lips. "Let's not argue, baby. We have bigger things to attend to," she whispered as she inched her hands down his chest to his leather belt, unhinged the buckle, and slid the zipper down as slowly as she could while sliding her tongue round and round her lips.

"Not here, babe." The timber of Robert's voice deepened with each word.

"Why not here?" Stella grasped onto his hands while gently lowering herself to the puffy white rug in front of the fireplace.

Robert followed her, pushed her down until she lay flat on the rug then straddled her.

She knew what he liked, and as sickening as it felt to please him, she took advantage of his arousal in all the ways he enjoyed until they lay side by side, his breathing heavy and loud in her ear as he slept.

How many more times would she have to do this? How many more years would she be jailed in this marriage cell before she'd be able to escape? And please God don't call me back, Kat. She hadn't had time to hide the burner phone yet.

I'll try again tomorrow, Katrina. I swear I will.

I can't live like this any longer.

Chapter Three

The twins, Loreen and Gabriel, would arrive home in a few hours. Robert returned to campus, where he taught afternoon classes five days a week. Stella had a lot to do before her husband came home for dinner. Shop for his favorite ingredients (a mixture of zucchini, onions, mushrooms, and tomatoes scooped over white rice) and hide the burner phone before he found it.

She watched enough true-life movies to know, if he found the phone and called the number for Monarch Manes and Katrina answered, he might recognize her voice. Of course, he'd wonder why she was calling her sister, since he forbade Stella to have anything to do with her sister almost ten years ago.

Robert had never liked Stella's sister. He thought Kat's bleached blonde hair, cut short with died black roots, the many tattoos that graced her arms and shoulders, and the "horrendous" nose ring (his words) would be a bad influence on Stella as well as the children. Robert believed Kat's non-conformist behavior would "rub off" on Stella, somehow turn her against him. Little did he know Stella didn't need any prompting or suggestions from anyone in order to come to the decision, her husband was a horrible human being and she should get out of the marriage.

No matter how many times Robert said he was sorry, Stella had endured too many trips to the E.R. with stories about falling down the stairs at home or backing the car out of the garage just as the electric door came down on the windshield, and on and on… Stella would not and could not forgive him for the physical and psychological harm he continued to inflict on her.

And by familial osmosis, the emotional damage inflicted on the twins as well.

Stella drove to the grocery store to pick up the necessary items for the night's dinner, during which time she contemplated the best plan for hiding the phone. In the event Kat *did* phone Stella back, Stella didn't want Robert to hear the ringtone or the vibration. She'd shut it off, then hide it "where the sun don't shine," as the old expression went. And where would that be? The basement, of course.

Robert would never suspect Stella of *ever* going to the basement. She was deathly and unbelievably afraid of spiders, and there were always spiders down there. She refused to even open the basement door, no matter how many times Robert promised he'd venture down there with her and protect her from any arachnids that might, literally, be hanging around. But Stella had a plan to help with her arachnophobia in order to hide the phone.

In this case, she convinced herself to run to the basement, not look around, put the burner phone in a spot at the very back, underneath the window located at ground level on the side of the house, then rush out… holding her breath the entire time. All she'd be able to think about was finishing the task and taking her next breath. The whole deed would take less than a minute, she told herself. She'd crack the window open slightly and that way, when she needed to call Kat back, she'd walk to the front yard, reach inside, and grab it… and never have to return to the basement ever again. She shivered. Just the thought caused goosebumps to pop out up and down her arms.

In the meantime, given the fact Kat had not hung up on Stella, she hoped her sister would be her savior. That she and the twins would be able to abandon their lives in Corvallis and head to Monarch Bay where Kat lived. They'd stay with Kat until Stella got her feet firmly on the ground, then she and the kids could get a place of their own.

Meanwhile, Stella had to make sure dinner was ready to eat by the appropriate time Robert wanted… or more appropriately, that he demanded. The kids would both be home soon as well. They, too, knew the penalty for arriving home late. So at four o'clock they'd march in the house, expecting a snack before dinner arrived on the table promptly at six o'clock.

Stella unpacked the groceries, began rinsing the veggies, then sliced and diced them. She heard the front door open and glanced at the clock—3:59 p.m. Right on time. She hated that her kids had to grow up living under the same roof with a tyrant like Robert, as if they were in boot camp for the marines. Oh, yes, Robert could be sweet and gentle and caring. He had the ability to laugh and talk like a "normal" father. But in between those infrequent times when he was on his best behavior, there lurked an angry, vicious, violent, foul-mouthed bastard who enjoyed beating his wife and yelling at his kids for some ridiculous made-up reasons that made sense only to him.

"Mom! Hey! Wassup?" Gabriel sauntered into the kitchen, jeans hanging so low on his hips, she could see the top of his maroon boxer shorts.

Robert continuously told Gabe not to wear his pants "slipping half-way off his ass" —Robert's words. Stella hoped he'd pull them up and use a belt before Robert returned home for supper.

Gabe also wore his dark hair way too long for Robert's liking — straight and often pulled into a pony tail or a man-bun, which irked Robert to no end. Stella wondered if Gabe wore it that way on purpose to make Robert mad.

Tiny wisps of dark hair grew above Gabe's lip. Not exactly a mustache, it made Gabe look even more "unkempt." Robert's words again. But for some reason Stella couldn't fathom, Robert never followed through with his threats of taking a hair trimmer and shaving off Gabe's hair and mustache if Gabe didn't "toe the line," another one of Robert's favorite expressions. Perhaps he was afraid Gabriel would retaliate? Seventeen years old, Gabe had shot up like a pistol in the last year, in weight and height. At 6 feet 2 inches, 185 pounds, Gabe now outweighed Robert and was taller than his father.

Loreen followed Gabe into the kitchen, a pink Hello Kitty backpack hanging over her shoulder. Stella always wondered where Loreen got her white-blonde hair. Robert's hair was dark brown, Stella's auburn and wavy. Many times Robert accused Stella of having a lover, that Loreen wasn't his child. No matter how many times Stella offered to take a DNA test, Robert refused. and she knew why. He just enjoyed criticizing Stella in whatever ways he could, his love of contention and dissension overwhelming and consistent.

The one compliment Robert deigned to give to Stella was that his gorgeous daughter took after her mother in the "looks department." Loreen had huge brown eyes, a wide pouty mouth, and high cheekbones, as did Stella. Too bad Robert enjoyed smacking Stella's face so often. One day Stella wouldn't recover from his backhanding her and break all the bones in that "beautiful" face. And then what? He certainly wouldn't pay the expense for plastic surgery.

He was miserly when it came to handing over his money for things that didn't benefit him directly but thought nothing of buying himself a new car or suit for work. He always shopped at the best department stores in Portland for his clothes, whereas the rest of the family could damn well go to Shop and Save in Corvallis. His selfishness knew no bounds.

Stella's heart squeezed when she looked at her children. She loved the twins more than her own life. They were always so upbeat and affectionate. With her. Never Robert.

She had to get them out from under Robert's influence before he did irreparable harm, all the while knowing harm already had been sorely meted out. However, Stella stayed hopeful and prayed for the possibility the harm would vanish with time, once she got them away from their father.

Stella turned toward her son, wiping her hands on a towel as she leaned closer to him. He kissed her on the cheek. Stella winced and quickly turned back to the sink. She'd covered the bruises on her face with a ton of very expensive make-up. Funny how Robert never mentioned the fifty-plus dollars on the credit card statement she had to spend on facial accoutrements to hide his "handiwork."

He meticulously perused every receipt. Why had she paid so much for avocados? Though he knew dam well they were expensive any time of the year and he had to have his guacamole with chips for a snack …or else. So what was she supposed to do? Damned if she did and damned if she didn't. But fifty dollar make-up? Hmm. He never mentioned that.

Gabe looked at the pile of vegetables on the sideboard. "Again, Mom? Jesus H. Christ. Can't we ever be like a normal family and have pizza or mac and cheese or something?"

Stella shook her head, then took a quick look in Loreen's direction. "How're you doing, honey? Did you take that Calculus exam?"

Loreen hugged her mom from behind and grabbed a baby tomato from the colander. "Aced it. Least I'm pretty sure I did. Gabe, I like this ghoulish shit Mom makes. I eat enough pizza over at Mario's house."

Stella turned and leaned her backside against the lip of the sink.

"First of all, the shit, as you call it, Loreen, isn't ghoulish. It's goul*ash*. And who is Mario?"

Loreen fiddled with the pocket of her backpack, seemingly searching for something, though Stella felt it was Loreen's way of gaining time enough to think of an explanation for Mario's identity.

"Mo-om. He's just a friend from school. He and I sometimes take lunch breaks together. Go to the pizza place down the street from the high school. Nothin's goin' on. Don't worry. I'm not pregnant or anything."

Stella puckered her lips. "I never said you were having sex with the boy. I asked you who he was."

Loreen slung her backpack over her shoulder and looked her mom in the eyes. "Well I'm not fucking him, and I have no intention of doing so. Can I go study now?"

Stella placed the towel she'd been holding on the kitchen table and walked slowly toward Loreen, standing an inch from her face. "If your father ever heard you talking like that, he'd have a conniption fit. Please be careful, Lo. His anger frightens me."

Loreen smirked. "What's he gonna do, Mom? Hit me like he does you?"

Stella drew back, feeling her face slacken. Yet she'd known this was coming, hadn't she? There was no way her kids hadn't either surreptitiously seen Robert hit her or they'd heard her muffled screams when he was forcing himself on her behind closed doors. Or… come on, Stella. They weren't blind. Make-up couldn't cover everything, and her kids were anything but gullible and stupid. Teenagers these days were a helluva lot more savvy than Stella had been at their age.

They knew.

And Stella hated that they knew.

She'd better talk to them soon about her plans for their future. She guessed they'd dislike moving, leaving their friends and prom night and all the festivities still to come in their senior year. But if everything went according to Stella's plan, they'd be out of Corvallis way before end-of-year senior activities. Hopefully, only a few days from now.

"Your father does not hit you, Loreen." Stella leaned in and hugged her daughter, hard.

"But he does hit *you*, Mom." Loreen glanced at her brother then pointed in his direction. "He knows too. We're not fucking stupid. Just cause we're only seventeen doesn't mean we're blind."

Gabriel joined them and put his arm around his mother's shoulders. "I'm getting to the age where I could be the, quote unquote, man of the house, Mom. I could deck that son of a bitch with my bare fists. Which is what I'm gonna do the next time I hear him using you like his personal fucking punching bag."

Stella opened her mouth. It was time to tell them her plans. But, no. There wasn't time. She'd need at least fifteen minutes of uninterrupted time in order to explain it all to both of them.

"Stella! Stella!"

The sound of Robert's bellowing grated on Stella's ears like cats squalling in the middle of the night. It hurt her ear drums… and her soul. He knew exactly where she was at this time of day. Hovering over a boiling hot oven, no matter the weather. The house didn't have A/C since in Corvallis it was usually raining or… raining.

Stella hated living here. But Robert accepted an offer he stated he "could not refuse." So they'd moved out of gorgeous Monterey, near Carmel-by-the-Sea, to Corvallis, Oregon! Nothing against Oregon, but Stella grew up in Monterey with her foster parents, Fiona and Nason Dominguez. It was paradise on earth compared to this wet burg.

But she didn't have time for reminiscing about the loving home Fiona and Nason gave both Stella and Katrina after their parents were killed. Robert was home, and dinner was expected on the table at six o'clock. Sharp!

"I'm in here. With Loreen and Gabriel," Stella called out.

"Where the hell else does he think you'd be, for fuck's sake?" Gabe grumbled.

Stella gave him "the eye" and turned toward her husband as he waltzed into the house carrying a bouquet of sunflowers in one hand and a box of chocolates in the other.

He bent his head to kiss Stella on the lips, then widened the kiss and practically stuck his tongue down her throat.

Stella pulled back, almost gagging, and swiped at her lips with the back of her hand. "Robert, for goodness sake. The kids!"

Robert laughed out loud. "I think our kids, at seventeen years of age, know what a French kiss is. How do they think *they* got here, if their parents weren't having mad and passionate sex?"

Gabriel and Loreen both stood behind Robert and mimicked puking while pointing down their throats with their index fingers.

Robert shrugged and placed the sunflowers and candy on the kitchen table then turned and grabbed Stella, pulling her in close. He ground his hips into her groin and bent for another kiss.

Stella could not do this. A sick feeling bubbled inside her stomach, nausea imminent. She wondered what he'd do if she actually threw up in his mouth. The thought made her even more nauseated, and she pulled away.

"I have to tend to dinner, Robert, otherwise we won't eat until seven, if that."

"You should have started prepping sooner then, my darling. We need time alone, Stella." He lowered his voice to a near whisper. "The kids are always hanging around at night, either in their bedrooms with the doors open or in the family room. There's never any time for lovemaking. They'd hear every sound we make." He shifted his eyebrows up and down.

Stella wanted to laugh in his face. He reminded her of Charlie Chaplin. Did he really think the kids couldn't hear Stella crying out in pain? Even though Robert waited until the middle of the night to fulfill his sexual fantasies and Stella tried to muffle her cries into a pillow, their "lovemaking" was never quiet. She was almost sure the twins heard them sometimes.

Stella thought of what Robert meant by "making love." What a crock of you-know-what. She hadn't "made love" to her husband for more than ten years. Right around the time he felt comfortable throwing her around, hitting her with his hands, punching her with his fists, forcing himself on her when she was exhausted from taking care of the twins all day, having his meals prepared on time, mowing and watering the lawn, tending the garden, keeping a tidy house. He was a complete narcissist. *Her* life had to be all about *him*.

And she had to get out.

Sooner rather than later.

She didn't want to go to jail for murdering her husband. Not that she'd ever do such a thing. But murderous thoughts had begun to invade her mind. When he was having his way with her, whether sexually or physically abusing her, she wished he were dead. She'd imagine hiding a ten-inch serrated knife under a pillow, reaching for it as he grunted and heaved above her late at night. She'd grasp the knife handle and plunge it into his back over and over and over, blood spurting from his wounds, covering the bed sheets, dripping onto her spread legs. Psycho Part 3.

She dreamed of him not living here any longer… or rather *living at all*.

But… he wasn't going anywhere.

She was.

Chapter Four

Back to dinner at the Walker house.

Since the beginning, Stella loved spending time with her kids. Robert had marveled at their birth. At the hospital, in the nursery, he was amazed he could love two little human beings so much. But truth be told, the moment they departed the Corvallis Medical Facility and crossed the threshold of their home, well… everything about them seemed to irritate him.

Twins meant double duty—for everything. Invariably at the same time. They would both wake up every two hours and want to be fed. Stella needed help, because she'd nursed both of them. So Robert had to hold one and walk the hallways in the middle of the night until Stella finished nursing the other and put him (or her) back into the crib. Then she'd grab the baby from Robert and nurse him (or her) and let Robert go back to sleep.

Robert complained about the disruption to his sleep schedule. He had to be at the university to prepare for classes, and his mind wasn't clear, he said. He needed his rest, he complained.

Robert abruptly forced her to stop nursing, even though she had enough milk for both the kids for many more months. He insisted they learn to drink formula, then insisted they begin eating jar baby food at an earlier age than the doctor suggested. And so it went for the first year. Until the twins slept through the night. Robert wanted their life back, he said. And the sooner the better.

So when the twins began to walk and talk and disobey and get into trouble as all kids do, the thrill was far, far gone… for Robert. He was not enthralled about being a father. And it showed. He punished both of them constantly. Not in a physical way but rather an emotional one. He never spanked them. In fact, he never touched them at all. He didn't want to pick them up and hold them and cuddle them. He didn't like to be drooled on. He didn't enjoy feeding them baby food. Too messy. He thought it looked like vomit, and he didn't want to mess up his clothes. He refused to help Stella at the twins' meal times.

As the years passed, Robert's interest in the twins waned more and more. By the time they were teenagers, the thrill had been gone for a long, long time. He refused to talk to them about their days. He definitely would not allow any arguments. He laid the law down concerning whatever he wanted them to do—what time to be home at night, whose houses they were allowed to visit, where they could hang out, what restaurants and stores he felt were appropriate to eat and shop. And his word was law. Period. No discussions. And they better abide by every single one of them. He was the penultimate dictator. He never got physical. In fact, he almost never yelled either. And he wouldn't tolerate being yelled at or talked to in a disrespectful manner.

Or else.

And the "or else" consisted of taking away privileges. The kids knew if they didn't agree to his demands, they would have to stay home on the weekends, return home from school early, drop out of any team sports they'd signed up for. Basically, Robert believed in education in the book sense only. No field trips. No watching high school baseball or football or basketball games. The twins weren't allowed to just be teenagers. And Stella knew they resented him for that to the core of their being. Perhaps they resented her as well for not sticking up for them… and for herself.

The twins wanted a dog. Robert wouldn't allow it. He said he'd be the one to care for the pet when they got bored with it, though it was obvious that job would default to Stella, and everyone knew it. And Stella wouldn't have minded. She'd grown up with chocolate labs once she and Kat moved in with Fiona and Nason. It was an experience Stella believed every child (every person actually) should have. But Robert disagreed. All he could envision (you guessed it) was poop, vomit, pee, missing shoes, chewed up slippers.

In fact, when Stella gave the situation thorough thought, Robert felt the same about the twins as he did about dogs. The difference was it was human poop, human vomit, his missing shoes, chewed up kid toys that his hard-earned money had purchased. Stella felt he wished he could return the twins the same as he would have returned a puppy to the shelter. And it distressed her every single day that her two amazing and beautiful children would grow up feeling Robert's dislike and inattention.

So… Stella treated the twins special every day of their lives, to make up for Robert's negligence bordering on outright dismissal of their existence. Robert called Stella's behavior going "overboard." Said she spoiled them to death. In Stella's mind, she was acting as any loving mother would. She would do anything for them. Did anything and everything for them. Maybe she did spoil them. But, who else would do so, if not for her?

Robert was a neglectful parent. He "brought home the bacon" — his words—but that was the extent of his involvement. Except for setting down his never-ending rules and regulations for them to follow, he didn't have much to do with them. He was an absent father, not literally but figuratively. Which was worse, in Stella's opinion.

Naturally the twins didn't like all the rules governing their every move. And Stella guessed they didn't much like their father either. So when the beatings started when the twins were around seven years old… and continued to the present… the twins grew to hate him. And Stella didn't think it had taken them ten years to hate him either. They just didn't say anything outright until recently—grumblings and swearing that Stella heard when they thought she wasn't near. So she tried to intervene. Make excuses for Robert's behavior. But the older they got, the less she was able to make her point appear even the least bit believable to either of them. It was useless.

All Stella wanted was a peaceful and loving home atmosphere, but Robert's way of parenting, if it could be called that, did nothing but foment more arguments as the twins got older. After they entered high school, arguments escalated to the point of no return, making Stella wonder if physical beatings would soon be the norm, since Robert's words were meaningless and stupid to the twins at that age and, little by little, they'd become vocal in their resistance.

She wanted her children to have a fun and happy youth, and if it were Robert's decision they'd both be sitting in their rooms studying, come to the table and eat without speaking, then return to their rooms for more studying then go to bed as soon as possible.

Stella had to get the three of them out of there before more damage was done.

Back to dinner at the Walkers's house.

Stella stopped at the bottom of the stairs. "Dinner, kids!" She returned to the kitchen and set the table and transferred bowls of rice and goulash to the middle of the table for easy access.

Robert walked in, washed his hands at the sink, and sat down at the head of the table.

Stella sat at the other end across from him and placed the cloth napkin Robert insisted they use in her lap, then looked at her husband and frowned. "What's wrong, Robert? You seem angry."

He didn't wait for the kids and scooped a pile of rice and goulash onto his plate. "Did you make garlic bread?"

Stella closed her eyes and sighed. "I knew I forgot something." She placed both hands on the table and was about to stand. "It's not too late. I have a loaf of French bread that I—"

"Never mind, Stella. If you had a brain, I think you'd play with it."

Stella shoved her chair back and stood. "No need to talk to me like that, Robert. I've had a lot on my mind lately."

"Where were you this afternoon when I phoned?"

Stella grabbed the loaf of bread and a serrated knife (oh, how she'd love to use it to cut off something else!) and began cutting individual slices. "Right here." She found the bottle of garlic spread and a butter knife and went to work preparing the bread for broiling.

"I asked you a question, Stella. Where were you?"

Stella opened the oven and shoved the tray under the broiler. "I was right here all day long. Oh, wait. I did go to the store; but that didn't take long. Why do you ask?"

"Where's your phone?"

The twins bounded down the stairs, their heavy footfalls sounding like a herd of cattle crossing the plains. They sat down and began ladling food onto their plates.

"In my purse, I would imagine, Robert." She shrugged. "You can go look if you so desire. It's right over there." She pointed to the side of the counter near the front room doorway.

"What's going on?" Loreen said.

"Yeah, what's the big deal with your phone, Mom?" Gabriel asked.

"No one asked for your opinion, Gabriel," Robert said. "This is between me and your mother."

Gabriel took a forkful of food and didn't look up from his plate. Loreen did the same. They knew something was brewing, knew when to shut up.

"Bring me your purse, Stella," Robert said in a monotone.

Stella grabbed the oven mitt and pulled the garlic bread out from under the broiler, set the pan on top of the stove, then grasped her purse, shoved her hand into both sides. "It's not here. What the heck happened to it? No wonder I didn't hear your call. I don't know where my phone is."

"Do you know how much that cell phone cost me, Stella? Six hundred dollars. And sixty dollars a month for service. Find it."

"If I knew where it was, we wouldn't be having this discussion."

She felt movement behind her before hands grabbed her shoulders and twisted her around. The look on Robert's face told her everything she didn't want to deal with tonight.

"I pinged your phone, Stella."

"What do you mean, you pinged my phone?"

"If you weren't so dumb, you'd know what I mean."

"Don't call her dumb," Gabe shouted, pushed his chair back, then walked toward his father.

Stella shook her head. "Keep out of this, Gabriel. This is between your father and me."

"The hell it is," Gabe snarled. "I'm tired of watching the way he treats you, Mom. You've gotta be sick of it too."

It suddenly dawned on Stella. How very, very much Gabriel had grown. Robert had met his match.

Robert threw out an arm toward Gabriel to fend him off, and Gabriel swiped it away, then shoved Robert in the chest. Robert stumbled backward, regained his balance, then powered forward, head down, and blasted Gabriel in the stomach with his head, knocking him to the floor.

Stella grasped wildly for a piece of Robert's clothing to pull him off Gabriel but only met with air.

Gabriel must have gotten the wind knocked out of him. He lay on the floor gasping for air.

Stella rushed to his side, knelt down next to him. "Gabriel?" She took his face in her hands, looked into his glazed eyes. "Are you okay?"

He struggled to sit up, shaking his head side to side. "I'm okay, Mom." He stood and faced his father. "You can't treat her that way anymore. Do you hear me?"

Robert smirked. Smirked! Stella wanted to slap him across the face, she was so angry.

"Everything that happens between your mother and me is between the two of us. She's not your wife. She's mine."

"You don't own her. And she'll always be my mother. Whereas I hope someday she won't be your wife any longer."

Robert's nostrils flared, fists balled into rock-hard masses of anger. She grabbed Robert's bicep and squeezed. "No more, Robert. Please. Let's just finish dinner and forget this ever happened."

Gabriel stalked out of the kitchen, clomped up the stairs. His bedroom door slammed shut.

Robert jerked his arm out of Stella's grasp and glared down at her. "He can't get away with speaking to me that way. Where does he get off saying he's hoping for the day you and I won't be together any longer. Where did he get that idea, Stella?"

Stella seethed, as if her insides were boiling, her stomach a fiery cauldron of hatred. He could beat up on her, but he damn well could *not* beat up on Gabriel. She took a deep breath and ignored him, slowly sat back down in her chair. She took hold of her fork with shaking hands and dipped it into her food. Her hand wobbled so badly she was surprised any goulash made it into her mouth.

She wished to God she had the inner strength to tell Robert how much she hated him. How she wished Gabe had pushed him to the floor and Robert had smashed his head into the corner of the doorway, killing him instantly. Instead, as always, Stella remained quiet as a mouse, knowing it was best for everyone she remain submissive, if her plans were to come to fruition.

Loreen remained silent during the dinner debacle. Stella hoped she'd continue to keep her mouth shut. Stella just wanted everything to stop. She wanted off this train. It was derailing, headed for disaster.

Robert was so unbelievably angry Stella couldn't find her phone. But what did he mean, he'd pinged her phone? Thank God she'd hidden the burner phone. There was no way she could explain having a burner phone in her purse.

Robert tucked his napkin into his shirt underneath his chin and picked up his fork. "No answer, Stella? Where did Gabriel get that idea?"

Loreen stood. "Excuse me. I'm not feeling well." She put her plate in the sink and walked out of the room.

Stella lifted her gaze to stare into Robert's eyes. "I have never wanted to leave you, Robert. Gabriel was just angry. Ignore him. Let's eat our dinner, okay?" She smiled at him, amazed at her ability to not spit in his face.

"Your phone is in this house or at least near the house somewhere, Stella," Robert announced.

Stella swallowed. Would this inquisition ever end? "I didn't realize it was missing."

He took another bite of food, chewed slowly, dabbed at his lips, set his napkin in his lap and stared at her. "I call you every day. You didn't find it odd you didn't hear from me."

Stella took in a deep breath and let it out slowly. "Frankly, Robert, I didn't notice. I had other things I was busy with, and I have more to worry about than whether my phone rings."

He leaned back in his chair, arms crossed over his chest. "Find it."

"I asked you how you know it's even around here."

"You've not heard of Find My Phone, Stella?"

She shook her head.

"It's an app on your phone which allows me to pinpoint its location through GPS. I told you, it's around here somewhere."

"I wasn't aware of that. I'll have to ask the kids about it. They're always so helpful with that type of electronic stuff."

"You're a moderately intelligent woman, Stella. I'm sure you can look it up on the internet. It will tell you everything you need to know."

Stella put down her fork. She couldn't eat any more. This conversation was making her stomach hurt. Every time she talked with her husband about anything, he made her feel ignorant and useless and a complete idiot. She'd gone to college. Monterey University was a reputable school. Not exactly a place for dummies. She'd aced all her classes. She loved to learn. But when it came to Robert, he thrived off putting her down and making her doubt her intellectual abilities.

"I know I could look it up on the internet, Robert. But I love engaging the kids in conversations about something they know so much about, that's helpful for me personally. Plus, it's a great way to get them to open up and talk about other subjects. Our talks almost always segue into other things that are important to them."

Robert shook his head, staring at his dinner plate.

"What is it, Robert? What have I said this time to piss you off?"

He looked up at her. "No need to talk like an angry teenager, Stella. 'Pissed off' isn't something a forty year old woman should say."

"Oh, for goodness sake. I'm sorry my vocabulary doesn't meet your strict standards of propriety."

His jaw muscles twitched, and his temples pulsed. Uh-oh.

"You certainly know how to push my buttons, Stell, because it appears you're purposely trying to make me mad. Again."

Their "talk" was heading downhill, and if she didn't want it to escalate further, she knew what she had to do. If ever there was an example of "kissing ass," this was what she'd need to reach a more peaceful state.

"I'll look for my phone, Robert. I'm sorry I missed your calls. I'll make sure to keep it in my pocket at all times from now on. I apologize. I should be more thoughtful, and I know you're just concerned."

"You do that." He pushed away from the table. "I have some papers I need to grade. I'll be in my office, if you need me."

"Didn't you enjoy your dinner? You didn't eat much."

"I'm not one of the kids, Stella. No need for you to be concerned about my eating habits. And the garlic bread wasn't broiled enough. It's inedible."

"It's not just the children I worry about, Robert. You're my husband."

He sat back down. "The children have always been your priority. Ever since they came into this house, I've taken second place. It's sick, Stella. I'm your husband."

What's sick, Robert, is the way you treat your wife when your kids aren't around, she wanted to say. And often when they *are* around and can hear you, for that matter. But she wasn't going to start another argument. She'd keep her mouth shut, as she always did.

It was important she get the burner phone in the basement and call Kat, then explain her plan to the kids and get out of Corvallis as soon as possible. Thus, it was imperative to maintain peace right now. More imperative than getting her point across to her abusive husband.

"I'm sorry you feel that way, Robert. I love you more than life itself." Speaking those words made her want to puke. She took a big gulp of water, endeavoring to quell the urge to run to the bathroom and throw up her dinner. She needed to keep calm. This marital charade was coming to an end. She needed to relish that. Look forward to it. What happened right now was important in order to reach her goal. She must keep her mouth shut.

"You love me more than life itself." He laughed out loud. "Those are nice words, Stella, but as the old saying goes, 'actions speak louder than words.' And you don't act like I'm that important to you, but it's glaringly obvious the kids are your focus, the be-all end-all of your entire life."

"You know, Robert, at this age they'll be concentrating on college applications and will be so busy they won't have time to speak to either of us. They're growing up so fast. I can't even believe how time flies."

He clenched his fists at the side of his dinner plate, flexing them, his breathing quicker than normal. Something was brewing and Stella braced for whatever negativity bubbled under the surface.

"I want them out of here, Stella. As soon as they reach eighteen. They can do exactly what my parents did to me. We'll hand them a suitcase and an umbrella, and they're on their own. They can get part-time jobs for awhile, then work full-time after they graduate high school. They can get financial aid for college once they establish their financial independence, which will take a couple of years. During that time, they can save up, become more independent of their mommy. They're adults already, Stella. Not kids, as you keep calling them."

Stella couldn't believe what he was saying. The world wasn't like it was when she and Robert were growing up. Rents were sky-high. College tuition had soared to unacceptable levels for many, if not most, parents to afford. The twins weren't financially or psychologically ready to fly the coop. And deep down, Robert knew that. He just wanted to assert his authority, show them who was boss, and ultimately have Stella all to himself. *That* was his prime directive, and he was fooling no one with this false speech about the twins becoming responsible adults.

All this didn't matter anymore. Her plan didn't include Robert. It was all about getting out of there, being safe out of this house, out of this town, out of this state, and away from the physical and mental abuse. Especially after what happened between Gabriel and Robert this evening, Stella didn't want to see Gabriel in the hospital for whatever injuries Robert might inflict upon her young son.

And they were just hours from escaping. Hopefully. She had to reach out to Kat the next day, and, God help her, Stella and the twins would be gone before Robert returned home from work tomorrow evening.

Chapter Five

Stella finished cleaning up the kitchen, then climbed the stairs to Gabriel's room and knocked lightly on the door.

"Yeah?"

"Can I come in, honey?"

"Yup."

Stella entered the room and found Gabriel sprawled on his bed, computer on his lap.

He glanced up at her. "Sup?"

She sat on the edge of the bed next to him and took his hand in hers. "Gabriel, I have to tell you something." She stood. "Let me go get your sister first."

He sat up and set his computer aside. "What for? I'm sure it's something about Dad. Is he kicking me out of the house? I wouldn't be surprised."

"Nothing like that, Gabe. Hold on a sec, okay?" Stella walked across the hallway to Loreen's room and knocked.

"Yeah, Mom?"

Stella opened the door a few inches and whispered, "Could you come join your brother and me in his bedroom. I'd like to talk with you both without your father hearing."

Loreen appeared in the doorway in a matter of seconds and they slid into Gabriel's room. Stella lightly closed the door, making as little noise as possible.

Loreen joined Gabriel, sitting several feet away from him with her back against the wall, legs crisscrossed. Her two kids. Hopefully about to be saved from this "sick house," which was how Stella thought of it. It was not a healthy environment for anyone—not her and not her two teenage kids.

Stella pulled a chair over and sat, facing both of them. "I know things have been… uh… not healthy, here at home… with your father."

"Ya think?" Gabriel snarled. "He's an abusive, wife-beating asshole. And I wish he were dead."

Loreen nodded, eyes glassy with unshed tears.

Maybe Stella had waited too long to act. Lately it had become obvious the kids knew more than she imagined. But it had taken her this long to save enough money. She'd hidden it in the pocket of her puffy down ski jacket. Where would she have worn that jacket anyway?

She and Robert never went on vacations to the snow anymore. Not since the twins were born. She recalled the time Robert and she rented a chalet in the mountains for a romantic getaway. They'd gone out to dinner after a full day skiing the slopes. She'd worn a simple, scoop-neck, black dress with five-inch black leather heels. Other men had taken notice which fomented Robert's never-ending jealousy.

And who had born the brunt of that? Stella. After they returned to the chalet that evening. It happened once and once only. From then on, she and Robert stayed home on the weekends, watching sports or old movies. They led the life of retirees.

Her mind wandered. She earned the money she saved from crocheting afghans in her spare time and selling them on Etsy for hundreds of dollars. She could now afford to get out of this town, away from Robert, and keep her children safe. Hopefully live with her sister Kat. And, if not, they'd find somewhere else to hide safely with no worries about Robert finding them.

"I hid my new burner phone from your father."

Gabe glanced at his sister and laughed. "Mom's got a burner phone?"

"I didn't want him to know I called my sister Katrina," Stella said. "Your Aunt Katrina. You might remember her from when you were little kids."

They both nodded.

"It's been awhile," Gabe said, "but I remember her pushing us on the swings at the park when I was five or six years old. Could that be right?"

Stella nodded. "Yes, that was her. And you, Loreen?"

"Me, too. I remember she always had these wild tattoos on her arms. I loved touching them. I thought I could rub off the color then use crayons or ink pens to draw new ones."

Stella laughed. "Yes, that's your Aunt Kat." She cleared her throat. "She and I haven't spoken for almost ten years because your father-"

"He definitely didn't like her," Gabe chimed in. "He said she was a bad influence. Too hippy, radical, whatever. Wasn't she a barber or something to do with hair?"

Stella nodded. "She wanted to cut your hair, Gabe, but you were afraid it would turn out like hers. You know, white with black roots? You were horrified."

Gabe chuckled. "True dat."

Stella moved her chair closer to the bed. "Okay, guys, I better say what I have to say before your father gets curious why it's so quiet and comes looking for me."

The twins rolled their eyes.

Stella cleared her throat. "I spoke to Kat yesterday, but my call was interrupted because your father came home early, and I had to hang up. I told her not to try to contact me, but to wait for my phone call. That's why I hid the burner phone. Anyway, I'm going to call her tomorrow and ask if we can stay with her for awhile."

"For how long?" Loreen said.

"Well, I'm hoping it's temporary," Stella said. "We can't live with her and her husband forever."

Loreen and Gabe glanced at each other, frowning.

"So when are we leaving? Before senior prom and shit?" Gabe said.

"I know you'll be missing out on all the senior activities planned for the end of the year. "

They looked at each other again, then Gabe shook his head. "It doesn't matter, Mom. You have to get out of here, and so do we. Fuck the senior activities. It's not safe for any of us living with that asshole."

"Yeah," Loreen said. "Don't think for a minute that Gabe and I don't see the bruises, Mom. We know he beats you when we're not here, cause we can see all that pancake make-up you use to try to hide the swelling on your face. And we don't believe the b.s. story that your eyes swell up because you have conjunctivitis. We're not babies, Mom. We know he beats you when we're not here."

Stella cradled her forehead in her hand and mumbled, "And he beats me when you're here, too."

"We know that too, Mom," Gabe added. "We know what's goin' on. The guy's a bastard."

Stella's head popped up, and she patted Gabe's knee. "Don't worry about all that now. If everything goes as I want it to, we'll be out of here tomorrow."

"Tomorrow?" the twins shouted.

Stella's eyes widened and she pressed her index finger to her lips. "Shhh. Yes. There's a major truck stop outside of Corvallis," she whispered. "I've been there many times to check out the place. I talked with the waitresses, who know our situation, and they spoke with several of the long-haul truckers. We can hitch a ride with one of them to probably anywhere we want to go. We can't take a train or bus or a plane, because your father would be able to track us. We can't afford to do that.

"That's the reason I ditched my cell phone. I can't use it because he checks it every night to see who I've talked to. That's why I buried it in the backyard underneath the hydrangea bushes. My own personal 'screw off' to him because I'm so sick of him monitoring my every move. He'll go nuts when he finds it, because he must tell me every day how much it cost him to buy me the top of the line 5G cell phone and the monthly service charges.

"But I didn't know he could ping it. Luckily it just shows it's somewhere at this address. But when he does find it, if he ever does, he'll know I put it there on purpose." She covered her mouth. "Very childish of me, I know. But I couldn't help myself. I've wanted to retaliate for so many years that—"

Gabe grimaced. "Stop it, Mom. I'm surprised you haven't kicked him in the nuts a long time ago, so he wouldn't be able to get it up anymore."

Stella blushed. "Let's forget about all that right now and focus on our upcoming freedom."

"You've been hard at work on this plan, Mom," Gabe said. "Why didn't you say anything to us? We could have helped."

"Yeah," Loreen added. "What about money? Gabe and I both have money saved up from odd jobs we've picked up in the last year or so. We can help out."

Stella shook her head. "Not necessary. I've got us covered. At least for awhile. What I'm hoping is to be able to stay with your Aunt Kat until I can get us on our feet."

"Where's she live?" Loreen said.

"In a place called Monarch Bay. It's located in California between Morro Bay and Pismo Beach. It's a small place. Twenty thousand people."

Gabe's dark eyebrows drew together. "And Dad won't be able to find out? He can search for Aunt Kat on the internet. He can search for us too. He'll find us, and then what?"

"Not gonna happen," Stella interjected. "Look. We don't have time for me to explain everything, but trust me. Everything's going to be okay. Without going into it, I filed name change forms for all three of us last year."

"What?" Their eyes practically popped out of their sockets.

Stella leaned toward them. "Listen," she whispered. "Believe me, it took months, but it's now complete. I had to file a Petition for Change of Name, which took about three months, then three months later the court order came through. I had to file an Order to Show Cause, which was published in the newspaper. Then I submitted a Decree Changing Name Form for the judge to sign. Of course there were no objections, because your father didn't know anything about it. There was a court hearing, which I attended, and the name changes were granted. People actually do it all the time, but I never knew that."

Gabriel and Loreen smiled.

"So what're our new names, Mom?" Gabe asked.

Stella smiled. "Well, you get to keep your first names because that's not a problem if your father was to search for us. Your new last name is Jensen." She stood. "I just heard your father downstairs, so I better wrap this up."

"Loreen and Gabriel Jensen," Loreen said, glancing at her brother. "We can live with that, right, Gabe?"

Gabe nodded. "Yep." He smiled. "Now what, Mom?"

Stella moved toward the door. "As I said, I'll call your Aunt Kat tomorrow. In the meantime, fill your backpacks with as much stuff as you can fit inside them and we can leave at lunchtime tomorrow. I'll text both of you to let you know if it's a 'go'. If it is, I'll meet you in front of the school at noon and we can walk to the truck stop. Pray everything goes as planned, you two." She twisted the door knob. "Are you both okay with this? I know I'm springing this on you and never asked for your input, but—"

"Mom!" Gabe interjected. He looked at his sister then back at Stella. "We're both happy about this, right, Lo?"

"Absolutely," Loreen answered. "Bring it, Mom."

Stella tilted her head and stared at her two amazing children. "You two are the bomb."

Gabe rolled his eyes. "Yo, Mom. So are you."

"Fasho," Loreen added, grinning.

"Okay then. Tomorrow it is. Fingers crossed all goes according to plan." Stella exited Gabriel's bedroom with a smile on her face, something she hoped to be able to do more of in the near future.

Stella tip-toed down the stairs to Robert's office and tapped lightly on the door.

"Come!"

Stella leaned around the edge of the door and smiled. "It's getting late. Will you be long?"

Without lifting his gaze from the papers on the desk, he let out a loud sigh. "I have a lot of work to do, as you can see, if you'd open your eyes. I'll be another hour at least."

"Can I get you something? A cup of hot cocoa?"

He slammed his pen on the desktop. "No, I do not want any cocoa, Stella. Please shut the door after yourself. You're breaking my concentration."

"I'm sorry." She inched the door closed and let out the breath she'd been holding. She needed two minutes, tops, to hide the burner phone and this was her chance.

She walked into the kitchen and stopped dead still in front of the basement door, slipped off her shoes and toed them to the side. How could she ever venture into that dreaded spider-filled, damp, musty-smelling pit to hide the phone? But she had to face her demons. She had no choice. And she'd surely feel so very proud of herself afterward.

She reached out and grasped the door knob, squeezed. And her hand instantly slipped off, her palm covered in sweat. However, she'd planned exactly how she'd pull this off and she was not changing her mind. No turning back now. It was her only chance.

After wiping her hand up and down the side of her pants, she took a deep breath and held it, opened the door, reached up to pull the chain for the light, shut the door behind her. Rushing down the stairs as quietly and safely as she could, she held the air in her lungs, swiping away spider webs as she ran to the window, placed the phone underneath it, pushed the window open, then ran back up the stairs without making a sound. Ten seconds of sheer terror but totally worth it.

Chapter Six

The next morning Stella pulled back the covers and stretched her arms above her head. She could hear Robert in the shower, so it was time for her to get up and fix him breakfast. Later she'd grab her burner phone and call her sister. She shivered just remembering last night's experience, hiding the burner phone in the basement. However, now she'd simply reach through the basement window from the outside of the house and grab it. Hopefully Katrina would answer.

Then Stella's plan could go into action. And when they arrived at Kat's house she'd throw the damn thing away and buy the three of them new cell phones under their brand new names: Stella, Loreen, and Gabriel Jensen. She liked the sound. It rolled off her tongue. And it didn't carry with it all the bad vibes she associated with the name Walker. Robert Walker would soon be part of her past. She'd no longer have to live in fear every… single… day. What a glorious vision.

Stella could barely sleep a wink that night. She'd gone to bed early, pleading a migraine. She didn't want to deal with more of Robert's inquisitions concerning the whereabouts of her phone or how she raised the kids. Oh, not kids. How she raised her "young adults," who were too old to be living at home and should be out working hard like their father, living in their own apartments. At eighteen years old. Just because Robert's parents had kicked him out of the house before he graduated high school didn't mean it was the wisest parental decision, especially given the current unaffordable housing and exorbitant living costs. In Stella's opinion, eighteen-year-olds these days would have a long way to go before they'd have the judgment to live on their own anyway.

Last night, when he came to bed, she pretended to be snoring. Just to make extra sure he didn't try to make any amorous moves. She wouldn't have been able to stomach them. Her anxiety about pulling off this escape without a hitch almost launched her into the worst state of panic she'd experienced in years. She'd gotten almost no sleep at all, lay in bed looking at the ceiling, daydreaming of the moment she and the twins would walk into Kat's house, free of Robert and out of this hell hole of a living situation. She could sleep later, after she arrived in Monarch Bay.

Her mind wandered, hoping the name Monarch stood for the butterfly itself, an insect she was particularly fond of. Half-asleep, she thought of their beauty and remarkable capability to float like a cloud through the sky so slowly, no care in the world but to flit from one flower to the next, alighting like tiny feathers from the sky.

The twins left for school as usual, both giving her a tiny grin as they walked out the front door. She cooked Robert his usual breakfast—scrambled eggs with two slices of lightly buttered toast and a side of Jimmy Dean sausage—two sausages, lightly grilled, no salt or pepper—a glass of freshly squeezed orange juice from their orange tree, and a cup of decaf coffee, no cream and only a half-teaspoon of sugar. Oh, and a cloth napkin folded in a triangle with the edges perfectly matched.

He'd lift his chin for Stella to tuck the napkin under the collar of his perfectly-pressed shirt, another one of her many chores. While most men preferred their shirts taken to a professional laundromat, Robert insisted she iron his—with just the right amount of starch and folded in the exact manner he'd taught her. "Yes, master. Whatever you want, sir."

Robert left for his morning class, and she made a beeline to the side of the house, reached through the basement window, grabbed the phone and scurried up the stairs. She stood in front of the lace curtains that covered the front room windows, watching the street, in case Robert happened to return unexpectedly. She didn't want to be taken by surprise as had occurred the other day, caught unaware, and have to make up some lame excuse for talking on the phone to anyone but him. Then she'd have to explain having a burner phone if he accidentally saw it in her hand before she hid it in her pocket. Oh, the intricacies of having to escape overwhelmed her.

She pressed the most recent outgoing call number and listened to it ring one, two, three, four, five times then go to voicemail. She tried again, just in case Kat recognized the number from when Stella called her the day before. Stella hoped then her sister would answer it.

The next thing Stella heard was Katrina's voice.

"Is this you, Stella?"

Stella immediately burst into tears, finding it hard to believe this whole thing might actually happen. She'd longed for this day.

"Yes." Stella's voice hitched on another sob. "It's me, Kat. God, I've missed you."

Katrina laughed.

It was so good to hear her overly loud guffaw. It had been years and Stella missed everything about her sister.

"What's wrong, big sister? You crying? What the hell is going on, girl?"

Stella closed her eyes, wanting to get this all out in one fell swoop without having to tell Katrina about her life with Robert over the last fifteen plus years. "I don't have a lot of time, Kat, and I'm sorry about that. But I'd like to explain if and when I see you."

"You're actually gonna come visit me? I'll be damned. So what've you been up to for the last… oh, ten or so years? I'm dying to know, you bitch." Katrina laughed once again. "I'm fuckin' with ya, Stell. I've missed you, too."

Stella let out a long breath. "I'm so happy you're even talking to me, but there really is a reason for my silence over these past years. It's all about Robert. He's controlling and abusive and—"

"Say no more. I never liked that prick. He always had to know every move you made even back then. And I only saw the two of you a couple of times. Did it get worse?"

"Much worse. But let's leave that for another time, okay? We need a place to stay. Just for a short while. I know you're married. That's why it was so difficult to find you."

"You've been looking for me? Well, yeah, I guess that would be pretty impossible. I'm no longer Katrina Montgomery. It's Katrina Swanson now. Married a damn long-haul trucker. Marcus. Fuckin' A, Stell. But he's a gem, Sis. Honestly, he's more a diamond in the rough." Kat laughed again. "Treats me like a fuckin' queen."

Stella smiled. "I'm so happy for you, Kat. And I know this might be too much to ask, and that's okay. I didn't expect—"

"Of course you can stay with us. Don't worry one second about that part. When can you get here?"

Tears coursed down Stella's cheeks as she sighed. "Oh, my God.

That's fantastic. We don't expect much. We'll sleep on the floor. And just until I can get a job and enroll the kids in school. And I can pay you rent and—"

"Will you freaking stop with all that shit. Here's my address. Got a pen?"

"I'm ready. You're in Monarch Bay, right?"

"You got it, babe. 1716 Monarch Lane. How're you gonna get here without Robert following you or finding out about me?"

"There's a huge truck stop near where we live here in Corvallis. I was planning on meeting up with the twins at their lunch break and walking there. I talked to a few of the waitresses, and they're going to help me. Hook me up with one of the long-haul truckers so we can hitch a ride to your place. I'm hoping it all works out. You said Marcus is a long-haul trucker too?"

"Kind of unbelievable, isn't it? Too bad he's not in the area. I could ask him to pick you up. But he's somewhere in Florida right now, so that's not gonna happen. Keep in mind, all truckers are tracked with GPS and they're not allowed to veer off their route. But as long as they get an okay from the company, it's allowed. And they're not paid for the mileage they drive that's not on the way to their destination."

"I'll keep that in mind when I talk to whoever's taking us to your place. I'll want to ask him about that and reimburse him for the mileage. That is so weird. Here I am for the first time in my life looking to hook up with a long-haul trucker to take me to your house, where I'll meet another trucker, who's your husband. Life can't be more unpredictable."

"Man, I've missed you, Stella. I guess I'll see you today or tomorrow then?"

Stella swiped the tears from her cheeks as she gazed out the window at her favorite view. It would be the last time she'd ever see the garden in her front yard. All the time and effort she'd put into planting rose bushes and geraniums. And the willow tree. How she'd miss that. But all that didn't matter. She and the twins would soon be free. Maybe she could do some gardening at her sister's place.

"It'll probably be tomorrow, Kat. However long it takes, the minute that truck leaves the truck stop, we'll be free. I'll call you when we get there. I love you."

"I love you too, Sis. And I can't wait to see you and the kids. We'll have a blast."

Stella closed the burner phone and stuffed it in the side pocket of her jeans. She'd packed quite a few things in the backpack she purchased months ago on sale. By this evening, the three of them would be sitting in an eighteen-wheeler with another man—ha! Screw you, Robert. She grinned. I'm finished doing your bidding, you shit. Freedom, here I come! Better yet, freedom here "we" come.

She had only a short time to wait until she walked to Corvallis High School to meet up with the twins. Then they'd be on their way to the truck stop on the outskirts of Corvallis, where she planned to hang out until her waitress friends hooked them up with the long-haul trucker. They'd told her most of them were on their way to California anyway, and Stella hoped they'd be able to hitch a ride all the way south along to Highway 1 and make it to Monarch Bay without having to hitch another ride.

One waitress in particular, Maisie, told Stella there shouldn't be any problem. A good majority of the truckers drove from the state of Washington to the Port of Los Angeles, and the waitress was sure one of them wouldn't mind making a detour off Highway 5 to Highway 1 along the Central Coast of California. Stella was prepared to offer a good sum of money for that detour. She'd be saving a ton of money by not taking a plane, train, or bus, and she'd been hiding cash and change for years.

This was going to be the trip of a lifetime.

At 11:30 Stella grabbed her backpack, patted her front pants pocket to make sure she had the burner phone, walked to the front door and turned.

"This is it. I won't miss you, house. You hold too many bad memories for me to reminisce fondly about all the years I've spent under your roof." She glanced around at the potted plants she'd so tenderly taken care of for years, stretched out her hand to fondle the homemade crisp, white lace curtains covering the front room window. She listened to the hum of the heater that always kept it so toasty during the interminably wet, cold weather that pervaded every inch of this town. She wouldn't miss that part either.

"Monarch Bay, here we come," she whispered, turned and walked out the front door. She wondered what Robert would think when he found the house empty when he arrived home. He'd probably suspect she'd hustled to the grocery store to pick up something special to make for his dinner. Not!

Maybe after an hour he'd begin calling her cell phone. Perhaps, depending on where he was sitting, he'd hear the special ring tone he'd set—"Chances Are," by Johnny Mathis, on her cell phone. Then he'd rush through the back door, trying to locate the phone. He'd wonder where the hell she would have gone and why she wasn't answering his calls. His temper would begin to simmer, almost reaching the boiling point.

And if he found her cell phone, he'd know. He'd have to know she'd buried it on purpose, but he'd still ask himself why. Why would Stella leave the wonderful life he'd created for her and the kids? They had every amenity possible—a nice house, clothes on their backs, food in their stomachs. What more would a wife and kids expect? He was such a self-centered idiot!

When the twins didn't walk in the door before five o'clock, anger would take precedence over confusion as to their whereabouts. He would have absolutely no idea what was going on or what had happened to them. That would irritate the crap out of him. He'd toy with the idea they'd been in a car accident. Then he'd realize Stella's car stood in the driveway, and there was no reason for her to go for a walk or go anywhere for that length of time. And that didn't account for where the kids were at five o'clock either. He'd be very bewildered and pissed off. Surely not deeply concerned about their welfare, that's for sure. The narcissist!

And, oh boy, Robert was a classic narcissist through and through. The most important person in his life was himself. And keeping her with him meant more to him than money or his job or his kids, for that matter. The only reason he'd want the kids was because he knew Stella would never, ever leave them. Robert knew the twins took precedence and importance over him. He knew it. He felt it. And he deeply resented her for that.

Stella wondered how long it would take before he phoned the police. He'd wonder if perhaps Stella had explained what was going on that evening and he'd simply forgotten. With that uppermost in his mind, he'd probably have a drink. His first drink. And not just any drink. Certainly not a carbonated drink or fruit juice or sparkling water. He'd grab a tall glass that held ten to twelve ounces, fill it to the top with his favorite, and also very expensive, Scotch, and guzzle it down in less than a half-hour. By the time seven o'clock rolled around he'd be so sloshed he wouldn't be able to see straight.

After his second ten ounces of Scotch, he'd fall asleep in front of the television until the next morning. And when he awoke he'd know. Oh, yes, he'd know. Nothing had befallen Stella and Gabriel and Loreen. If they'd been in a car accident, someone would have called him. The truth would hit him like a hammer.

Stella had left him. Finally.

And he knew goddamn well why too.

Chapter Seven

Stella, Gabriel, and Loreen practically skipped to the truck stop on the outskirts of Corvallis. All three of them talked about what an exciting journey this was going to be. None of them had ever been passengers in an eighteen-wheeler, had never taken such a long drive either—783 miles. So very, very far away from home to… what? Their new home in Monarch Bay, California.

"How long has Aunt Kat lived in Monarch Bay, Mom?" Gabriel asked.

"You know, Hon, I have no clue. Your aunt and I stopped talking about ten years ago and—"

"Why's that?" Loreen interrupted.

Stella sheltered her eyes with the palm of her hand and gazed down the road. "We're almost there, guys. The truck stop's right ahead."

"Yeah, Mom, why haven't you talked to your only sister for ten years?" Gabe added.

Stella paused, giving a few seconds of thought to whether she should diss their father or let them harbor a smidgeon of false gratitude for Robert having gone to work every day of his life "to put food on the table and clothes on their backs"—Robert's words. Or should she be honest with them? After all, they were seventeen years old. They'd turn eighteen before graduation—too young to be mollycoddled, as Robert would say.

But in this instance, Stella felt she owed them the truth. They were definitely old enough to handle the truth. So she made up her mind to stop hiding the excruciating honesty she owed them about her life with their dad. As hard as it was going to be to tell them the sordid details, it would be harder for them to understand this violent shift in living situations, if Stella didn't own up to how difficult it had been to have Robert as her husband for almost twenty years.

Actually that wasn't totally true. He was a perfect gentleman and partner for the first… oh, year or so—until the twins were born. Stella knew it had been hard on Robert. They never really had a "honeymoon phase" due to the fact they married soon after Stella discovered she was pregnant. He never got over the fact it would never be "just us"," at least not until *after* the kids left the house. And with the financial times being what they were in the U.S., the twins weren't going anywhere anytime soon.

So, over the years, Robert became more and more disgruntled—more like angry—that it was not just the two of them. And he took all that irritation and rage and anger out on Stella. He began drinking every night, which segued into drinking first then forcing himself sexually on Stella, which segued into drinking, pushing her around, then sexually assaulting her. Which segued into drinking too much, a little slap here and a little slap there, then raping her while she tried her hardest to fight him off. Then one day the backhanded hits and misplaced kicks ended in several visits to the E.R. Until such time as Robert became more proficient in learning how to hurt but not break—bones, that is. A little bruising never killed anyone, he said. And a bloody nose or mild concussion never killed anyone either.

And so it went for the rest of their marriage. Of course there were weeks—well, more like days, if she were honest—when serenity actually flowed through the house. But that was attributable to Stella's unexpected sexual overtures toward Robert, which he found the ultimate turn-on—Stella's way of saving herself from the constant torture. And it would please Robert to no end when Stella farmed out the twins to friends' houses for sleepovers on weekends, which would not only make for a pretty peaceful week prior to the weekend, but the entire weekend itself would be harm-free for Stella's body. Well, as far as bruises were concerned. She'd still have to suffer through Robert forcing himself on her, even when she asked if they could forego having sex for whatever reason Stella made up.

Now Robert would finally understand. Stella hated him enough to want to leave him and not leave any clues as to where she or the twins had gone. He would know Stella had faked interest in him, that she'd done it to make him suffer, all the more knowing that their "happy times" together had been a charade to keep the beatings to a minimum. Oh, would he be outraged.

Which was why Stella had to be very precise and calculating in her plans for leaving. Everything had to be perfect. She would need to cover her tracks in order to pull this off without a hitch. No receipts for anything she'd purchased then hoarded away for months prior to her getaway, no notes or errant scribblings concerning the private investigator, no calls on her cell phone, no bus rides to the truck stop in case the driver could identify Stella and the twins. Nope. Nothing that could lead Robert to Stella or the kids. And the waitresses at the truck stop told Stella it was a common fact, those who worked there, along with the truckers, lived by the mantra "if asked, don't tell." They'd never reveal they'd seen Stella or her kids, no matter who wanted to know. "Lips sealed" was the unwritten rule.

Thank God for television and library books, where Stella learned all she needed to know about how to disappear and not be found.

"So, Mom, what's up with you? We asked you why you didn't talk to Aunt Katrina for ten years."

Stella shook her head free of mental musings over her embarrassingly distasteful life with their father and looked at her two kids. "Your father wouldn't allow it."

"Did you even try to get in touch with her behind his back?" Gabe said.

Stella nodded. "Many times. But your dad always found out. He went through my calls every night. He wouldn't allow me to travel. Other than to the store and back. He checked the odometer! I had no money. I couldn't do much. And I wasn't about to run away and leave the two of you alone with him. He didn't know the first thing about being a father. I had you two to make my life full of happiness. I sure didn't get any happiness from him."

"But that's no life, Mom," Gabe said. "That's sadder than shit."

"Yeah. You deserve better than that." This from Loreen.

"I think I knew that back then… maybe all along. I certainly know it now. He did a fabulous job of making me feel like a piece of… shit. That's the best word for what he did to me over the years. It took me long enough to mastermind a plan that would get both of you two and me out of there and not be found later. I hope I did everything I needed to do to accomplish that."

"Doesn't matter anymore, Mom," Gabe said. "None of us, including you, is ever going back to Corvallis to live with Dad."

"No frickin' way," added Loreen. "We're a team now."

Stella lifted her arm in the air. "To the new Jensen family!"

The three of them laughed as they entered the vast parking lot in front of the Corvallis truck stop, where they entered the Truckers Only Restaurant and took a seat in the nearest booth by the door.

Maisie, the waitress whom Stella had spoken with more than the others, arrived at their table and set three laminated menus in front of them.

Maisie chewed gum like a typical teeny bopper while staring at Stella. "These your kids you been talkin' about?"

Stella grinned. "Yes, this is Gabriel and Loreen. They're twins."

"Coulda figured that out, Stella." She smiled at the twins and grabbed the pencil hidden behind her ear. "What can I getcha? Ya hungry?"

The twins nodded.

"Burger and fries and a coke for both of us," Gabriel said.

Maisie's penciled eyebrows lifted toward her hairline. "You order for your sister all the time, young man? Maybe she wants somethin' different?"

Loreen shook her head. "One of the perks of being a twin, ma'am. I don't need to think for myself. My brother makes all the important decisions for me." She nudged Gabe in the side—hard— with her elbow.

"Jesus, Lo. That hurt." He glanced up at Maisie. "I know what she likes to eat, ma'am. I'm actually being polite by ordering for her."

Maisie shrugged. "Never been around twins before. Guess I'm not too old to learn a thing or two." She nodded at Stella. "Tom's here today. Talked to him already. Matter a' fact, he's goin' from here all the way to San Diego. Ya interested?"

Stella could hardly contain her surprise and good fortune. "Yes, yes, yes. I can't believe it. How did this happen today of all days? Wow!"

"Good things happen to good people, Stella." Maisie pointed the tip of her pencil in Stella's direction. "And you're good people. Told me enough of your story to know how important this is to you and them two kids a' yours." She winked. "And Tom won't say a word to anyone, if'n he was to get asked by a certain party 'bout you or where y'all got dropped off. He ain't much for talkin', mind you, but he's got a heart a' gold. He's happy to take y'all wherever ya wanna go."

Stella stood and wrapped her arms around Maisie.

Maisie stood stock still for several seconds before returning the hug then she pulled back and smiled at Stella. "What'll it be for you, Hon. Don't want the manager breathin' down my neck about talkin' to the customers for too long."

"I'll have the same as the twins." Stella's eyes teared up. "Thank you, Maisie. For everything. You don't know how much this means to all three of us."

Maisie nodded. "I think I have a pretty good idea." She turned to go, took two steps, then turned back around. "And you're more than welcome. I'll let Tom know which table you're at. He's hangin' out in his truck. I'll give him a call. Be right back with your food." She winked and walked away.

Gabe laughed out loud. "What a wacky chick."

"Don't make fun, Gabriel," Stella said.

"I'm not, Mom. I think she's pretty cool. She's the one who has a good heart, doing all this for us."

"Yeah," Lo said. "And she's not related to you or to us, and it's not like she's a close friend of yours, Mom. It's pretty amazing she'd set this up. She's cool."

Stella smiled and looked through the windows at all the gigantic trucks in the parking lot. "I can't wait to meet Tom."

Gabriel and Loreen gazed out the window.

"They're kinda scary," Loreen said. "So big. Can you imagine if you got hit by one of those things? You'd be dead instantly."

"Ni-ice, Lo," Gabe added. "What makes your mind always go to the dark side?"

"That's not what I'm doing, jerk face," Loreen said. "I just mean they're huge. I can't imagine driving something that big down the street. It's like a freaking house on wheels. But with brakes!"

Gabe chuckled. "I'd like to learn how to maneuver one of those things. It'd be fun to party in the container."

Stella shook her head. "Don't even think of asking him to teach you how to shift gears in that monster. All of them in the parking lot are about the same size. It's a wonder they don't crash into each other upon lift-off."

"They're not spaceships, Mom," Gabe added. "It's a freakin' truck. It's meant to be driven by a human being. Why not me?"

Stella stared into her son's eyes. "You heard me, young man. Hands off and don't bug this Tom person. I'm sure he'd love to talk to you about what it's like to be a long-haul trucker, but don't touch anything inside or outside of that thing without asking first."

Gabriel gave Stella a thumbs-up. "Gotcha, Mom. No harassing the trucker. No problem." He smiled.

Maisie arrived with their food and placed their plates in front of them. "Have a nice lunch."

"We should leave her a big tip, Mom," Loreen said. "For hooking us up with someone she knows and trusts."

"I will, honey," Stella replied. "I'll have to send her something nice in the mail, too, posted to this restaurant, so she'll be sure to receive it."

A man about fifty years old with a greyish-white mustache and a short-clipped beard of the same color approached the table, his red button-down shirt tucked into clean blue jeans, cowboy boots clicking on the linoleum. "Afternoon. Name's Tom. Tom Mizerany. You Stella?"

Stella smiled. "Yes, I'm Stella, and this is my son Gabriel and daughter Loreen. Would you like to join us?"

"Don't mind if I do," he said, sliding into the booth next to Loreen. Lo and Gabe scooted closer to their mom on the other side of the table.

"Hear you need a ride to the Central Coast of California. That right?"

Stella nodded. "First, would you like something to eat or drink? My treat."

Tom shook his head. "Just finished my biggest meal of the day. Two chili dogs with fried onions, side of spicy fries, large coke." He rubbed his flat stomach. "I'm fine for now. But thanks for offering."

"It's so nice of you to give all three of us a ride. And yes, we're headed to Monarch Bay. Have you heard of it?"

Tom nodded. "Right on Highway 1, south of Morro Bay, north of Pismo Beach. Both towns are pretty nice. Honest people. Good food in the restaurants. Stopped in both places a couple of times."

"My sister told me, the truckers aren't allowed to drive off their route without permission. I don't want to cause you any trouble with your boss and I'll pay you for your time and any pay you'll lose."

"You don't have to worry about that, ma'am. I'm getting a head start on this trip, so I can meet up with a buddy of mine. Already okayed it with the boss man. After that, I'll head to the Port of Los Angeles. I love driving down the 101 anyway. The 5 is a real boring drive, let me tell you. I'd rather go on the 101 and the 1 any day."

"That's perfect then," Stella said. "We'd love to join you, if you'll have us. And I'll of course pay you for gas, food, and your trouble."

"Awful generous of you," Tom said, winking. "I don't often get offers from young ladies any more. I don't mean that in a weird way. Nice to have company to talk to when I'm driving long hours."

Stella nodded. "I can't imagine driving as much as you do. All alone too. I'm sure after a few hours with the two kids in the back you'll wish you were alone though."

"Possible, I suppose. Doubt it. Got a couple of kids of my own back home. Miss them terribly on these long hauls."

"How many children do you have? What are their ages?"

"Two. Twenty and twenty-two. Wife's passed on. Few years ago. Cancer. Two boys still live with me. Dora, Missouri."

"Bet it's a pretty place to live. It's not a bustling city with too many people and cars and smog and such, right?" Stella said.

"That's right, ma'am. Got married in Dora. Raised the boys in Dora. Love going back there after a long haul. Peaceful."

"I bet," Stella said.

By then they'd finished their meals. Stella dabbed at the corners of her mouth, then put her napkin on her plate. "We're ready to go whenever you are, sir."

Tom glided across the leather seat and stood. "After you. I'll show you all my truck once we walk across the parking lot."

Stella paid for their meal, then hugged Maisie, promising to keep in touch. They crossed the parking lot, the deafening noise of truck engines idling so loud, Stella covered her ears with her hands.

They walked in front of an unbelievably shiny, cherry-red eighteen-wheeler (Stella counted them), where Tom stopped and pointed. "That's my girl. Becca Jane I call her. Had her almost ten years now."

"But she looks brand-new," Stella shouted.

"Could sell her today for more than I bought her for. Let me help you three into the cab, then we'll be on our way."

Stella and Loreen and Gabriel looked at each other.

Gabe chewed at his bottom lip. "How're we supposed to get up there?"

Loreen nodded. "I'll need a freakin' ladder, Mom."

"I'm sure it'll all work out, you two." Stella flipped her hand, moving them along toward the truck's doors. "This will be quite the adventure and I, for one, am looking forward to it."

"Onward and upward, Christian soldiers," Gabe added, chuckling.

Loreen just shook her head and took a deep breath. "I hope so."

Chapter Eight

Stella settled in the front seat and glanced at Gabriel and Loreen in the rear area. "You two comfy back there?"

"That was hella easy," Gabe said.

"I didn't know there'd be steps to get up here," Loreen added. "And I love this bed thing. Can I take a nap?"

"'Course you can. Just put clean sheets on too," Tom said. "That's what it's for. Plenty of room to kick back, listen to those head phone things. Chill… as you young people like to say."

Tom pulled out slowly and entered the freeway about a block from the truck stop.

Stella turned and looked back at the restaurant, saw a man in a suit the exact color and style as Robert's. Hair same color. Walked like him. Goose bumps pricked up and down her arms. She shivered.

Tom turned to her. "You cold? If so, I can turn up the heat."

"No, no. That's okay. I just got a bit of a chill. I thought I saw my husband walking out of the restaurant." She turned back around, saw no one. "I'm just nervous, I guess." She sat up straight, taking it all in. "Wow! It's a smooth ride, Tom. I thought we'd be jostled around with all the shifting gears."

"Automatic. Been driving over thirty years now. Used to drive trucks with the gear shift and such, but no more of that. This is pure luxury."

"I bet it is," Stella said. "So tell me about your truck. Is it yours? The company's? Do you sleep in it every night or drive to a hotel?"

"That's a lot of questions, young lady. But we got plenty of road to cover. Guess I got all the time in the world to answer them."

Stella scanned the inside of the cab. "It's amazing how huge the inside is. I've never seen one of these close-up like this. Neither have the kids." She turned around and found them both with earbuds in, eyes closed, legs crisscrossed, leaning against the back of the cab. Stella smiled. "Well, I guess we're on our way, Tom. I appreciate you taking us. You can't know how very much this means to the three of us."

"Maisie told me a little about your situation. Awful sorry to hear about your husband and all."

Stella tapped him on the forearm. "Tell me more about this truck. That's a much happier subject than my husband Robert."

"Alrighty then." He glanced in both side mirrors and shoved his cap back a few inches off his forehead. "Well, this here's what you call a big rig. Any truck weighs over twenty-six thousand pounds is considered a big rig. Has eighteen wheels, and it's a reefer."

"Isn't a reefer the slang name for a joint?"

Tom laughed out loud. "Yeah, but in this case I got a container filled with milk. Keep it at thirty-four degrees. Nice and cold."

"I didn't know there was such a thing. The outside of the truck says California Long Haul. So you haul other things besides milk?"

"Yes, ma'am. Anything that'll fit in a seventy-five foot container and needs to be kept cold. It's thirteen feet three inches high, so I can make it under the freeway overpass. But I check that anyway, in a little guide I got here, just to make sure."

"Can you imagine what would happen if this was too tall?"

"Seen it happen once or twice. Not a pretty sight. But I got Tom-Tom GPS, so I know where not to drive Becca Jane."

Stella chuckled. "Do all the drivers name their big rigs?"

"I believe so. When you drive the same rig five, ten years, you get sort of attached. Like a car."

"Makes sense. What about a bathroom? Do you shower somewhere? And do you have to pay to stay overnight at the truck stops?"

"There's truck stops all up and down every freeway in the U.S. Most of the time, if I fuel up with more than sixty gallons, I get a free shower. Been to a couple of stops that charge twenty or so bucks to park overnight, but most let us park for free."

"How many gallons of, what, diesel, does this hold?"

"Three hundred gallons. Yep. Diesel. Right now it's going for about three dollars and thirty-one cents a gallon. Company pays for it, though."

"It doesn't seem fair any truck stop would make you pay to stay overnight. America would literally shut down if it weren't for men like you. We wouldn't be able to eat or drink or do most anything without the goods the truckers haul in these big rigs. We'd be lost without you."

Tom nodded and smiled. "Thank you for that, ma'am. That's kind of you to say. Can be a lonely life on the road. But I love it. Wouldn't do anything else, even if I had the choice."

"You obviously enjoy driving and seeing the U.S. I bet you've been to more states than I'll ever have the opportunity to visit."

"Four weeks on the road then maybe five or seven days at home with the boys. Makes for a different life, let me tell you. But I pull in some serious dough. Enough to send my boys to college."

"When your wife was alive, did she ever accompany you on your trips?"

"Back in the day, yes. Then the kids came along, and she couldn't do it any more. Now she's gone, so." He shrugged. "On my own now."

"Well, you must have a lot to talk about when you come home to your sons. You must see a lot of beautiful scenery… and interesting people, right?"

He chuckled. "Sure do."

Stella cleared her throat. "I hope you don't get offended but… I saw a movie once where girls, women, went from truck to truck and they make money by—"

"Sex. That what you're talking about?"

"Yes. Yes, it is. I was just wondering if that really happens. I mean, it sounds so risky and dangerous, especially with all the sexually transmitted diseases and such. Plus, sex trafficking is a really scary thing."

"Never once in my life have I let one of those girls in my rig. They'd be as welcome as a porcupine in a balloon factory. Scares the crap out of me, to think what diseases and such they're all carrying."

A horn honked and Stella jumped half-way out of her seat, twisted her head to look out the window, saw a car exactly like Robert's. Covering her mouth with her hand, she held her breath and squinted, trying to see the license plate.

"Damn fool," Tom grumbled. "Course, he's got a California license plate. Crazier than a crow on a power line."

Stella let out a sigh. Of course, Robert's car had Oregon license plates. Boy, she was more nervous than she thought she'd be. Then again, until she reached Monarch Bay, her stomach would probably be tied up in knots. She'd dreamed of this escape. It was finally happening. But her luck in life had not been that impressive so far. She carried a load of pessimism on her back like a twenty-pound bag of rocks.

Tom continued. "I've seen some of those girls drive off with truckers. Don't know where they're going or what they're doing but you have to be stupider than a cow on a freeway to do something like that."

Stella's eyebrows drew down sharply. "Or badly in need of money to buy food for yourself or your children. I feel sorry for those women. And as far as the young girls are concerned, they must be horribly desperate to go off with some man they don't know."

"Sometimes they're hungry, I suppose. Sometimes it's for drugs. Sad whichever reason it is."

"How's truck stop food anyway? Is it as horrible as I've heard it is? Personally I've only eaten at a truck stop a couple of times in my life."

Tom changed lanes and stepped down on the gas pedal, honked his horn as he passed another truck, waved, and continued in the fast lane. "Food's not too bad. Breakfast is always the best meal, in my opinion. Can't mess up eggs and toast too terribly. Some of the stops have great dinners, though. When you drive as much as me, you know which ones are good."

Stella yawned.

"Boring you?" Tom laughed under his breath.

"No. Not at all. I've discovered there are so many professions most of us know nothing about. It's fascinating to learn what people do for a living, other than the typical nine-to-five jobs."

"What about yourself? Have time to do more than raise those twins back there?" He took a quick glance behind him and chuckled. "What would they do without cell phones?"

Stella shook her head. "Die a sad and lonely death, I would imagine."

They both laughed out loud.

When was the last time she'd laughed? Had it been months?

Years? Certainly a long time since she and Robert had shared a good belly laugh. There wasn't much that was funny about having your face slapped and your stomach kicked with the pointed toe of his shoe.

Stella leaned her head back and stared out the window. "Well, Tom, I haven't had it as bad as many women with…" She glanced back at the twins. Both looked asleep. And she knew for sure they listened to their music so loud, they couldn't possibly hear her. "There are lots of women who live with abusive husbands. Worse off than me, I'm sure. But I have to think of my kids. They deserve better than a father who ignores them and treats their mother badly. And I didn't realize until recently, the twins have been aware of what's been going on."

Tom shook his head and swore under his breath. "Guys like that oughta be shot. If they have to hit something, then go out and join a gym with a punching bag and go for it. Just doesn't make sense to me. If you love someone, why would you treat them like that? And if you don't love her, then get a divorce. Simple as that."

As far as the eyes could see, green pastures went on and on with the occasional herd of cattle. The hum of the truck's engine and the setting rays of the sun lulled her into a calmer state than when she was back at the truck stop. Her dream of freedom looked and smelled divine.

"I don't know. If I had the answers to those questions, maybe I'd understand. And if men like Robert felt the way you think they should feel, there wouldn't be so many of us women around, bruised and battered and feeling like shit." She touched her lips with her fingertips. "I'm sorry. I shouldn't swear. Not very ladylike."

Tom took a quick glance at her and she believed his eyes glistened.

"Sorry you've had to live like that. Even though I don't know you, your story kicks me in the gut. I'm happy to be the one taking you away from him. Makes it all worth it."

"Thank you for saying that. You're a kind man."

She shut her eyes on a sigh. When she next opened them, the lights on the dashboard glowed in the dark. A full moon hung in front of them like a medallion on a chain. She glanced at the clock in the middle of the dash. Eight p.m. Her stomach growled.

"You must be awful tired. You were snoring like a hibernating bear."

Stella sat up, scrubbed at her face with both hands, chuckling. "Sorry about that. I haven't been sleeping well."

"Plan to stop for a late supper. Park for the night. Next truck stop has a clean motel. Kids and you can stay there. I can drop you three off in Monarch Bay tomorrow."

"That sounds fabulous." She leaned around the side of her seat. Both kids still had their earbuds stuffed in their ears, but they were sound asleep. "Loreen. Gabriel. Time to wake up." She reached out and shook Gabe's ankle.

He stirred and lifted his head. "Wassup? We there yet?"

Loreen sat up abruptly. "What the heck?" She glanced around, eyes half shut. "We're in Monarch Bay already?"

"Not until tomorrow. But Tom's going to stop at a truck stop. We can grab a bite to eat or not. Stay at the motel for tonight. Tomorrow will be here before you know it." Stella smiled at her two kids. "I can't wait."

"Me, too, Mom," Gabriel said, glancing at his sister.

"I am, too, Mom," Loreen grinned. "You finally did it."

Stella nodded, let out a deep breath, glanced back at the twins, their earbuds already back in place. She smiled.

"Don't worry about me opening my mouth to anyone who'd ask me about you and your kids." He made a gesture of zipping his lips with his finger. "I never saw the three of you."

"Thank you for that, Tom." Stella stared at her hands clenched in her lap. "I still can't believe we're actually in a big rig, hurtling toward a new future for the three of us. I'm still worried Robert will find us. That I didn't cover my tracks or that I missed something that will lead him to us."

"You have your own money? A phone he can't trace? Somewhere to stay after I drop you off?"

"Yes on all counts. We had a joint savings account. Not much in it, but I withdrew all of it today. I have a burner phone he knows nothing about. And we'll be staying with my sister in Monarch Bay." She grabbed her purse from the console between them. "I want to pay you for gas and your dinner this evening."

Tom patted her hand. "No need to do that. I'm going to take a bit of a break in L.A. after I drop you off, so it's not like I wasn't going to travel this road anyway. Save your money, because if you don't already have a job lined up, prices in Cali are through the roof. Costs a bunch to live there, let me tell you. My friend I'll be visiting? He tells me how much housing and groceries cost in this state? Woo-eee! Glad I don't live here."

Stella swooped her head from side to side, gazing out the windshield. "We're already in California?"

"Crossed the border hours ago. You were sleeping, remember?"

"You're right. Geez. This rig really can go far in a short amount of time."

"Straight freeway the whole way. No traffic to speak of this time of night." Tom chewed on his bottom lip with his top teeth, looking serious. "Sorry about your husband, ma'am. Woman like you? I don't mean anything by saying this, but you're a beautiful gal. Got a nice personality too. He's gotta be some fool to treat you bad like you told me."

"Thank you for the compliment. I struggle sometimes, you know? Wondering if I bring it upon myself? That I say or do things that irritate him and make him treat me the way he does… or did."

"Don't matter if you did irritate him, ma'am. No one hits a woman for no good reason… or bad reason. It's not right. Lord didn't put you on this earth to be a man's punching bag. You're the delicate side of our species, meant to be taken care of, loved, treated with kindness for everything you do for us. Cooking and cleaning and having babies." He gestured with his thumb behind him. "Those two seem like good kids too. Something to be real proud of, if I was your husband. Sounds like he's got a screw loose, if you were to ask me. Which you didn't."

"I appreciate you saying it. And it makes me feel a bit better to hear it too. Thank you, Tom."

He pointed straight ahead. "Next stop right up there."

"The kids and I will check into the motel and maybe have dinner once we get settled in." She took a quick look at the twins. She motioned for them to take their earbuds out. "We appreciate you taking us to Monarch Bay." She nodded to her children.

"Thank you," Gabriel said. "You saved our asses."

"Gabriel!" Stella shook her head.

Tom chuckled. "You're welcome, son."

"Thank you," Loreen added, digging her elbow in Gabe's side. "You really helped us out of a bad situation."

Tom nodded. "It's nothing."

"Oh, it's something," Loreen said. "I don't know how Mom did all this, but here we are." She gazed out the side window. "California," she whispered. "Never thought I'd be living here. Cool."

"Fasho," Gabe said. "Can't wait to get a skateboard, yo. Supposed to be real sunny."

"That it is, boy. Been visiting around Central and Southern Cali for years. Sun's always shining, even when it's cold."

Tom pulled into the truck stop and parked. The four of them made their way down the stairs.

"What time should we meet you here at the truck tomorrow morning?"

"Plan on leaving around seven in the morning. After breakfast. Suit you?"

"We'll have breakfast here at six, if they're open," Stella said.

"Open twenty-four hours a day. I eat around that time too." He tipped the brim of his baseball cap. "Sleep well. They serve a good dinner here too."

Stella glanced at the twins. "Maybe we'll catch a bite in a bit. I'm exhausted. Maybe we'll just snack and go to bed a little early."

The kids were both fiddling with their phones.

Tom walked toward the restaurant, waving as he departed.

Stella's head popped up and she gasped. "Oh. My. God." She stretched her hand out. "Both of you. Give me your phones." She grabbed Gabriel's out of his hand. Loreen gave up her phone willingly.

Loreen's eyebrows drew down in a vee. "What's wrong, Mom?"

Gabe squinted. "Yeah, what's up with taking our phones, Mom?"

"I have a burner phone so your father won't know where we are or where we're going or anything. He can't track a burner phone. But I forgot about your two phones."

Loreen shook her head. "I totally didn't think about that."

"Shit," Gabe mumbled.

"He's probably already pinged both your phones. God, I'm stupid. I was so intent on not leaving any tracks so he could find us, I forgot about your phones too. Stupid, stupid, stupid." Tears rolled down Stella's cheeks.

"It's not too late, Mom," Gabe said. "Give me both phones. I'll stomp on both of them, then throw them in the trash." He took both phones out of Stella's hands and walked to the big green dumpster at the side of the restaurant. It took only a few minutes for him to crush them with his shoe and dispose of them.

"But he can see where we are if he pinged them before you stepped on them," Stella said.

"*If* he already did that, Mom," Loreen said. "Or he might have gotten so drunk, he's passed out on the couch in the front room, asleep. Then he'll try tomorrow, and it'll be too late."

Stella stared at the ground, shaking her head. "God, what is wrong with me? Forgetting that is just—"

"Come on, Mom," Loreen said. "We'll be on our way by tomorrow at seven in the morning. Let's just cross our fingers and hope he lives up to his reputation and he's blitzed right now."

"He'll figure it out tomorrow morning," Gabe said. "But it'll be too late to ping our phones by then."

Loreen turned to her brother. "And he won't necessarily drive all the way to California looking for us. He won't have any idea where we're headed. I think he would have tried calling you or me by now, Gabe." Loreen turned to her brother. "Did he call you?"

Gabe shook his head. "Looked at my phone. No calls."

"And he can't call Mom, cause she only has her burner phone," Loreen said. "And he didn't phone me."

"You're probably right, Loreen," Stella said. "There's nothing to be done now anyway. Once we're on the road again tomorrow morning, it'll be too late for him to find us." She glanced at her burner phone. "Not too many hours before we leave here. Let's check in, get some rest, and hope for the best."

With Gabe on one side of her and Loreen on the other, she made her way to the motel office.

Chapter Nine

Stella allowed the twins to go to the restaurant and order take-out which they brought back to the room. They watched a horror movie for an hour and a half and Stella fell into a deep sleep, waking with a start at five a.m. The twins were still sound asleep, and no one had knocked on their door. She showered and dressed, and by that time Loreen and Gabe were awake and ready to leave. The three grabbed their backpacks and walked the short distance to the restaurant next door. Tom sat in a large booth, giving them a little wave as they entered.

Stella explained about the phone problem and Robert's penchant for pinging their cell phones. She ended with their speculating he probably got drunk and fell asleep, but they had to get out of there soon after breakfast.

"Service here's quick as a snapping turtle. We'll be outta here in twenty minutes. Don't worry your head about it, ma'am. I think it'll all work out."

"From your lips to God's ears," Stella said, then let out a breath.

Tom patted her hand. "Eat a good solid breakfast." He glanced at the twins. "You too. Then we're outta here."

Thirty minutes later, the tension in Stella's stomach lessened as Tom pulled out of the truck stop. Once they entered the freeway, the rumble of the truck's engine and the soft music of the radio lured Stella into a meditative state. She sighed and shut her eyes, hoping to take a short nap, dream of Monarch Bay—what it would look like, the sunny weather ahead, seeing her sister for the first time in years. She smiled.

Stella catnapped for most of the final leg of the trip. They took a short break and stopped at a cafe to pick up sandwiches and colas, then ate in the truck, arriving in Monarch Bay at three o'clock.

Tom pulled into a small grocery store parking lot, letting the truck idle as he turned to Stella and the kids. "I want to wish you all good luck in your new home. Been a pleasure meeting you. If you ever need a ride back to Oregon, just let Maisie know. She'll get in touch with me."

Stella shook his hand. "You're a kind man, Tom, and we appreciate what you've done by taking us here. You're our savior."

He blushed, and Stella grinned, then flicked his baseball cap gently with her finger. "You pretend to be so tough, but you've got a heart of gold inside there," she said, pointing at this chest.

"Geez, ma'am. You're making me blush. Now go on outta here."

The kids thanked him, and they stepped down from the rig and waved goodbye. Stella watched Tom slowly make his way back to the freeway entrance, then she grabbed her phone.

"I told your Aunt Katrina I'd text her when we arrived. She'll pick us up as soon as she has a break."

"Can Lo and I walk over to that place across the street and get a Boba drink?" Gabe pointed to the little store in a strip mall.

Loreen bobbed up and down on her tip-toes. "Please, Mom. We've got our own money."

Stella smiled. It seemed her two kids were in better moods already. Back at home they normally were rather morose, especially if Robert was around. She'd done a good thing, escaping like this. Sometimes running away from your problems was a bad thing. Stella knew that. How many times had she pleaded with Robert to go to marriage counseling. She'd loved him once. Back in the day. But this? Running away like this was definitely a good decision.

"I'll sit right here, under this tree. Go get your Boba drinks. I'll watch you from here. I'll just sit and enjoy being outside. And, hey, don't ever separate. Stick together. Just in case. None of us has ever been here before."

"Gotcha, Mom," Gabe said.

Loreen nodded.

Stella sat beneath a tall tree with tons of shade, faced the Boba cafe where the kids were headed, laughing and running across the street. She suddenly realized it was as quiet here as it was on the block where they lived. Past tense. Where they once lived.

She glanced up when she heard a tiny chirp. A small nest sat cradled amongst the leaves about six feet above her. Two small heads popped up over the side of the nest, which couldn't have been bigger than a matchbox.

"A hummingbird," Stella whispered. "An omen." Once upon a time a hummingbird made a nest on the side of their front porch in Corvallis. There'd been a red hook made for hanging a plant on the ceiling, and one morning Stella noticed pieces of what looked like cotton and little twigs surrounding the hook. After several days the cotton and twigs morphed into a nest, and the mother hummingbird spent most of her day flying back and forth from the nest to somewhere. Stella guessed she was searching for food for her babies.

One day, once the mother bird had left, Stella pulled a short ladder over to the hook and peeked over the side. Two itsy-bitsy baby birds looked up at her, their little mouths opening and closing, opening and closing. Stella had jumped down from the ladder, knowing the momma bird would be returning soon. Sure enough, she flew to the nest with what looked like an insect of some sort dangling from her beak. Meal time!

Stella closed her eyes, vividly recalling that day. She held a few good memories from living in Corvallis. It hadn't all been bad. She'd met Robert in Monterey soon after both Fiona and Nason—her and Katrina's foster parents—had passed away. Fiona and Nason had been in love with each other since the day they'd met. They decided to become foster parents, and Stella and Katrina were their first "children." Stella was fifteen and Katrina, ten. Of course, the two girls missed their natural parents, but Clark and Rosemary Montgomery had had an odd marriage, as opposed to the warm and loving marriage Fiona and Nason shared.

Clark and Rosemary had died in a boating accident off the Monterey coast, leaving the two girls without parents at a crucial time in their growth. Not that there was ever a good time for parents to pass away. Stella was old enough to know what was really going on. Kat? Not so much. And the disappointment was astounding. After hearing her father on the phone telling another woman he loved her, Stella figured it out. Which led her to wonder if all marriages—or most of them—were like her mom and dad's. How sad! In the movies it was always "Till death do us part," and Stella realized that was all a fantasy, like a Hollywood movie—for entertainment purposes only, not the truth.

Just as her own marriage had been a fantasy—or rather, a nightmare. Although in Stella's case till death do us part would have come true one day or another. The beatings had escalated year after year. She was afraid one day he'd knock her out and she'd never wake up. She tried to keep peace by doing everything right. But Robert would constantly fabricate something and blame her for not doing what he'd specifically asked her to do.

Everything was always her fault. He blamed her for the tiniest things no "normal" person would even bat an eye at, like the color of his toast. It was a bit too brown on one side. The toaster had malfunctioned, she guessed, and she hadn't noticed a slight differentiation in shading from one side to the other. Oh… my… God. Disastrous!

On that morning, thank the Lord, the kids had already left for school. Robert grabbed Stella by her pony tail, her feet slipped out from under her on the linoleum, and she landed on her bottom on the floor, smashing the back of her head on the ground. She'd seen stars, then everything went black. Next she knew she felt him inside her, and when she looked around they were in their bedroom having sex. Well, that wasn't exactly the right word. Rape would be the correct term. It wasn't making love, that's for sure. That hadn't happened in a long time. The love Stella once felt for Robert had dropped by the wayside after the second or third time he'd slapped her around for some ridiculous, silly reason that only made sense to someone who had mental problems.

Stella guessed from the get-go marriage counseling would have been a charade. Robert needed more than "sharing his feelings" in therapy. He needed some serious behavior modification. Along with medication. No one who truly loved and cherished their spouse got gratification from physically and mentally abusing her month after month, year after year. Stella grew to hate him and knew she had to get out. But it had taken years to mastermind a plan, and even then she'd messed up with her kids' cell phones.

That was not the only thing she'd screwed up. She'd obviously failed in the marriage department and hadn't picked the "right one." Sometimes it seemed she screwed up constantly. Maybe Robert had been right. She *was* a screw-up. Although she didn't deserve to be beaten because of it. Couldn't he have approached her and talked to her kindly about all the things he wanted her to change. She would have done her best to make him happy.

But talking wasn't his style. He got his point across with his hands and his feet. Not with words. How had she gotten herself into such a horribly dysfunctional marriage? She only had herself to blame for *that* mistake. So, yes, maybe she was a fuck-up, as the twins often used that term. Call it like it is, she guessed. Maybe Robert was right.

Chapter Ten

"Mom. Mom," Loreen said.

Stella jerked her head in the direction of her daughter's voice.

Gabe grasped Stella's hand. "What're you doing, Mom?"

"Sorry. Sorry." Stella shook her head. "I was daydreaming." She pointed. "Look at the hummingbird nest. Just like the one we had on our porch that year. Remember?"

Loreen and Gabe both shaded their eyes with their hands and stared up into the tree.

"Yeah, I see her," Loreen whispered. "She's beautiful."

"Are there babies?" Gabriel asked.

"Two of them," Stella answered. "And the momma bird has flown back and forth a couple of times since I've been sitting here, searching for food for her babies."

"Did you call Aunt Kat?" Gabe asked her.

"Dang it!" Stella grabbed her phone and began writing a text to her sister.

Loreen sat beside Stella and put her arm around her shoulders. "Are you okay, Mom?"

"Space cadet!" Gabe said, laughing.

Stella gave him "the eye." "Just reminiscing. Gimme a break. I didn't sleep very well last night."

Loreen rubbed Stella's back. "Leave her alone, Gabe." She gave her brother a look that said he'd better not mess with Stella—one eyebrow cocked upward and her lips drawn in a straight line.

Gabe looked immediately contrite. "Sorry, Mom. I was just kidding. I didn't mean anything by calling you a space cadet."

Stella reached out to her son, held onto his hand and squeezed. "Don't worry, baby. I know you weren't trying to hurt my feelings." She held up her burner phone. "Let me finish texting Kat."

The twins sat down with their Boba drinks, sucking on their straws. Stella finished texting, then pressed the send button. And waited.

It only took a minute for her sister to respond.

"You're only a couple of minutes from my house. Go left at the corner which is Sand Lane—toward the ocean—turn right on Monarch Lane. Number 1716. I left a key in the potted plant to the left of the front door. I pushed it down into the dirt on the right side of the plant. Easy peasy. See you in a couple of hours. Make yourself at home. Love you all."

Stella smiled and stood. "Let's go. She lives not too far from here. She said it's a short walk. She'll be home a little later."

The two kids nodded, walking next to Stella as she followed Kat's directions. In less than five minutes Stella saw 1714 and knew the next house was her sister's.

In a few feet a beautiful Craftsman home came into view, and Stella let out a sigh. "It's so beautiful. Look at the pergola, the flowers, the stone walkway leading to the front door."

"The front yard's bigger than ours back in Corvallis," Loreen said.

Gabe pushed on the latch of a three-foot high gate and walked underneath the trellis. "Hope it's got enough room for all of us."

Stella nodded. "Maybe she has an extra room we can share."

Gabe frowned. "The three of us? Are you kidding, Mom?"

"Beggars can't be choosers, Gabriel." Stella put her arm around his shoulders and squeezed. "It's not forever. Just until I can secure gainful employment."

"We're gonna enroll in Monarch High school or something?" Loreen asked.

Stella smiled at her daughter. "As soon as possible." Stella bent over, poked her finger in the plant pot and pulled out a key. She wiped the dirt from the grooves and inserted it into the keyhole and turned. The latch opened, and she swung the door wide.

Gabe entered before them. A short hallway led into a good-sized front room to the left with a fireplace on the far wall and a huge glass window looking out onto the front yard garden. A curved doorway led to a nice kitchen with windows all around and a work place in the middle with a granite top and sink, a kitchen table to the side with plenty of room to hang out and eat meals. The stove and refrigerator lined the wall, and at the rear was a sliding glass door leading to the backyard.

Stella slid the door open, and her jaw dropped. A huge redwood deck stood between the door and yards and yards of dark green grass. A fountain sat in the middle of the yard, water trickling down two-tiers, making a soothing, tinkling sound in the balmy afternoon air. A barbecue, picnic table, and numerous chairs with pillowed seats graced the deck.

Suddenly a deep "woof" echoed through the air. Stella's gaze shot to her right, where a huge chocolate lab danced toward them, wiggling his butt, making him look like a worm on a fishing line.

Loreen and Gabe bent low to the ground, hands out to pet him.

Loreen grasped his muzzle and kissed his nose. "What's your name, boy?"

Gabriel fiddled with the dog's collar. "It says Remy, and there's a phone number." He ran his hand down the dog's back, and Remy licked Gabe's face. "Hey dude! His fur is hot. He must have been lying in the sun."

"Your aunt and I always wanted a dog, but when we were young our mom was allergic. Then when we moved to Fiona and Nason's house, they didn't have room for another dog. They had a chihuahua. Who was cute but growled and snapped at everyone." Stella knelt on the deck and reached out her arms and hugged Remy to her chest. "This guy's a love, don't you agree? He came to us immediately."

"He must know we're related."

Stella stood and swung around. "Kat," she whispered.

Her sister stood in the doorway, looking not that much different than the last time Stella had seen her. Short, thin, with cropped white hair and dark black roots, a silver nose ring on one nostril, a smile that reached from ear to ear with the straightest teeth like those in a toothpaste commercial. God, Kat was beautiful.

Katrina rushed toward Stella and engulfed her in her arms, squeezing tightly. "I've missed you, Stell. So much." She leaned back and perused Stella's body from the top of her head to her toes. "Same gorgeous long auburn hair, hazel eyes, pink lipstick, big boobs!" She laughed. "You're a looker. Always were." She lowered her voice. "And way too good for that asshole Robert."

Stella smiled and shook her head side to side. "You never change, Kat. And you are the same beauty you were way back when. I love your hair. Always have. It's totally you. Kind of hippy California, I guess you'd call it."

Kat pointed to the round picnic table. "Sit down. I'll get you something to drink. But I want to at least talk to my niece and nephew for a second before you and I get down and dirty."

Loreen and Gabriel appeared a bit shy. They sat next to each other, across the table from their aunt, sipping their Boba drinks, quiet, reserved. But they hadn't seen their Aunt Kat in ten or so years, which meant the twins had been seven years old.

Kat stood, hands on hips. "You two are drinking," she tilted her head to read the side of the cups, "Boba? I've had that before. It was really the weirdest drink I've ever had. All those squishy round balls of tapioca. But it's probably good for you. Better than drinking colas or that drink uber popular in Appalachia. What's it called?"

"Mountain Dew," Gabriel said. "But, hey. It's popular in all the high schools too. Lo loves it. Don'tcha, Lo?" He nudged her with his elbow.

Loreen nudged him back even harder. "Stop it, will you?" She glanced at her mother. "Will you make him stop, Mom?"

Stella closed her eyes and smiled. "Oh, the joys of having twin teenagers."

"Would you like something to drink, Stell?" Kat said. "I've got sparkling water, soft drinks, coffee, you name it."

"I'd love some sparkling water, Kat. I'm kind of thirsty."

Katrina made her way to the kitchen, and Stella looked at the twins. "Is this okay? Are you two all right with staying here with your Aunt Kat?"

They both nodded, sipping their drinks, not saying a word.

"Then why are you being so quiet?"

Gabriel set his cup on the table. "I'm just really tired. Plus it kinda just hit me. I don't have any friends, yo. I'm a senior in high school, and I just left everyone I've been hanging out with for almost four years."

Loreen put her arm around her brother's shoulders. "Totally. I didn't get a chance to even see Natalie. She's my best friend, and now I'll never be able to talk to her again. It's really weird, Mom."

Katrina set a glass of sparkling water in front of Stella and took a seat at the picnic table. "What did I miss?"

Stella patted Kat's forearm. "The kids are already missing their friends. I knew this would happen, but, really, I didn't have a choice." She leaned her forehead in the palm of her hand. "I'm sorry, Loreen… Gabe. I didn't want this new life for you. But-"

"Mom, you gotta be shittin' me," Gabe murmured. "We get it. Right, Lo?"

"Of course." Loreen grasped her mother's hand. "We love you, and neither of us wanted to live with Dad anymore. You know that. We don't say this stuff to make you feel bad. You did the right thing."

Gabe nodded. "The only thing you could do, Ma. I mean, you don't think Lo and I knew he busted your lip a bunch of times and slapped your face? We saw the bruises."

"I know you tried to hide them." Loreen glanced at her brother, then back at her mom. "We might only be seventeen, but we knew. As much as you tried to hide it, me and Gabe talked about what we could do to help. But we couldn't think of anything. You never talked about it, and we'd never confront Dad. We were scared he'd beat on us too."

Stella dropped her hand from her forehead. A lone tear dripped down her face. She swiped at it with her fingers. "I didn't want you to know. I didn't want anyone to know. I didn't have anyone to talk to about it. Your father monitored my every move. He called me several times a day to make sure of my whereabouts. He looked at every receipt to make sure what I was buying with *his* money. He wouldn't let me work, so I had nothing of my own." She covered her face with her hands. "I'm weak and didn't have the guts to stand up for myself."

Remy walked over to Stella, nudged her elbow with his nose.

Stella glanced down and laid her hand on his head. He whined, lifted his head and nudged her again.

"He knows you're upset, Stella," Kat said. "I've never been around a dog who's so empathetic. I swear to God, he can tell whenever I'm having a bad day."

Stella cradled Remy's muzzle in her hand, leaned down and kissed him on his furry cheek. "You're a good boy, Remdog."

Remy licked her chin and face and Stella chuckled. He plopped down on the floor next to her with his head draped over one of her feet.

Katrina curled her hand around her sister's forearm to get her attention then looked her in the eyes. "You're not weak, Stella. Look around. You're here in Monarch Bay, aren't you? That took a lotta balls to get up and leave that asshole behind. Don't ever put yourself down again, Big Sista. I didn't know this was going on, obviously. But now that I do, I… I can't believe it, Stella.

"You must have been so afraid. And for good reason. That fear held you back. He was abusing you. And maybe mind-fucking you as well. Excuse my language, Loreen and Gabe, but it's true. Emotional and physical abuse can fuck a person up, big time."

Kat swiped away the tears on her sister's cheeks. "You're brave and you're strong, Stella. But, you know, it might be a good thing for you to see a therapist. I see a really good one every week. She's helped me a lot with the issues we probably both have with regard to our parents' marriage. Maybe not as horrible as what Robert did to you, but I think Mom was scared of Dad in some ways, you know? Scared of him leaving her. And we both know he lied to her, so there was a trust issue goin' on there. "

"What're you guys talking about?" Loreen said.

"Yeah, which parents?" Gabe chimed in. "The real ones or Fiona and Nason?"

Kat's face flushed. "I'm sorry, guys. I really spoke out of turn about our parents' marriage. It's not my place to reveal family secrets. You two aren't my children. That's your mom's job, if she chooses to tell you anything about our real mom and dad."

Stella leaned over and hugged Katrina. "I never said anything to them since they were so young. I just didn't think it was necessary to discuss."

"And you don't have to do that now either." Kat covered her face with her hands for a few seconds. "Just because I opened my big mouth doesn't mean you have to *do* anything about it. I'm sorry. Sometimes I speak before I think."

Stella chuckled. "You were always more outspoken than me. You'd never have stayed with a man like Robert for more than two seconds. I should say, you'd have left after the first slap across your face. But me?" She shook her head, then took a sip of water. "I'm an idiot."

Kat grasped Stella's hand. "No. You. Are. Not. And that's why you should see a therapist. Someone who could help you out with some of the similar issues Mom had to deal with in their marriage."

"Hey!" Gabe interjected. "What is it me and Lo aren't supposed to know?"

"Yeah," Loreen said. "I feel like an outsider in my own family, since our real grandma and grandpa died before we got to know them. It's *not* like we're gonna be devastated by anything you tell us."

Stella grabbed a napkin and dabbed at her cheeks. "You're right. I should have said something long ago." She turned to Kat. "We can tell them now, can't we?"

"Your call," Kat said.

Stella cleared her throat. "Our parents had an odd relationship. Dad travelled all over the country. He took care of jewelry sales for the southern California franchises of Bonfaire Jewelry stores. He'd be gone for weeks at a time. And Mom was left at home and… she didn't enjoy being a single mom. It wasn't what she signed up for. At least that's what I heard her say many times."

Katrina sat up straight. "She'd say that over and over during their never-ending arguments after our father returned from his trips. And the arguments were always followed by mumbled conversations where your mom thought our father must have explained everything and our Mom must have trusted he was telling her the truth, because the days following were filled with roses and candy and kisses and date nights. It was scary for your mom and me. We didn't understand what was going on."

Stella sighed. "Both Kat and I were afraid they'd get a divorce. And back in those days we'd have been pariahs at our school. People in our community didn't get divorced willy-nilly like they do these days. The divorce rate wasn't as high then as it is now."

Kat folded her hands on the table. "Your mom's right. And one day your mom heard our father on the phone saying something like 'I love you, baby," and he wasn't talking to our mother. So he was cheating on her. But we couldn't do anything about it. We had to keep our mouths shut because Dad had obviously convinced mom he was being true to her whenever he was away." Kat waved her hand as if swatting a fly. "Anyway, we were both scared they'd get a divorce and we'd have to live at two different houses and we'd never be a family ever again. Everyone in town would be looking down on us." She glanced at Stella. "Then…"

Stella continued the story. "Then one evening they had a huge row… again… Mom confronted Dad about this other woman. I remember it clearly. She, too, heard him on the phone with someone else. Our dad admitted what he'd done, swore it happened only once and would never happen again."

"Until it did," Kat interrupted.

Stella nodded. "Yeah, until it did. Over and over again." She shrugged. "So their marriage was on the rocks way before they both died."

"What a sad story," Loreen whispered.

"Yeah," Gabe said. "That's messed up."

"How'd they die?" Loreen said.

Stella glanced at Kat and nodded.

Kat cleared her throat. "They went out with a friend of theirs on a boat, and the fog came in fast. That's how it was explained to us. And their boat ran into another boat that I guess had GPS but it had broken." She stared at the table.

Stella continued. "And their bodies washed onto shore the next day. It was absolutely devastating for your aunt and me."

Kat and Stella looked at each other.

Katrina swiped at her eyes. "Then we had the most fortunate thing happen to us, right, Stella?"

Stella sniffed then smiled. "Fiona and Nason Dominguez fostered the two of us. And I've never seen two people as kind-hearted and sweet and loving in my life."

"We were lucky," Kat added. "Very lucky." She smiled at Stella.

Stella nodded. "They had been in love with each other since the day they'd met, pulling broccoli in the fields of Salinas. They'd both come from Mexico in their teens and worked hard and long before Nason secured a job as a journeyman electrician after studying in the program for several years. He ended up making more money than he ever dreamed possible and immediately asked Fiona to marry him." She turned to Kat.

Kat sighed. "Then Fiona and Nason moved from Salinas to Monterey, bought a small house, and settled down to have kids. Which never happened, for whatever reason. They decided to become foster parents, and Stella and I were their first 'children.'" Kat stood.

"Yup," Stella said. "I was fifteen and Katrina was ten." Her eyes glistened. "Fiona died suddenly one day of a brain aneurysm at sixty-nine, and Nason passed away a few months later of a heart attack. In my mind, yes, it was a heart attack, but I believe it was brought on by loneliness." Stella got up and put her arm around Kat's waist. "And that's the story. The end."

"Wow!" Gabe and Loreen said at once.

"Are you mad I didn't say anything until now?" Stella asked.

Loreen and Gabe shook their heads.

"Pizza for dinner tonight?" Katrina said.

Gabe and Loreen nodded. "Sure," they said at the same time.

"Holy shit," Kat muttered. "Twins."

Stella walked over to her kids, put her arms around both of them and squeezed. "I love you two more than life itself. And I'm hoping and praying that our new lives here will be happy and full of positivity."

Gabe smirked. "Heav-y, Mom."

"Yeah, Mom." Loreen glanced up at Stella. "Positivity, man."

"Children shouldn't make fun of their mother," Kat said with a grin. "My therapist talks about positivity and all kinds of woo-woo stuff."

Gabe and Loreen picked up their drinks and stood.

"Can we walk around for awhile?" Gabe asked his mom.

"Yeah," Lo added. "I want to see where we're going to school. Can you tell us how to get there Aunt Kat?"

Stella patted her pockets. "Darn. I forgot I need to buy all three of us new cell phones."

Kat nodded. "That makes sense."

Stella pursed her lips, thinking. "Your dad would have called both of you as soon as he couldn't get in touch with me. He's probably already gone to the school, asking around, talking to your friends."

Gabe and Loreen rolled their eyes and sat back down.

"First thing we'll do is buy you two new cell phones under your new names."

"Yes!" Gabe shouted.

"Thank you, thank you, thank you," Loreen added.

Stella held up her index finger. "But… you have to promise not to call your friends."

The twins' smiles morphed into frowns.

"You know as well as I, your father will go to any lengths

necessary to find us. That means he'll beg, steal, lie, do whatever he has to in order to get the information he needs to find us. We can't take that chance."

The twins faced each other and nodded.

"We promise not to call any of our friends," Gabe assured his mom.

Stella tilted her had at her daughter. "Loreen?"

"We promise not to call anyone we know," Loreen agreed.

Stella stared at her two kids. "I'm sorry, you guys. But I have to make absolutely sure there's no way he can find us. You understand, right?"

"We understand," the twins said at once.

Katrina tapped Stella on the shoulder. "So you three have new last names?"

"It took months, but, yes, our new last name is Jensen. No more Stella, Gabe, and Loreen Walker. This way I can get a job with a new Social Security number, and I can enroll the kids in school."

"I never thought of all that stuff, Stell," Kat said. "How did you know what to do in order to pull this shit off anyway?"

"I read it in a book I got at the library," Stella said. *"How To Disappear and Not Leave A Trace.* There was so much to learn. But I started my research a long time ago. Watched movies and documentaries and such too."

Gabe frowned. "Why didn't you ever tell us what you were planning, Mom?"

Stella stared off into the distance. "I wasn't sure I'd be able to do it." She turned back to her son. "After everything with your father, I didn't have much faith in my ability to …uh… to do much of anything, actually. And to disappear without a trace? I thought I'd for sure mess it up big time, make things worse for all of us when he caught us and made us go back home with him."

"I'm sure that's why your mom is being uber-cautious about this whole thing, Gabe, Loreen." Kat folded her arms over her chest. "I don't think I would have had the patience to wait years to get all my ducks in a row. I would have screwed up somehow, missed an important piece of the puzzle that I needed in order to disappear. All of us leave a footprint in this society. And we don't realize how easy it is, especially with the internet, to find someone no matter how much they want to go unnoticed."

Stella gulped the rest of her water and walked to the kitchen.

Kat leaned toward the twins and whispered. "Go easy on your mom, guys. She's been through a lot. Not that you two haven't had it rough too. But you know what I mean. This is a huge deal, trying to hide from your dad in plain sight. Let's all do whatever we can to ease her worry that Robert will find you. K?"

Loreen and Gabriel nodded.

Kat smiled. "So let me tell you how to get to Monarch Bay High School."

Chapter Eleven

The twins watched Netflix with Remy in the family room at the back of the house off the kitchen. Remy snuggled between the two kids, upside down, snoring. Kat and Stella settled in the front room in lounge chairs to share a bottle of wine.

Stella took a sip and sighed. "Tell me how you met your hubby Marcus."

Kat laughed out loud. "Nothing all that romantic, and when I first saw him he wasn't much to look at either. I'll have to tell you the story. But first you. I want to know about you, Stella."

Stella swirled her wine glass, watching the sunflower-colored liquid swish along the inside of the glass. "You mentioned at first you didn't think Marcus was much to look at. Well, believe me, looks mean nothing as far as I'm concerned. Robert was the most handsome man I'd ever dated, and look what he turned out to be. I'd much rather have someone who treats me kindly and loves me for who I am. Not a man who forced me to be who he wanted me to be. Which turned out to be nothing more than a slave to his sexual whims. Someone who knew how to cook a hot meal and bake cakes and cookies." She lifted her index finger. "All at the appropriate time, mind you, not one minute late. Otherwise, look out! The axe would fall. Mostly on my head… sometimes my stomach… I sure as hell don't miss that, and I wouldn't wish it on anyone, especially my favorite sister."

Kat reached for her sister's hand. "I'm sorry you had to live through that for so many years. I can't imagine, Stell. What a fucking nightmare. But I understand it must have been damn hard to get yourself out of that hell hole. You had two young kids to think of."

Stella grasped the handle on the side of the lounge chair to raise the footrest. "Robert wasn't happy about sharing me with the twins. I just can't understand a man being jealous of the attention and love children need in order to thrive. I didn't stop loving *him*. Not right away. And we still had sex and everything. But he wanted all my attention. I mean all of it.

"He hated that I rocked the kids to sleep every night and read them bedtime stories. He didn't act like a father their entire lives." She leaned her elbow on the armrest and cradled her head in her hand. "I should have left a long time ago. I could see it coming once the ball started rolling downhill. I should have had the guts to split, right then and there. Jesus, what have I done, Kat?"

Kat shook her head. "Look at me." She waited for Stella to turn in her direction. "Under very fucked-up circumstances you did the best you could. Stop the what ifs and the I wish I'd done thats. Okay? You can't turn back the clock, as the old expression goes. No regrets. You did nothing wrong. Robert did. And now you're free."

"Onward and upward, Christian soldiers?"

Kat laughed out loud. "Remember when Nason used to say that to us after we'd fuck up somehow? He'd have a talk with us about the shit we did wrong, then we'd say we were sorry, then he'd say— "

They burst out together, "Onward and upward, Christian soldiers," and laughed and laughed until they were out of breath.

"Ohhhh," Kat continued on a big sigh. "I miss Fiona and Nason."

"Me, too, Kat. Enough about me and my sorry *past* life. Tell me about Marcus."

Kat grinned. "Well… I moved to Monarch Bay to get out of Monterey, where all my memories of Fiona and Nason were just too much. Every street and restaurant brought vivid pictures to mind of when they were both alive. Their laughter. Nason's jokes. He was so damn funny. 'Why does a duck have tail feathers?'"

Stella smirked. "To cover its butt quack."

They burst out laughing again.

Kat continued her story. "So anyway, I came here to Monarch Bay. You remember how much I love butterflies. Well, every year the Monarchs fly to Monarch Butterfly Grove in Pismo Beach. And they stop here on their way. Thousands and thousands of them. And there's a festival here at the beach boardwalk with a street faire and food and everything 'butterfly'." She made air quotes with her fingers.

"It's a happy place to live, even though I know that sounds trite and kinda goony. But there's a sense of community here. I have neighbors who look out for me. Store owners know my name. You know what I mean? So I applied for a job at Monarch Manes as a barber. She hired me on the spot, and I've been there ever since. I make my own hours, have my own clients, and I make damn good money."

"And Marcus came in for a haircut?"

Kat grinned. "One day I was cutting this woman's hair. She wanted a buzz cut and a dye job. Bright pink. I thought, hey, I can do that. No one else thought they'd be able to pull it off." She took a deep breath. "This woman was a kick in the pants, I'm tellin' ya. We're still friends. Maybe you'll meet her someday. But anyway… so I finish with this gal, and the owner, Samantha, asked me if I had time for a walk-in. My next client wasn't for another half hour, so I thought, sure, I have time. Samantha said it was a guy who wanted his beard trimmed and a haircut. Nothing big.

"So I clean up my work station and turn around to tell her I'm ready, and over walks this dude, six-foot four, beard down to the middle of his chest. Looked like Jesus Christ the way they portray him in church, you know? His hair? Oh, my God. Dreadlocks to his shoulders. I couldn't tell if he was ugly or handsome. But he sure as hell was scarier than shit.

"So, I say hi, and he says hi, in this big deep, I gotta admit, sexy voice. My toes curled in my shoes, man. Tells me he wants the beard totally gone but to leave a bit of stubble like, you know how the guys do these days, like Ben Affleck or whoever? And he wanted the dreadlocks totally gone and maybe an inch-long buzz cut. So I say 'no problem,' grab my scissors and begin, right?

"He's quiet the entire time. Doesn't say a fuckin' word. I asked him where he was from, and he says Monarch Bay. I hadn't seen anyone around town looking like this dude, but whatever. I asked him where he worked. He tells me he's a long-haul truck driver. Gone for weeks at a time then comes back to his apartment for a few days, then on the road again for another few weeks. What's that look on your face, Stell?"

Stella waved her hand. "Oh, it's nothing. You remember how I told you how we got here? Tom, the long-haul trucker?" Kat nodded. "A waitress named Maisie at the truck stop in Corvallis hooked me up with him, and he drove us here. I'd never met a trucker in my life.

So, when I meet Marcus, this'll be my second time. That's all. Just strikes me as kinda weird, after never having met a trucker before, you know? But go on… continue your story."

"That *is* pretty bizarre." Kat took a breath. "So, anyway, I start with the beard, give him the, quote unquote, stubble look. He's got a jaw to rival any movie star, great complexion underneath all that mass of yucky-looking hair. Then I snip off the excess hair on his head and bring out my clippers and give him the buzz cut he wants." She smiled while she gazed at the ceiling. "He was so damn handsome. You would never ever have suspected what was hiding underneath all that hair, I swear to God."

"And you fell in love."

"And I fell in love. Hard." Kat giggled like a kindergartener. "He asked if he could take me to dinner at the end of my shift. I thought, why wait? I didn't want to lose sight of this dude. No way! So I gave my next client to Samantha, and he and I left together right then and there, walked down the street to Amorio's Italian Restaurant, sat, and talked for four hours, then he brought me home. That was the beginning of a whirlwind romance. When he came back from his next trip, he and I got engaged, and after he returned the next time, we got hitched."

Kat gave Stella a sideways glance. "I wish you'd been there, Stell. But when I phoned to invite you to our wedding, your number had been disconnected. I searched for you, couldn't find anything." Kat shrugged. "So what could I do?"

Stella chewed on her bottom lip. "First of all, you couldn't find me, because everything was in Robert's name, and after we moved, he placed the ownership of the house in the name of some fake company for tax purposes. Don't ask me to explain it. I still don't understand. Plus he changed our cell phones and numbers constantly, so we'd have new numbers every year and never under either of our names. It was under that company name. It was really, really weird."

Stella waved her hand in the air. "To answer your question, Robert didn't like me talking to you. He'd been around you a couple of times, and his impression was that you had a wild streak and you'd be a bad influence on me or some crap. He just didn't want me to have anyone else in my life but him. I mean, I think that time we had dinner with you in Monterey, all he could talk about afterward was your bleached hair and black roots and long fake fingernails and black kohl around your eyes, as if you were some Goth teeny-bopper who smoked crack and would lead me down a path to destructive behavior."

"I've never done drugs, Stella."

"I knew that, and I told him as much. He didn't believe me."

"He's a prick. I'd never touch crack. I never even smoked marijuana, for God's sake. And I drink on occasion. Don't touch beer. I'm like Sister Catherine Marie. Remember her in grammar school? We both had her in fifth grade?"

Stella chuckled. "I remember her. Yeah, you sound a bit like her. Pure as the driven snow."

"Nason used to say that all the time."

"So, when do we get to meet this Marcus guy?"

"He comes home tomorrow."

"Cool. This'll be fun. And I want you to know, as soon as I find a job, we'll be out of your hair."

Kat rolled her eyes. "Are you freaking kidding me, Stell? Do you know Marcus is literally gone for four weeks at a time for each long-haul, and then he's home for maybe five, seven days, and he's usually so tired he spends a lot of time sleeping because I can't take off work for an entire week anyway. We don't see each other much, when I think about it. But we make the best of it. I knew what I was getting into when I fell for the guy."

Kat shrugged. "It's worth it. To me. Both of us are pretty independent people, and when we get together after he's gone for a month? Good golly, Miss Molly, do we have a good time in the bedroom. And the living room. And the kitchen." She chuckled. "And we tell each other stories about what's been going on and… you know what? We're really close. I mean, we're super best friends. For us, it makes the relationship more exciting, because each of us has time to be alone, which is something that means a lot to both of us, and then our time together is really, really special. And Marcus has so many stories. And I mean totally whacked stories of shit that happens on his hauls.

"So my point is, you're not gonna be interfering in our lives, if that's the way you're looking at it. You'll be working soon, I'm sure of it, and the kids will be at school. And in the evening we can have family dinners together. Marcus and I don't have kids—yet. Family means a lot to him. And to me. And I enjoy being around kids, especially teenagers. So it's a good situation all around."

Kat took a sip of her wine and rubbed her finger round and round the rim of the glass. "Then again, if you need to have a place of your own, I totally get it. It's your call, Stell. But don't move out because you think Marcus and I want you to. Cause that's not what's happening. You and I have always gotten along. That's not gonna stop. And I know you'll like Marcus. And he'll like you too." She glanced over at Stella. "Please don't leave. Not soon anyway. Promise?"

Stella finished off her glass of wine and reached for the bottle, tipping it toward her sister. Kat nodded, and Stella filled her glass half-full then poured the remainder of the bottle into her own glass. She sat back, took another sip, then inhaled deeply. "What you just said? About not wanting us to move out? I think that's the kindest thing I've heard from anyone in years. I'm not kidding you. Robert was the most negative person I've ever met. He wasn't like that when we first met, but he morphed into Mr. Negativity after the kids were born, and I already explained how having kids was not what he dreamed of, at all. It got to the point where I felt Robert didn't like me anymore. And he wanted the kids out of the house too. As soon as they reached eighteen and would be considered adults he wanted them gone. It was almost like the three of us were interlopers in our own home.

"That's how Robert made us feel with his cutting remarks about the kids' behavior and little jabs about everything I did that was not up to par—which was pretty much everything. I could do nothing right. Nothing. It was his domain, his house. And we just lived in it. So to hear you say that you actually want us around and family means a lot to you… well, it warms my heart, Kat." Stella dabbed at her cheeks with a tissue.

Kat got out of her chair and knelt next to Stella, reached for her hand, and held it between hers. "I love you, Big Sis. I've missed you more than I let on before. I cried myself to sleep many nights when you stopped calling, and then I guess you moved and I couldn't find you. I was devastated. And meeting Marcus? That's when my life turned around. I found happiness again. He wanted me. I missed that because I felt like you didn't want me anymore. You didn't need a sister anymore. Otherwise you would have reached out. I was only a text or a phone call away. And I never heard from you."

Stella pushed the foot rest down and swiveled toward her sister, stared into her eyes. "I am so, so sorry, Kat. Yes, Robert didn't like you for no good reason. And for a while, I'll be honest, he convinced me you were a bad influence, because of the drugs and stuff. He checked my calls every day after he got home from the university. He tracked my every move by pinging my phone, and he demanded I take it everywhere I went. But really? When I realized after several years that he'd been screwing around with my mind, I tried to find you. I went to the library, Googled you, and… nothing. I didn't know you'd gotten married and changed your name." She bent her head back and stared at the ceiling. "How could I have been so stupid? I really am an idiot. I know you. Better than Robert ever did. But why did I let him convince me you were a bad person?"

She stared at Kat. "How did I let that happen? Because I'm weak, Kat. And just plain stupid. But day after day, hearing him berate me about literally every single thing I did …" She shrugged. "He broke me." Tears spilled down her cheeks, but she was too distraught to wipe them away. "I hate myself for letting him do that to me. And for allowing the kids to be privy to that abuse. God, Kat. I need help. Some serious help." She started to sob, deep gulping sobs. And she couldn't stop.

Kat squished into the seat of the chair next to her sister and wrapped her arms around her tightly. "It's okay, Stell. People are brainwashed all the time. People who are held captive whether it's a stranger or a husband or whatever. Happens all the time, honey. It really does. And it doesn't make you stupid or silly or an idiot, like you're calling yourself. You're a beautiful, kind, generous individual. He beat you down, both physically and mentally. But look at your kids. They're fucking resilient as hell. It's so obvious they've turned out to be really cool people.

"I'm mostly worried about you, Stella. I truly believe you can be helped. I can ask my therapist, Roslyn, if she can refer you to someone. Please give it some thought. You realize you need help, and you can get it. Right here." She grasped Stella's hand in hers. "And it's up to you right now whether you look for a job or not. On the one hand, maybe you need to take some time to regroup, think about life or whatever. Or maybe you want to feel more productive and getting a job will do that for you. I don't know. It's your call. Whatever you want to do, Hon. I want you to be happy again. Like you were before you met Robert, the shit bag."

Stella reached for another tissue and blew her nose. She turned to her sister. "You forgive me for ignoring you for so many years? I swear to God, Kat, it wasn't on purpose. You've gotta believe me."

Kat smiled. "Of course I believe you. I understand now why I never heard from you. You couldn't find me, and I couldn't find you. But you're my sister. You'll always be my sister. And I love you. Forever and a day."

"Forever and a day. Remember when we used to say that when we were kids?"

"Yep. And nothing's changed between us, Stella. The only thing that's different is years have passed, but otherwise, we, as sisters, remain the same. For always."

Stella took in a huge breath and let it out slowly. "Well, this conversation was cathartic."

Kat chuckled. "For both of us. I'm glad we talked."

Chapter Twelve

The following morning Stella, Kat, and the twins ate breakfast together outside on the deck. It was sunny, and the deck sheltered them from the breeze. The sweet scent of freesias filled the air, and Stella sighed. "Your backyard is really lovely. So this is what the weather's like in September? It's absolutely beautiful this morning. None of us is exactly used to a morning with no rain."

Kat glanced around, smiling. "It's generally in the low seventies in September, sometimes gets up to eighty, eighty-five, depending on the Santa Ana winds, which really warm us up. But it's truly a Mediterranean climate. I love it. You kids should go to the beach. It's just a block down the street."

"Can we, Mom?" Loreen and Gabe said.

"I thought you wanted me to take you to Monarch Bay High so we can get you enrolled and you can start school?"

Gabe smirked. "We can put that off for a couple of days, Mom."

Loreen sat up straighter. "Gabe and I walked to the school. We know exactly where it is. Only a few blocks from here. It's Friday. Why don't we do all that stuff on Monday."

"Yeah," Gabe added. "We can take the weekend to gear up for returning to school and take advantage of this weather, Mom. It's never like this in Corvallis. Pleeeeease."

Stella glanced at Kat.

Kat smiled. "They can take Remy, if they want. He loves going to the beach."

"Ohhh-kay, you two. Go do your thing. I'm sure it won't make that much difference if we enroll you today or after the weekend."

"Yes!" Gabe and Loreen high-fived each other. They grabbed their dishes, brought them to the kitchen, rinsed them off and put them in the dishwasher then headed for their rooms upstairs. Remy followed right on their heels.

"Guess that's settled then." Stella grinned at her sister. "When do you go in to work?"

"Not until noon."

"And Marcus arrives home today, right?"

Kat nodded. "Sometime today. I'm not really sure when. He usually texts me when he's about an hour away. It's usually late in the afternoon. Gives me time to do what I need to do. I try not to schedule late appointments on the day I know he's returning. I like to take a bath, put on some sexy underwear. Get ready for a fun evening alone together."

"We can stay in the family room and watch TV or hang out in our bedrooms, so you two can have a romantic evening alone. This house is huge, Kat. Four bedrooms and two-and-a-half baths? It's gigantic."

"Marcus's dad passed away from prostate cancer several years ago, and Marcus is an only child. His mom's gone, too, so he inherited this house when my father-in-law died. He was a nice old man. Lived to be ninety-two. Neither of us ever dreamed we'd live a block from the beach. It's like a dream come true."

"You're lucky, Kat. You have a wonderful husband, a gorgeous home in a great area of California, a great job you like. What more could you ask for?"

"I'm happy, Stella. But I'd like to have kids. At thirty-five the cliché' fits. My clock is ticking. I don't have forever to get pregnant. And it ain't happening so far."

"Have you seen a fertility specialist?"

"Yes, we have. A few weeks ago before Marcus left on this last trip."

"Are you thinking IVF? It's expensive, isn't it?"

Kat nodded. "Yeah, it is. But we have the money in savings from his inheritance. A part of me is scared to go on fertility drugs. What if I have quadruplets or some shit? I am not mentally prepared for *that.*"

"I hear you. It would make a big difference in your life even having twins. But having kids changes you, Kat. In a good way, in my opinion. I love raising the twins, influencing their lives, even though it's been really rough on them having Robert as a father. I tried my best to mitigate his bad influence as best I could."

"Looks like you did a fantastic job then, Stella."

"I'll babysit for you whenever you need me."

Kat burst out laughing. "Don't get ahead of yourself, Sista. Marcus and I have a second appointment scheduled. I'm scared to death if we decide to do IVF and it doesn't work. I'd be devastated. I've heard about lots of couples who go through it over and over again. Sometimes it just doesn't work."

Stella reached out and covered her sister's hand. "Think positive. It'll make a big difference."

"We're gonna head to the beach. That okay, Mom?" Loreen called out.

"That's fine. See you at lunch time," Stella yelled.

"Yup. Bye, Mom, Aunt Kat! Remy's with us too!" Gabe shouted.

The front door slammed shut, and silence returned.

"They'll have a good time, Stella. Remy'll watch over them. Lots of kids down there too, even though it's a school day. People vacation in Monarch Bay all year round. There's usually a volleyball game going on and surfing. It's a cool place to live."

"When does that Monarch Bay Faire happen?"

"It's coming up. It's always held in September." Kat grabbed the newspaper off the chair next to her, found the ad, and laid the paper in front of her sister. She pointed. "Read that. It tells you everything you need to know with times of when bands are going to play and what food they have and all about the booths available. It's a big thing. The *biggest* thing each year for this small town. Twenty-thousand people is relatively small for California."

Stella perused the news about the Faire, moving her finger along the descriptions. "This'll be really something special to look forward to. I can't wait."

Suddenly the sound of an engine burst through the silence of the morning's tranquility. Kat's eyes grew wide, and she smiled. "It's my main man. And he's early!" Kat stood. "Looks like I'll have to cancel all my appointments after all."

"I'll make myself scarce."

Kat frowned. "You'll do no such thing. I want you to meet this guy. You can wait a few minutes, can't you? You can hide away afterward." She raised her eyebrows. "He and I will excuse ourselves and head to the bedroom upstairs in a bit anyway. You don't have to do anything but make yourself at home down here. We'll exit before nightfall for dinner." She grinned. "Maybe."

Stella laughed out loud. "Afternoon delight."

"And evening dessert." Kat chuckled.

The front door opened, then slammed shut. and Kat ran to the front of the house.

"Hey, babe," a deep voice rang out.

Then silence for at least several minutes. Stella smiled to herself. She'd experienced that anticipation of seeing Robert and the subsequent sexual need for such a short of amount of time during their marriage. She admitted she was jealous though happy for her sister. She wondered if she'd ever feel that way again for any man. Or was she already too cynical about the whole "falling in love" thing? Once burned, twice shy? She wasn't sure. Stella set the newspaper aside. She'd look for a job after Kat and Marcus fled upstairs for their reunion.

"Stella," Kat said, holding onto Marcus's hand, pulling him toward the back deck.

Stella caught her first glimpse of Marcus and let out an inner sigh. He was as handsome as Kat had described him. His smile couldn't have been wider and she could tell he was in love with her sister—big time. Stella grinned and stood.

"This is my sister Stella, Marcus." Kat looked from Marcus to Stella. "Stella, this is my hubby, Marcus. The love of my life."

Stella walked toward Marcus and stretched out her hand.

He took it with a firm grasp and squeezed lightly. "Nice to finally meet you, Stella. I've heard a lot about you."

Stella nodded. "And I, you. You look exactly as Kat described. I find it hard to picture a full beard and dreadlocks, though."

Marcus let out a belly laugh. "All that went with the Harley Davidson. Got rid of the hair. Kept the Harley."

He took a seat at the picnic table with effort. He was basketball player tall with long legs and a muscular build and just as handsome as Kat described him. They made a beautiful pair, and it was obvious they cared for each other. They couldn't stop glancing at each other, staring into each other's eyes.

"So you have a Harley?" Stella asked him.

"If you ever wanna go for a ride, I'm not reckless. We'll go slow the entire way. I'm not in it for the thrill of going fast. I just like the feel of the wind on my face and the freedom of not being constricted by the doors and windows of a truck."

Stella nodded. "Sure. One of these days I'd love to go for a short spin around the block."

Kat sat down and smashed up against her husband across from Stella. "Marcus drove straight through on the last leg of his trip, so he could get home early. He's pretty beat."

Marcus turned to Stella. "I can't wait to meet the twins. I hear they're very well-behaved teenagers. I sure wasn't. This'll be a nice change."

Stella chuckled. "Robert wielded a firm hand when it came to discipline. I'm more of a softy. He liked to scare the bejesus out of them." She shrugged. "He thought that would make them toe the line, I guess."

"Sometimes it works the opposite way," Marcus replied. "My dad was what you'd call a pretty rigid dude, but I couldn't be controlled. I was totally out of control. Took meeting your sister to calm me down, I have to admit. I didn't want to do anything to make her walk away from me." His gaze returned to Katrina. "The love of my life, I gotta tell you."

"And you're mine," Kat replied, holding his gaze. "I'm suddenly really tired." She stood and yawned. "I think a nap is in order."

"Don't mind if I do." Marcus grinned and stood, reaching for Kat's hand.

She grasped it, giving Stella a sideways glance. "See ya' later?"

"I'll be here. I'm going to look for a job in the paper. If you need anything, I'll be right here."

Kat chuckled. "I think I have everything I need right next to me."

Marcus rolled his eyes, then shot Stella a quick glance. "See you a little later, Stella. I look forward to getting to know you better."

"Likewise," Stella replied.

The two lovebirds headed toward the stairs, and Stella couldn't help but grin. She was happy for her sister. A handsome man. A kind man. A man interested in having a family. Treated her sister well. Worked hard.

A twinge of jealousy ripped through her. Would she ever find someone like that, or would she be single for the rest of her life? She thought of Kat's suggestion that she see a therapist, that her sister could get a referral from her therapist, Roslyn. What would it be like to talk to someone about her life, her past with Robert, her future?

Chapter Thirteen

Marcus had the next week off. He and Katrina spent most of their time away from the house, having picnics, going to the beach, hiking, biking, riding the Harley to bed-and-breakfasts, taking Remy on long walks.

Stella enrolled the twins in Monarch Bay High School with no problems. So far, Loreen had made a couple of friends, and Gabriel met some boys who liked to play guitar and were teaching him how to play bass, since he only had experience with classic guitar. They were hoping to form a garage band, and so far they'd been practicing at one of the boy's houses, thank goodness.

There were few jobs available in Monarch Bay itself. Stella had no mode of transportation to Morro Bay or Pismo Beach, the nearest cities, which also had few opportunities available. Stella's B.A. degree was in English, which was how she'd met Robert. She'd need to get her state credentials if she wanted to teach in a school setting. If she didn't find a job soon her money would dwindle slowly but surely.

Kat and Marcus offered to support her no matter how long it took her to find employment, but Stella was sick of being "supported". It reminded her too much of her marriage to Robert. He never wanted her to be out of the house. He needed to know her every action—who she spoke to, who she met, where she went. It was Robert's nightmare that Stella would meet another man who'd whisk her away from the abuse.

To be honest, Robert was right to worry. Stella often dreamed of meeting someone who would treat her kindly and believe in her and help her make something of herself. Instead, she was a college graduate with a Bachelor's degree in English, but she'd wanted to continue, perhaps get her Master's degree, hopefully in Psychology, since that was her minor. Instead, she hadn't been allowed to work outside the home even after the kids were no longer "kids." Now here she was, perusing the small town paper, and the only openings to be found were at the local burger barn or taco haven.

Stella discovered a small graphic on the front page of the newspaper, requesting volunteers for the Monarch Bay Faire, so she called the number. They told her one of the businesses with a booth at the street faire would get in touch with her within twenty-four hours. Stella didn't relish spending her days lounging at the beach every day while her sister worked at Monarch Manes and the kids were at school. She needed to feel useful, after years and years of feeling Robert's shoe on her neck, literally and metaphorically speaking, holding her down, keeping her from any sort of gainful employment, forcing her into a life of uselessness--making cookies, getting dinner on the table at the appropriate hour, bringing him lunch at the university whenever he was too busy to step away from his desk.

The next day, while everyone was gone, including Marcus, who left on another trip to Florida, her cell phone rang.

"I'm looking for Stella Jensen."

"This is she."

"My name's David. David Crockett. My wife Patti and I own Patti's Pastries on Butterfly Street in Monarch Bay. We'll have a booth at the Faire next weekend. I was told you wanted to volunteer to help one of the small businesses. Would you be interested in joining us?"

Stella could hardly contain her excitement. Not only did she love baking, but she was good at it. She looked forward to meeting people, perhaps making a few friends, if that were possible. She'd spent so many years alone, not allowed to have a gal-pal. Robert forbade it. So it had been years since she'd had a buddy to hang out with. Now that she'd reconnected with Kat she was in "hog heaven", being able to share experiences and talk about meaningful subjects. She hoped volunteering would lead to brighter and fuller days ahead.

"Yes! Oh, yes, I'd be honored to volunteer at your booth. I've been baking pies and cookies and cakes for my family for years, so I know a little bit about what makes for delicious baked goods. I'd love to help you in any way I can to make this a profitable experience for you and your wife. I'm so happy you called me."

He chuckled.

Stella hoped she hadn't made a fool of herself, chatting like a child and not knowing when to shut up and listen, as Robert always told her.

"I don't think in the years we've had our booth at the faire, I've ever encountered anyone so excited to volunteer to help us out."

"I just moved here to Monarch Bay, and I'm living with my sister, Kat Swanson."

"I know Kat and her husband, Marcus. Good people. I have a Harley too. Marcus and I go riding sometimes, when he's not on the road. If you're anything like Kat, customers will love you. You sound like you have a sense of humor, and your excitement is contagious."

"Well, thank you. It's Dave and Patti, right?"

"I go by David. And yes, Patti's my wife. But she can't work the entire day, so I need someone to help out, then take her place in her absence. Having three working the booth is actually ideal. And maybe she'll be having a good day and be able to stay until closing, but I don't want to push her. Do you have a set number of hours you want to volunteer to help or—?"

"Oh, I can work the entire day. I've been sitting around for several weeks since we arrived, looking for a job in the newspaper. I'd like to stay a bit more active than that. I'm going crazy being inside the house all day. I'd feel guilty lying on the beach while everyone else is working and my kids are in school."

"So you're living with Kat and Marcus? And you have kids?"

"My twins, Loreen and Gabriel, are seniors at Monarch Bay High School. We'll be with Kat and Marcus until I get on my feet, which requires securing gainful employment somewhere in the area. So far, no luck in that department."

"Sounds like a plan. So can you meet us this Saturday morning at seven-thirty? The Faire starts around nine, and we don't need to train you or anything. Patti and I will need help setting up the baked goods, putting up little signs how much each item costs. We have a small cash box full of change and such. Nothing you can't handle, I'm sure."

"I know all about making change. I have a B.A. Granted, it's in English, not Math, but I'm still able to count." She chuckled.

"D'accord, Stella."

Stella laughed out loud. "You speak French?"

"Just enough to get by. Say hello and such. But, don't ask me how to say a cupcake costs a buck-fifty or anything. That's a bit much for my level. I studied for one year in college, back in the day."

"Don't worry. I don't think you'll have to speak any French in order to sell baked goods in Monarch Bay. Does your wife speak it as well?"

"Yes. She studied French at U.C. Santa Barbara. That's where we met. But I was an Engineering major."

"So you became a baker?"

"Ha! You caught me. Not much of a segue from Engineering to baking, eh?"

"I guess there could be. You have to know about ovens and temperatures and… and—"

He laughed. "Nope. Not making the connection as far as I can tell. But thanks for the effort."

Stella smiled. David seemed like a really nice man. She wondered how old he and his wife were and why his wife couldn't handle an entire day of working the booth at the Faire. Perhaps she was pregnant, expecting their first child? She'd find out soon enough, after she talked to Kat. "So will I be able to find you easily enough when I arrive this Saturday, promptly at seven-thirty in the morning?"

"We're booth number nine. If you walk toward the beach from Marcus and Kat's house, turn right when you hit the boardwalk. We'll be the ninth booth on the right. The booths go down along the boardwalk in both directions, so remember to go to the right. I'll see you then. It's Stella, right?"

"Yes. Stella. It'll be nice to meet you and Patti. And thank you."

"No. Thank *you*. See you then."

They ended the call, and Stella couldn't stop grinning. She was going to be doing something social. That was a first for her in years. Something to look forward to. And since David and Patti obviously were friends with Kat and Marcus, perhaps she could make friends with Patti as well. Go shopping together—after she found a job, of course—go out for coffee. She pictured the three of them—Kat, Patti, and herself—walking the streets of Monarch Bay, shopping for clothes along Main Street.

Stella clapped her hands. She couldn't wait to share the news with her sister and the twins. It felt so good, being able to talk to Kat in the short time since they'd arrived in Monarch Bay. Stella had missed out on so many years of friendship and camaraderie with another woman, especially her sister, with whom she'd shared a close relationship growing up together in Monterey.

After their mom and dad passed away in the boating accident, Stella had been like a mother to Katrina, being five years her senior. At fifteen, Stella didn't take the place of a mom for Kat, but she was better than having no family member with whom to share her grief and devastation when they'd lost both parents in one fell swoop.

Stella heard the front door open and shut then Kat humming a song that was on the radio every time Stella wanted to listen to some music to dance to when she was all alone at the house. She recognized Bruno Mars and the tune "Uptown Funk," which always made Stella want to jump up and boogie.

Stella connected her new cell phone to a tiny boom box. When Kat entered the room, Stella held up a finger, then pressed the song title on her phone. "Uptown Funk" blared out of the speaker, the music surrounding them. The things they were able to do these days!

Stella grabbed Kat's free hand, and they danced around the room, singing at the top of their lungs.

"Too hot," Kat sang, shaking her hips, waving her arms above her head.

"Hot damn," Stella shouted, mimicking John Travolta in *Saturday Night Fever*.

They danced until the end of the song, then threw themselves into the chairs in the kitchen, laughing until their sides ached.

Kat let out a breath. "Whew! What brought that on?"

"I just volunteered to work a booth at the Monarch Bay Faire."

"Oh, wow. How fun! Which one?"

"I'll be helping out Dave, I mean David, and Patti. They own Patti's Pastries. David said he and Marcus ride their Harleys together. Are you friends with his wife, Patti?"

Kat frowned.

"What's wrong, Kat?"

Kat shook her head. "Patti and I are good friends, yes. She's one of the sweetest people I've ever met. David named their bakery after her. They're like young lovebirds. It's so cute. And they've been married since they graduated from Monarch Bay High School. I don't think either of them ever had another boyfriend or girlfriend."

"I feel a 'but' coming."

Kat stood and walked to the refrigerator. "I made lemonade with lemons from our tree in the backyard. Want a glass?"

"Sure. Thanks."

Kat poured two glasses, set them on the kitchen table, and plopped herself into the chair. She took a sip, scrunched up her face and stood. "Sugar?"

Stella took a sip, squinted her eyes. "Please."

Kat brought back the sugar bowl with a tiny silver spoon sticking out the side, sat down again, and let out a sigh. "Patti was diagnosed with breast cancer about a year and a half ago. She's only thirty-seven years old. She didn't want to go through chemotherapy. She's so skinny already, she knew she'd be a bag of bones in a matter of weeks, and the prognosis after chemo would have given her, maybe, a few additional months."

Stella waved her head slowly, side to side. "Oh, my God. How devastating."

"Well, she blames herself. And I can understand why. She hadn't gotten a mammogram in, like, ever. And she admitted she'd had some discharge from one of her nipples. I don't know a lot about breast cancer, but she told me she was going to make an appointment soon. Then I guess she got busy getting the bakery going and running in the black. It's a lotta work starting a business. Takes years. Anyway, so she's on pain meds, and she gets acupuncture and totally revised the way she eats and drinks. She's made it past the year mark already but …" Kat grabbed a tissue from the box on the table and dabbed under her eyes.

Stella grasped her sister's forearm. "That is so sad. And it could have been prevented?"

Kat nodded. "She knows it. Everyone knows it. But, of course, she's the only one who would ever actually say the words. She realizes how very stupid she was not to see a doctor immediately. She wasn't exactly being pro-active."

"The poor woman. So does she still work in the bakery?"

"Every single day. But in the last month David told Marcus Patti's getting really tired. She's finding it hard to wake up at four in the morning to turn on the ovens and start baking for hours and then stand at the cash register while David takes over in the back with everything that has to be done. He needs help, but Patti feels guilty making him bear the burden alone, you know? It's too much for one person."

"He told me on the phone if Patti's having a good day, she'll be able to stay until closing at the Faire, but he doesn't want to push her. I didn't query him what he meant by that, but it all makes sense now."

"Yeah. This may be her last Monarch Bay Faire, and the thought of that …" Tears flowed down Kat's cheeks, and she dabbed them with the tissue.

Stella's eyebrows scrunched together. "Wow. That's really sad. I look forward to meeting her. She sounds like an amazing woman. Working so hard every day when she's dying of cancer. God dang."

"For real."

"Well, hopefully this weekend we'll have nice weather. But as far as I can tell, the weather here's perfect all the time. Granted I've only been here for a short while, but I see the sun every day, which is a totally novel occurrence, having spent so much time in Oregon."

"But it's so green in Oregon, Stella. People say it's lush and gorgeous and breathtaking."

"That may be true. However, you have to see it through the windshield wipers of your car. It never fricking stops raining, Kat. It's depressing. At least to me. I can only speak for myself, but having come from the Monterey and Carmel area, I was shocked. I'm a spoiled brat as far as weather is concerned."

"Here in California, we're all spoiled brats. I wouldn't move away from here unless there was a life and death situation that called for it, and I can't think of one."

Stella stood and brought her glass to the sink. "This lemonade is really good, once I added sugar."

Kate let out a guffaw. "Far as I can tell, it looked like you added about a cup."

Stella rinsed out her glass and returned to the table. "Probably did. But it sure was delicious. Thank you. Maybe I can help out a bit, pick some more lemons. I can make lemonade too."

Kat stood and took another sip. "That'd be great, if you have the time. There's a ladder for the lemons that are high up, but Marcus usually picks those. He's always worried I'm gonna fall and lie there for four weeks while he's on the road. He's scared he'll return one day and find my decaying body underneath the tree."

"I won't pick any lemons I can't reach from the ground then." Stella glanced out the sliding glass doors. "Looks like there are enough for several pitchers of lemonade from just the ones right above my head. I'll do that now."

"And I'm gonna take a shower. Get all this hair offa me."

"Don't you wear a smock or something?"

"You'd think that would work, but it doesn't. Ask any person who cuts hair for a living. There are these hairs we call splinters. They're tiny hairs that actually penetrate your skin, kinda like when you get a wood splinter. They're irritating, and they hurt. I have to take tweezers and pull them out. I get them on my arms, and I had one on my face the other day. You can't believe where I find those suckers. You find them on your skin under your clothes, too, not just on exposed skin."

Stella took a sponge and wiped down the table, then dried it with a towel. "The things the customers never find out about, right? How bizarre."

"You'll have to come in sometime for a trim. I wouldn't want to cut off too much of that gorgeous auburn mane of yours."

Stella lifted her hair off her neck, pulled a scrunchie from her pocket ,and wrapped her hair into a ponytail. "It's getting kinda long. I'll come in soon and have you take off a couple of inches."

"I'll have to use a step stool, you're so much taller than I am."

"Yeah, I'm five-foot six and you're how tall?"

"Five-three, I think. And my hair is about an inch and a half long these days."

"It suits you, Kat. I've always loved the dark roots look against the blondish-white hair. It's bleached, right?"

"Right. The roots are dyed black, and the ends are bleached. I have Camilla do it for me once every two months or so."

"It really is the perfect hairdo for you, in my opinion. With your beautiful heart-shaped face and the red lipstick, you're a poster girl for Monarch Manes. It's probably one of the reasons the owner hired you."

"Thanks for the compliment."

"You were always the one with the boyfriends in high school, Kat. I never had one."

"Cause you were too shy. You were sort of a loner."

"Yeah, I was. I liked studying and reading books."

"I sure didn't. Which is why you went to college and I didn't. But as far as boyfriends, I believe your self-esteem has always been on the short side."

Stella stared outside at the lemon tree. "That speaks volumes for why I wasn't able to extricate myself from my marriage to Robert, right?" She turned to Kat. "Just say it."

"You just did, Stell. But you're thinking about calling my therapist, right?"

"I think that's a good idea, yes."

"Good. Gonna jump in the shower."

"And I'm going to pick some lemons."

Chapter Fourteen

The first day of the Monarch Bay Faire, Saturday, brought sunshine and a warm breeze that tickled the wind chimes hanging from almost every booth lining the boardwalk along the beach. Stella arrived at the Patti's Pastries booth at 7:25 a.m. She'd worn a hoodie, since it was a bit chilly in the mornings at the coast, and a pair of distressed jean coveralls. She'd gone barefoot for the first time in years, something she'd enjoyed when she lived in Monterey in her youth. She found it freeing, plus she hated it when sand got in her shoes.

As she walked toward booth number nine, she observed a very thin, almost anorexic-looking woman of indeterminate age, since her clothes were youthful—T-shirt with a pink Breast Cancer Awareness flag on the front and a long, flowing pink skirt. The woman's face appeared drawn tightly over high cheek bones, but there were no wrinkles. She looked rather pixie-like, cute, tiny. Stella assumed it was Patti.

A handsome man with a dark brown, chin-strap beard and a mustache, stood behind the woman, arms curled around her waist, fisted at her stomach. He rocked her back and forth and looked as if he were whispering something in her ear. She laughed, then cringed, and he turned her around in his arms and was speaking to her, a serious look on his face. She shook her head, and by that time Stella could hear her saying "No, I am not leaving" in a strong tone. Maybe Patti was in pain, and David wanted her to go home?

Stella reached their booth and stood in front of the couple. "Hi. I'm Stella. At your service for as long as you need me." She stretched out a hand toward Patti, and Patti's grasp was gentle —what Stella would call weak. But Patti had a beautifully endearing smile, and Stella could tell she had been a knock-out before all the weight loss.

"Hi, Stella," Patti replied. "We're so glad you volunteered to help us out this weekend. David told me you moved in with your sister, Katrina. She and I are good friends. How lucky for you and the twins, right? That you get a chance to get reacquainted after such a long time apart."

Stella could tell Patti was someone she'd instantly like. Her demeanor spoke volumes as she looked straight into Stella's eyes, making her feel as if she were the only person in the world she wanted to focus on at the moment. Stella hoped she'd get to know her better before it was too late. Then she felt guilty even having the thought.

"I am lucky indeed." Stella turned to David and shook his hand. "Thank you for allowing me to help you and Patti this weekend. This will be my first Monarch Bay Faire."

"And hopefully not your last," David said. Then he appeared to realize what he'd said and grimaced.

Stella assumed he was uber-aware this may be his wife's last Faire and felt he'd committed the ultimate faux pas, so she immediately grinned and spoke to Patti. "I hear your pastries are to die for." Then Stella realized what *she'd* just said and wanted to kick herself. What was wrong with her, using the word "die," especially after what David just said? Geez Louise. Rude! Yep, Robert was right. She couldn't do anything right.

Stella could feel her face heating up and looked down at all the baked goods covering the table at the front of the booth. "These look delicious."

Patti appeared not to have taken notice of either Stella's or David's comments and pointed at a huge, medium-brown croissant on a pink paper plate. "You're welcome to try one out."

"I didn't have time for breakfast, so, yes, I think I will." Patti picked up the plate, bent her head, and breathed in the aroma. "I absolutely love croissants. Why don't you show me what you want me to do today to help you out." She took a bite of the croissant and groaned. "Oh, man, someone knows how to make a true French croissant. Which one of you is it?"

Patti bowed. "I'll take the compliment, thank you. I was at the bakery this morning at four a.m." She took in a deep breath. "Which is why I won't be helping out for too long today. I think I'll go home a little later and take a short nap then return sometime in the afternoon." She turned to David. "If that's all right with you, sweetie?"

David kissed Patti on the lips, then hugged her. "Sounds like a plan, babe."

The morning flew by. Customers lined up ten-deep at times to select cookies, brownies, slices of banana bread, chocolate fudge cake. David and Patti encouraged Stella to taste-test most of them, so she'd be able to answer any questions people might have concerning the quality of their baked goods.

At around eleven, Patti excused herself and walked the two or so blocks home, leaving David and Stella to work the Patti's Pastries booth.

"Thank you again for helping us this weekend, Stella. It's nice to have someone I can trust with the money and know you won't eat all the merchandise while you're here." He laughed. "I say that because we know you're Kat's sister, so you're good people. Last year we had some young kid from the grammar school helping out. We ended up missing around a hundred dollars from the till along with a box of chocolate fudge brownies. I don't know how he did it without us seeing him." He shrugged.

"Thank you for trusting me, David. As much as I'd love to eat a dozen of those brownies, I don't need the added calories, if I'm going to be swimming in the ocean for the first time in ages. I need to fit into a bathing suit sooner or later."

David laughed. "Doesn't look like you need to worry about that. You're built like your sister Kat—naturally thin. But you two do not look like sisters in my opinion. The two of you have totally different hair color and haircuts. Kat's shorter than you are as well. And I know you had the same parents."

"You probably know a lot more about me than I know about you." Stella chuckled.

"Not too much. Just the basics." David grew serious. "And I'm sure Kat told you about Patti's cancer?"

Stella pursed her lips, took a quick look at the sky, then faced David. "Yes, she explained to me Patti decided to forego chemotherapy. But she's still here, longer than the doctor's expected. I'm so sorry this is happening to her… and to you. I don't know what to say. I'll admit, I've never known anyone personally who had breast cancer, David, but I'm certain this is an extremely difficult road Patti's walking. And she's such a sweet woman, so kind and generous. And I'm sure she's not feeling well. But you'd barely know it by looking at her, except for the weight she's probably lost over the last few months."

David nodded, lips drawn in a straight line. His eyes teared up as he looked at Stella. "It's been really, really hard on both of us. We wanted kids, but then this happened, and we're both devastated at what life has thrown at us." He stared at the ground. "We talked about adopting kids as well, since there are so many children out there with no one to love them. We didn't care if they were babies or teenagers. We just wanted a family.

"But Patti kept putting it off. Said she wanted to get the shop running in the black." He shrugged. "Now that'll never happen. Having kids, that is. The shop's doing excellent though. But the thought of not having Patti by my side is-" He abruptly stopped talking, turned his head to the side, took a deep breath then faced Stella once again. "Enough of this. You didn't come here to sell pastries *and* listen to my depressing story."

Stella laid a hand on David's shoulder and looked him in the eyes. "If you ever need to talk, I'm a great listener. It's probably the only personal trait I have going for me."

He pulled his head back. "Why would you say something like that? Kat speaks very highly of your intelligence and kindness and generosity and you've raised two great kids who aren't out smoking crack behind the bleachers at school or selling drugs on the street."

"Well, that's nice of her to say those things about me. But, believe me, if I was so smart I wouldn't be in the situation I am today."

Several people came to the booth, and David spoke with them as if they were friends of his, sold them a dozen mixed cookies, and said goodbye.

"What situation is that?"

"What did you say?"

"I said what situation were you talking about? You said if you were so smart you wouldn't be in the situation you are today."

"Oh, right. Well, without belaboring the point, in case Kat hasn't told you—"

"She only told Patti and me that you'd lost touch with each other over the years and you used to live in Corvallis, Oregon. You're no longer with your husband, so you came to Monarch Bay to start a new life."

Stella nodded. "That's pretty much it. Except for the part about no longer being with my husband."

"So you're still with him?"

"Well, that part's technically correct. It's just…" She looked to the side then back into his eyes. "I left without him knowing where I went, and I took the twins with me. I legally changed our last name to Jensen and took the money I'd saved for several years and got as far away as possible by hitching a ride with a long-haul trucker. I guess you could call what I'm doing hiding out. I've kidnapped his children and am running from the law, if he's reported me to the police."

"You must have good reason to do so."

"Yes, I have good reasons, plural."

"Don't feel as if you have to tell me anything. And what you've already told me I promise not to reveal to anyone, even Patti, if that's what you want."

"I know you're close friends with Kat and Marcus. I trust you." She cleared her throat. "Robert, my husband, was physically and mentally abusive. I left to save myself and my kids from further abuse."

"Did he ever lay hands on them?"

"They had a short altercation in our kitchen before we escaped. Robert rammed his head into Gabe's stomach and knocked him to the floor. One day that type of thing could escalate, and he could hurt Gabe, send him to the hospital. I couldn't take that chance. And both kids hate him at this point. They witnessed the aftermath of Robert's hands on me and were sick of it."

"Did he hurt you badly? Broken bones, concussion?"

"Mostly bruises, and he knocked me out several times. I went to the Emergency Room a couple of times, but he wouldn't allow me to stay in the hospital. That would have given me the opportunity to talk to people about the real reason I was in there in the first place. Most of the time he said I'd be fine and I'd heal on my own. I had no reason to leave the house, so he made me stay home until the bruises were gone before sending me to the store or outside to do my chores."

"What a tyrant. Man, I just can't imagine laying my hands on Patti like that. It's totally foreign to me. Impossible to imagine."

She smiled. "You're obviously nothing like him, David. Thank God. Plus I have to admit, I'm weak. Lots of women would have left long ago. But I felt trapped. He knew my every move, and he threatened to take my kids away, if I ever told anyone he hurt me. I just couldn't take that chance. I couldn't possibly leave. I'd never want them alone with Robert. God!

"But now that the twins are almost eighteen years old, they could leave on their own without his permission soon enough anyway. But I couldn't wait any longer. I had to get them out of that atmosphere. It was sick." She shrugged. "So here we are. Camping out at my sister and Marcus's house until I find gainful employment to be able to support the three of us and can move out."

David shook his head. "I'm sorry to hear this happened to you. Even though we don't know each other, it's difficult to listen to your story and not feel outraged. If your husband was in front of me right now, I'd knock him out with a few appropriately placed punches and leave him in the street."

"Lucky for him, he's not here then. And I wouldn't want to put you in that type of situation anyway. You have a sick wife, and she needs you. Way more than I need a hero to fight my battles for me. Patti is a strong woman."

David grasped Stella by the shoulders and looked her in the eyes. "You shouldn't think of yourself as weak because of the actions and threats of the sick man you're married to. It's not your fault he turned out to be abusive. You don't deserve that. No woman deserves that. But you stayed for good reasons. Two good reasons. Your two kids. It would have been dangerous to have them living under his roof without you there to run interference, in case he turned his anger onto them.

"And you're here, aren't you? It sounds like you made it to your sister's house by the skin of your teeth. That makes you strong. You should be proud of yourself. You're safe and sound. Hold your head high, Stella. I'm proud of you too. Consider me and Patti your friends now. Anytime you need an ear, someone to vent to, Patti and I will be here for you." Tears glistened in his eyes. "Well... one of us will still be here for you."

Even though Stella had just met David and Patti, she felt a connection with him after sharing her story and listening to his as well. She reached out and gave him a hug, then stepped back. "Thank you, David. That's very kind of you to say."

He coughed. "Let's clean up here. I'll bring the van around to the boardwalk and we can carry what's left and put it in the van. If you have the time."

"No problem." Stella began boxing the few bakery goods left on the table. "Not much to carry back, David. Today was fun. I enjoyed meeting so many people who live in Monarch Bay. Everyone treated me as if I'm already a part of this community. I didn't feel that way in Corvallis."

"I wonder why that is."

"Some cars and trucks have signs on their bumpers. 'Don't Californicate Oregon." Can you imagine? Rude!" She laughed out loud.

He chuckled. "That *is* rude. California is a melting pot for many people from around the United States, of different races and religions and sexual preferences. I enjoy meeting people different from me. It's ignorant to think if you're not white and born in a particular state or country, then you're an alien who better get outta town and go back home. That's total bullshit. Sorry for my French."

"No offense taken. Plus, you didn't sound very French to me. And you have absolutely no accent either." She grinned.

"Ahhh. She shows her true colors. Sarcasm befits you, Stella."

"No one's ever said that to me before. I'll take it as a compliment. You said you didn't want to be surrounded by people who were all the same as you, right?"

"Yeah, I guess I did. I sure don't have a sarcastic streak. Maybe I'll learn something from you."

She nudged him with her elbow. "Stick with me. You can teach me French, and I'll show you the fine art of mockery and well-placed ridicule."

He chuckled. "You got a deal." He paused. "And Stella?"

"Yeah?"

"Thanks for listening. And helping today. Patti and I appreciate it."

"It's been fun. I look forward to tomorrow, if you still need me."

He nodded. "Seven-thirty sharp, if that's okay with you."

She saluted, then carried several boxes to the van and loaded them inside.

Chapter Fifteen

Stella was exhausted from standing all day at the pastry booth. She'd experienced the most interaction with other human beings than she'd had in years. And she loved it, eager to return to the Faire on Sunday morning to help Patti and David again.

At six a.m. her cell phone rang, waking her from a sound sleep.

She rubbed her eyes, blinked, then searched for her phone. It had accidentally fallen to the floor, and she reached to pick it up and hit the answer key.

"Hello?"

"I'm so sorry to call this early, Stella. This is David."

Stella sat up straight and tried her best to wake up her mind. David was on the phone, probably cancelling on her, not needing her help today. She had probably messed up somehow and they'd lost money, which made her look like a thief. Dang!

"What's up, David? My alarm was going to go off soon anyway."

"I can't be on the phone for long. I had to bring Patti to the E.R. at two in the morning. They admitted her. Her organs are shutting down. She isn't doing too well."

Stella cradled her forehead in her hand, closed her eyes. Granted, she'd only met the couple yesterday, but from everything Kat told her and how the two of them welcomed her, Stella knew they were "good people" and she felt so sorry for Patti. Her life being cut short by a terrible disease that still had no cure.

"I am so sorry, David. Is there anything, *anything* I can do to help?"

"I don't want to disappoint Patti by closing down the booth today but of course I'm not leaving her, and it's really is too much for one person to handle, so I'm sorry—"

"Wait! David! I can do it. Really, I can. Maybe people will have to wait longer to be served, but I don't mind running it by myself. It was fun yesterday. The folks in Monarch Bay are so friendly, I almost feel like I've lived here for months already. I can do it. Please let me handle it for you."

Her speech met with a short silence. She heard David's breath hitch and surmised he was trying to control his emotions. What a terrible thing to happen to Patti… and to him. They were so much in love.

"I'm tempted to say yes. But you'll need to stop by the bakery first and load the van with the pastries Pascal is baking right now. He sometimes helps me out, especially when the Faire's going on. I'll call him now. He'll help you get settled, and you can drive the van to the Faire. But are you sure about this, Stella?"

"Absolutely. I'm getting up right now, and I'll be at the bakery in about twenty minutes. Is that okay?"

He let out a breath. "You're an angel sent from Heaven. I believe you *can* do this. But feel free to pack up early if you get overwhelmed or tired or whatever. And you can always reach me at this number. It's my cell. We'll probably be at the hospital for most of the day, but I'm not sure of anything right now."

"Don't worry about the booth, David. You tell Patti I send her my love and I'll take care of everything for you guys. I promise."

Stella closed her phone, showered, dressed, left a note for Katrina and ran to Patti's Pastries where she introduced herself to Pascal—an older, grey-haired Frenchman who spoke with a beautiful accent. He'd already boxed up the cookies, pies, brownies, breads, and cakes—more than they had yesterday. They'd sold out most of the pastries early on Saturday, and David told Stella he expected a larger crowd on Sunday. Stella geared up for a long and prosperous day for Patti's Pastries and zoomed off in the van with a smile on her face.

Stella spent all day at the Faire, from seven-thirty until four-thirty and sold every single pastry Pascal had baked. The till overflowed with bills and change, but she left that for David to count and returned the van to the bakery parking lot.

She walked home, slumped in the lounge chair on the deck, and closed her eyes.

The front door slammed shut, and Loreen's voice echoed

through the hallway. She wasn't alone, but Stella didn't recognize the male voice. It wasn't Gabe.

Loreen rounded the corner and jumped when she saw Stella. "Whoa! You scared me. Kat told me you'd probably be at the Faire all day."

A young man with short, spiked, dark brown hair, wearing black leather pants and jacket, moved next to Loreen and encircled her waist with his arm.

Loreen smiled at him, then turned to Stella. "Mom, this is Harley. He's a senior at Monarch High. We have some of the same classes."

Just then Remy bounded onto the deck, barking his head off.

Stella stood and pet Remy's head. "It's okay, boy."

He let out a deep, low woof, walked tentatively toward Harley, sniffed his legs, then wiggled his butt and tail and licked his hand.

Harley squatted down to Remy's level and looked him in the eyes. Remy stuck out his tongue and licked Harley's face from one side to the other, then placed his paw on Harley's knee and whined.

"Wow, is he a beautiful dog," Harley whispered.

Stella chuckled. "I think he likes you more than he likes us."

Harley stood and stretched out his hand. "Nice to meet you, Mrs. Jensen."

He had a firm grip, impressive for a teenager. "Nice to meet you, too, Harley. Is there a reason they call you Harley? I mean, does it have anything to do with the motorcycle?"

Loreen beamed. "He's the only senior at Monarch High who rides a Harley Davidson to school. That's where he got the nickname. He works on the bike himself too. It's a cool ride. Lotsa fun."

Stella frowned. "You mean you've already been on it, Lo?"

Loreen nodded. "He has a motorcycle license, Mom. It's legal."

Stella let out a deep breath. "I would appreciate if you'd ask before going on a motorcycle like that or a car with a boy I've never met. You know the rules." She glanced at Harley. "Nothing against you whatsoever, Harley. This is a rule Loreen has been aware of forever."

Harley took a quick look at Loreen, then turned to Stella. "No offense taken, Mrs. Jensen. Parental rules are made because you care. I get that."

Loreen rolled her eyes. "I'm almost eighteen, Mom. I could

move out of the house and be on my own soon. Then I won't need your permission. Harley's been riding that bike for years now."

Harley took hold of Loreen's hand, facing her. "Yeah, I've been riding that bike now for several years. But your mother's got a point. She doesn't know me. I'd like to start out making a good impression here, Lo, and that's not happening."

"Harley?" Stella said.

He turned to Stella. "Yes, ma'am?"

"Until I get to know you a little better, it would be best if Loreen walked home from school. I'd feel more comfortable."

He shrugged. "That's okay with me, Mrs. Jensen." He leaned toward Loreen and whispered none too softly, "Don't worry. I'll win her over in no time."

Stella laughed. "At least one of you understands."

Harley performed an exaggerated bow to Stella. "It was a pleasure meeting you, Mrs. Jensen."

"Likewise," Stella said. "I look forward to seeing you around. Oh, and please call me Stella."

"Well, Stella, I don't scare away that easily."

Loreen rolled her eyes at Stella, then pulled Harley toward the front room.

The front door opened then shut. Loreen returned and sat on the chaise lounge, wearing a deep frown on her face. "Why'd you do that, Mom? I am totally humiliated. You're treating me like a little kid when I'm gonna be graduating next June. I'm not a baby."

Stella sighed. "I'm not treating you like a baby, Loreen. You have always asked before you ventured out with your girlfriends and guy friends when we lived in Corvallis. Nothing's changed. *You* changed the rules. Not I."

"Well, they're stupid rules. I don't think I should have to follow the same rules I've been following since I was a freshman. Fuckin' A!"

"Don't swear at me, Lo. I'm not the bad guy here. If you think the rules need to be changed, then you should have come to me and we could have discussed it. But you unilaterally changed them without asking. That's not fair and you know it."

Loreen stared at the ground. "Sorry." She slowly lifted her head. "Do you think you could relax the rules a little then, Mom? I'd like to be able to go for a ride with my boyfriend sometimes."

"Your boyfriend? Since when did Harley become your boyfriend?"

Loreen bent her head back, looked at the sky, then let out a sigh. "For a while. We're exclusive now. I really like him."

Stella tried to recall her high school days, but she hadn't been popular like Kat, didn't have a boyfriend until after she graduated high school. She wondered if she needed to have the "sex talk" with Loreen, sooner rather than later. She recalled reading about a mandatory sex education class during junior and senior years at Monarch High and wondered if Loreen had already taken one in Corvallis or was enrolled for a class at Monarch High.

Stella cleared her throat a couple of times, then plunged ahead. "There's a mandatory sex ed class for juniors and seniors. Have you already taken it?"

Loreen rolled her eyes. "I'm enrolled in it already. But I already know all about that stuff."

"Oh, you do? And where did you learn all about having sex and contraceptives? From your girlfriends?"

Loreen crossed her arms over her chest. "As a matter of fact, yes. And I'm the only girl I know who was a virgin."

"Excuse me. *Was* a virgin?"

Loreen waved her hand in the air. "*Sor-ry*. I meant "is"."

Stella squinted at her daughter. "I hope that's what you meant, Lo. And Harley is how old?"

Loreen lifted her chin, looking defiant. "He's twenty-one. He got held back a few years cause he got in trouble a lot, but he said he's past all that now."

"Good to know," Stella said, then reached out and took hold of her daughter's hand, guiding her to the chaise lounge to sit next to her. "Look, Loreen. As of this one meeting with Harley, I'll be honest with you, he seems like a polite young man, respectful, funny." She stared into Loreen's eyes. "Will you please cut me some slack here, Lo. I'm doing the best I can as a single mom, and I need to know you're safe, that the guy you're with isn't violent like your father, that he won't take advantage of a virgin like you."

Loreen huffed out a breath. "He's not like that, Mom."

"You've known him for how long? Don't act like you've been friends for months and months because you haven't. You need to be careful."

Loreen nodded. "We've been hanging out together since the first day of school. And I get it, Mom. I promise to be careful."

Stella smiled. "I'm glad you shared that with me. I know I seem as ancient as a Triceratops to you, but I recall quite easily what it was like in high school."

Loreen gasped. "No way? No one's memory could possibly go back that far. Wasn't that the Pleistocene Age?" She grinned.

"You're treading on thin ice, young lady."

"I'm just joking. In fact, a couple of the guys at school asked me who the chick was who came to school with us that day you enrolled Gabe and me."

Stella pulled her head back sharply. "You have got to be kidding me. I'm forty years old. Lo. I hope you told them that."

"Well, I didn't exactly tell them how old you are, but I did agree with them. You're pretty hot."

Stella covered her face with both hands. "Oh. My. God. You didn't?"

"You're a total cougar, Mom. You got a rep now, so you better live up to it, yo."

Stella dropped her hands, then stared at her daughter. After a few seconds she chuckled. "I could be flattered… *yo*… but I choose not to. I'm your mother, and I deserve respect."

"Harley respects you, Mom."

Stella nodded. "It seemed that way. Let's wait and see. Just take it slow, Loreen. Promise me that?"

"Yeah." Loreen sighed overly loudly. "Can I go now?"

Stella lifted her index finger in the air. "Just one more question."

"Ye-es," Loreen strung out the word to two syllables.

"Have you met his parents?"

"He has no parents. They abandoned him when he was real young. He lives with his aunt and uncle somewhere south of here."

"I'm sorry to hear that. That's awful. Poor guy. There's not much south of Monarch Bay unless you're talking about Pismo Beach."

Loreen shook her head. "He lives in a trailer off Highway 101, kinda up in the hills. He needs transportation to get to school, and his uncle lets him borrow his Harley."

"Let's have him over for dinner sometime. I can get to know him a bit better. How about that?"

"Cool." Loreen stood and walked into the house.

Stella slumped back onto the lounge chair. "Teenagers," she whispered, watching her daughter walk away. Was she up to this job? Raising teenagers alone? "Guess I have no choice," she said to no one.

The front door slammed, and Katrina rounded the corner.

"Stella! Hey. I got your note. How'd it today go?"

"I just got back a little while ago. Have you heard anything more about Patti?"

"They're home now." Kat dropped into a chaise lounge, took off her shoes, then leaned back. "He called in hospice." Her bottom lip quivered.

Remy suddenly appeared at Kat's side and whined.

"Hey, Rem. I'll be okay, boy." Kat bent over and kissed the top of his head. He licked her neck then laid down on the floor next to the chaise lounge.

"Oh, man. I am so sorry about Patti," Stella said. "Is there anything we can do?"

"I don't think so. I talked to David. He's thinking of closing their shop." She covered her mouth with one hand, draped the other hand over the side and pet Remy's head.

"Geez, that's rough."

Kat stared at her sister. "I can't imagine how the two of them are feeling right now. I mean, we all knew this day was coming, but somehow, you know, you just stuff it in the back of your mind and ignore it. Pretend it isn't gonna happen. Which is stupid really, because I feel as if I've been hit by a truck. I can't even begin to imagine how David's feeling."

"Are we talking weeks or days? Do you know?"

"David said she might hang on for a few days. Once your organs start shutting down… well… They're not going to try to resuscitate her to keep her alive for a few more hours or anything like that. It sounded pretty imminent. Shit!" Kat pounded her fists on her thighs. "This is such bullshit. She's way too young. Why the hell didn't she go to the doctor? What was she thinking?"

Stella sat next to her sister and put her arm around her shoulders. There were no words to make the situation any better. Stella could only try to help out, do what she could to ease David's mind with regard to shutting down the bakery, which she suspected was his only source of income.

"You know what, Kat? Let me run this by you. I met Pascal, the bakery chef. What if he did the baking for Patti and I took Patti's place at the register up front, selling the baked goods? I could do that. I'd love it. Then David could take some time off to be with Patti. What do you think?"

Kat turned to her sister. "Are you serious?"

Stella nodded.

"That's fuckin' genius." She stood. 'Hold that thought. I need a cup of coffee." She walked into the kitchen. "Want one?"

Stella followed her and sat at the kitchen table. "Yeah, I need a pick-me-up right now. So what do you think about my plan for Patti's Pastries?"

Kat reached for two mugs, the box of coffee filters, and got the cream out of the refrigerator. "I think it's perfect, Stell. Do you want me to talk to him, or would you rather ask him yourself? I know you don't know him well, but I don't think I have to intervene. Do you?"

"I can call him. Or at least text him and tell him I'd like to run it by him. Then he can call me when he feels like it. What do you think? You know him way better than I do?"

"Text him. He'll call when he's ready to talk." Kat swiped at the tears on her cheeks. "I've gotta tell Marcus about Patti. I don't think he'll be able to return early from this trip. He's in Florida."

"I forgot about that."

Stella got her cell phone and texted David.

Kat set their mugs on the table and sat across from her sister.

Stella took a sip of coffee. "Do you know anything about a boy named Harley? He's a senior at Monarch High with the twins?"

"Rides a Harley?"

"That's the guy."

"Why do you wanna know?"

"He's Loreen's new boyfriend."

Kat shook her head, eyebrows scrunched together.

Stella's stomach dropped. "What?"

"If ever the expression 'he comes from the wrong side of the tracks' would fit somebody, it's that poor boy. You know he's twenty years old or maybe older. I cut his aunt's hair. I know she's into drugs.

She comes in all spaced out every time I see her, a total crack head. And the uncle's an alcoholic on top of everything else. That doesn't mean the boy's doing drugs though. I'd keep an open mind."

"Just great." Stella picked up a spoon and stirred her coffee continuously for no reason. "Anything else I need to know?"

"Just keep the line of communication open with Loreen."

Stella nodded.

"It wouldn't be right to judge the boy just because he's surrounded by people who use and sell drugs."

"They sell drugs too? Good God! Does it get any worse?"

Kat reached out and covered her sister's hand. "I'll ask Marcus what he knows. Harley may be totally fine. I don't know. But keep talking with Loreen. That's the best advice I can give you. But I don't have kids, so I may be talking out of my ass."

Stella shook her head. "It's good advice. And I'll do that." She stood. "I have to shower. It's been a long day."

When she exited the shower, she'd gotten a call from David, so she phoned him back.

"Stella, hi. I wanted to get back to you right away about your text. If you really are serious about working at the shop, I'll pay you the going wage and you can make your own hours. You don't have to open the shop at eight in the morning and close at five. Whatever hours you'd be available, I'll take it. I'd love not to shut down completely. Patti would be devastated if I did."

"No worries, David. Eight to five fits right into my not-busy schedule. I'd love to do it. How's Patti doing?"

"Hanging in there. The pain shot through the roof today. She's heavily medicated. Hospice says she won't last long." He paused, let out a deep breath. "Even though I knew what to expect, the reality of it is like someone punched me in the gut."

"I'm so sorry. If there's anything Kat or I can do—"

"You taking over the shop means more to us than I can tell you. I really appreciate it. You don't even know me. You have a heart of gold."

"Not according to my teenage daughter. Oh, sorry, I don't know why I said that. Let me let you go. And give Patti a hug from me."

"I'll expect an explanation about your teenage daughter sometime. Maybe if you come by and say hello to Patti we can talk about something other than what's really going on."

"Maybe Kat and I could come by soon. But you text me later and tell me if that's okay."

"Will do. Thanks, Stella."

Stella placed her phone on the dresser and sat on the bed, thinking of the randomness of life. Why Patti and not someone else? Why now and not ten years from now? How did it all fit together? It was like a puzzle, out of one's control. The pieces fit only one way and you couldn't force them to go in some other way.

She lay back on the bed and closed her eyes. This had not been one of the best days of her life. The Faire had been amazing, and she was proud of herself for keeping the booth open all day and making so much money for Patti's Pastries. But meeting Harley and being told he was her daughter's boyfriend threw her for a loop. Then finding out Patti was literally on her death bed? Total bummer.

She woke up hours later, and it was dark outside. She realized she hadn't had dinner. Had Gabriel come home?

Chapter Sixteen

The following day Stella arrived at the bakery at five in the morning. She wanted to talk with Pascal and ask him for any suggestions he might give her for doing the best job she could. She'd never come this close to "managing" a store of any kind nor had she ever had so much responsibility, and she didn't want to make any serious mistakes. Patti and David were counting on her, and she wanted to shine. It was a bonus she'd be getting paid too, since her funds were dwindling. But she'd have done this job for free because… well, because it was the right thing to do.

With Pascal's baking almost complete, trays and trays of baked goods on rolling carts lined the kitchen and the aromas woke her right up, since she was still tired from the past weekend. In a nutshell Pascal would bake and bake to keep up with what was needed, based on what sold the fastest that day and historically what customers bought each day of the week. Patti had kept meticulous notes.

Stella's job at the front was to make sure she used gloves to pull out the pastries then either bag them or place them on plates for the customers, then remove her gloves, ring up their purchases, put on a new set of gloves, and continue the same routine throughout the day. They also served coffee but not specialty coffee—no lattes or macchiatos. Customers would have to go across the street if they wanted the fancy stuff, though the coffee at Patti's came from Columbia. Stella had a cup, and it was delicious.

The day flew by with lulls interspersed with lines of five to ten people. She hung a small sign behind the cash register explaining she was an "employee in training," which led to numerous questions concerning Patti's and David's absence. Stella waffled about what best to answer and decided to tell everyone Patti and David were taking a short vacation. She didn't feel it was her place to reveal medical information about Patti's condition.

She texted David twice that all was going well, he had nothing to worry about concerning the shop. She closed up at five o'clock and walked the few short blocks to Kat's house. On her way, Stella heard music playing and slowed when she noticed a garage door open and speakers on tables in the driveway. At first she thought the sound was coming from a radio, but as she approached, a young kid, head bent, playing a guitar, swung his head up and down with the beat of the drums. Obviously a live garage band.

Inching closer, Stella caught sight of an Anderson Paak T-shirt and the side of a boy's face—Gabriel. He had a guitar pick in one hand. He angled his head over the guitar, flipping his head up and down to the music. To Stella, it appeared he might be playing bass guitar. Listening intently, she recognized the song, though she couldn't recall the name, their rendition amazingly identical to the original.

She approached the garage from the side and stood, listening and watching, completely in awe of the quality and togetherness of this boy band. Then she saw a couple lounging on a couch on one side of the garage, holding hands, laughing—Loreen and Harley. Glancing toward the street, Stella caught sight of Harley's motorcycle and shook her head. Dang it! She'd be surprised if Loreen walked here, and Harley rode his motorcycle alone. Though she guessed it was possible. However, not very plausible.

The song ended, and the four boys—bassist (her son), main guitarist, drummer, and singer—high-fived each other, grinning and shouting words Stella couldn't make out from where she stood.

Loreen suddenly saw her mom standing near the side of the entrance to the garage and ran to Stella. "Did you hear them, Mom?"

Stella smiled. "Amazing. I can't believe how much that song sounded like the original version. I'm impressed."

"For real. What're you doing here?"

"I'm helping out the owners of Patti's Pastries. You remember the couple whose booth I worked at the Monarch Bay Faire? Well, I'm working for them while Patti's sick. I was walking home and heard some really good music. Thought I'd stop by. And here you are. And Gabe too. I noticed Harley's motorcycle, Loreen."

"Don't freak out, Mom. I called him after Gabe invited me to watch them practice. Harley just got here, all on his own."

Stella stared into her daughter's eyes. She'd never lied to Stella before, as far as Stella knew. So Stella made the decision to trust Loreen as she always had, and hugged her daughter. "Thank you for doing as I asked, honey. I appreciate it."

Loreen gestured at Harley to join them. He hopped off the couch and stood next to Loreen.

"Hi, Harley," Stella said.

"Hello, Mrs. Jensen."

"Remember, it's Stella. If you'll be spending time with my daughter, I think that's more comfortable for both of us. Would you like to come over sometime for dinner?"

He stared at the ground, kicking a pebble with his boot. "That would be awesome." He glanced up at her. "You sure?"

Stella placed a hand on his forearm. "Of course, I'm sure. Loreen and I can figure out a good night, and she'll let you know. Do you want to walk to Kat's house together right now? Have something to drink? Chat for awhile?"

He stared at Stella, as if he hadn't heard her.

Loreen nudged him in the ribs with her elbow.

He blinked several times, then smiled. "Uh, sure, Mrs.… I mean Stella. Let me grab my jacket. I'll leave my bike here for now."

Stella held up her index finger. "Gimme a second. I want to say hello and goodbye to your brother."

It took her only a second to give Gabriel a hug. He was all smiles, so proud of himself for his ability to pick up the bass guitar, an instrument he'd never played before arriving in Monarch Bay. He didn't have time to talk to Stella right then, but she promised she'd watch them play at their first gig, which he said might be the next dance at Monarch High. Stella hugged him a second time, then joined Loreen and Harley on the sidewalk.

The three of them chatted about the great weather in Monarch Bay, mid-term exams, the upcoming Halloween dance, where they hoped Gabriel's band would be hired to play. When they reached Kat's house Stella searched through her purse for the front door key.

Remy barked on the other side of the door.

"Just a second, Rem." She found the key, opened the door and the three of them stepped inside.

Remy jumped up and put his paws on Harley's chest.

Harley grinned from ear to ear. "Hey, Remy! How ya doin', guy?"

The dog licked under Harley's chin.

Harley laughed out loud.

"Let's go sit at the picnic table outside," Stella said.

Stella brought out three tall glasses of crushed ice and three colas, then sat across from the two of them at the picnic table.

"So, Harley, my sister Kat told me you live with your aunt and uncle south of here?"

He nodded. "Yeah, I guess you could say that."

Loreen bumped shoulders with Harley. "You can tell my mom anything, Harley. She won't judge. Will you, Mom?"

Stella looked into Harley's eyes and saw something. She wasn't sure exactly what, but it was almost as if he was afraid whatever he'd reveal to her was a secret. And she certainly didn't know him well enough to make a promise and expect him to believe her. But she'd do her best to gain his trust. Obviously her daughter liked this young man, and she trusted her daughter's instincts.

"Harley, whatever it is you decide to tell me, I promise I will not tell anyone. You can trust me. It you trust Loreen's advice to trust me, that is."

He smirked. "Guess most people around here know all this sh-, stuff anyway." He shrugged. "My aunt's an addict. Pills, meth, I don't know what all. My uncle's an alcoholic. Been ticketed enough times for driving under the influence, they took his license away. Which is why I get to drive his Harley around. I couldn't afford one myself, that's for sure. I work at the local guitar shop in town and don't earn shi-... don't earn much money."

Stella tilted her head to the side. "I'm sorry to hear about your aunt and uncle. That sure doesn't sound like the easiest place to grow up. You probably love being able to escape from that environment by riding the Harley around."

He nodded. "It helps. I feel free when I'm drivin' around. Wish Loreen could join me sometimes though."

"I understand your feeling that way, Harley. And I'm sure she will. I wish you could understand that not only do I have a fear of motorcycles because one of my friends died in a horrible accident when she was eighteen, but I also don't know you. Yet. You're a stranger to me, so I'm a bit 'motherly' about my baby girl. I don't expect you do get that. You're only, what twenty, twenty-one?"

"I'll be twenty-one in a month."

"So you're still quite young. But a bit older than my daughter. She hasn't even graduated high school yet."

"Neither have I. But I'm supposed to, if I keep my grades up."

Loreen rolled her eyes. "He's being modest, Mom. He's gotten all As ever since he returned to Monarch High in his junior year. He's a genius when it comes to calculus and anything math-related. Don't let his aunt and uncle's reputation sway you."

Stella poured her cola over the ice, watched the fizz climb to the edge of the glass before she set the can back on the table. "I don't really care that your aunt and uncle are addicted to drugs or alcohol. I mean, I care in the sense that they're human beings, and I hate to see a life go to waste, and they obviously have problems that they're trying to hide from or forget about by using drugs. But that doesn't mean *you're* that way, Harley." She stared him down, eye to eye. "Does it?"

He took a long drink of his cola, swallowed. "People around here have been really kind to me. They haven't pegged me for a druggie or an alcoholic. I think they're all watching me though. But I don't touch that shit." He stopped. "Sorry. I should respect that you're Loreen's mother and not swear in front of you."

Stella swiped her hand in the air. "It doesn't bother me. That's not the type of thing I judge a person by. It's their actions. You can swear like a sailor, but if you're a kind person and don't hurt others, that's what I want to see in another human being. Especially someone who's dating my daughter, or whatever you young people call it now when you two are 'hanging out', quote unquote."

Stella paused, gathering her thoughts. "I want you to know, Harley, I don't judge you based on whatever your aunt and uncle do. All of us know how to get drugs or alcohol or guns or whatever these days. Everything is available no matter where you live. I'm not going to judge you by your aunt and uncle's actions simply because you live with them. And I won't judge you by the clothes you wear or if you say shit, damn, fuck or whatever. It's not what you say as much as what you *do*. That's what sways me in one direction or the other."

Harley smiled, and Stella's heart ached for the boy… man. What a complicated life for being so young. To have lost both parents, then be relegated to second or third place in importance to his aunt and uncle's addictions. Wow!

'Why don't I leave you two alone?" Stella said. "I'm going to go take a nap. I look forward to having you over for dinner sometime soon, Harley. How about next time we do Taco Night, Loreen? We won't try to impress you too much by making a roast with mashed potatoes and gravy. I'll save that for another time."

Harley grinned. "Thank you". He stood as Stella raised her butt off the seat. "I've never been invited to anyone's house for dinner. Lots of people wouldn't."

Stella smiled. "We're not 'lots of people,' Harley. I'll see you later." She glanced to the side, saw Remy and slapped her hand on her thigh. "Come with me, Rem. Let's go take a nap."

Remy stood and followed her up the stairs into her bedroom. He jumped onto the bed, circled round and round then plopped down with a groan.

Stella flopped onto her bed next to him, arms stretched out to the sides. Her upper arm muscles ached from carrying the pastry trays from the kitchen to the front of the shop. Then she thought of poor Patti, lying in bed, probably wishing she could have come in to work today and sold bakery goods to her "regulars". Stella had no right whatsoever to complain. She set an alarm on her cell phone for thirty minutes and closed her eyes.

Chapter Seventeen

Stella arrived at Patti's Pastries at five the next morning. David greeted her as he schlepped a tray of pastries to the glass cases at the front of the shop. Stella hung up her hoodie and purse and was tying an apron around her waist when he returned through the double swinging doors.

She looked up. "How's Patti doing? You didn't have to come in to—"

"She's gone, Stella. Couple of hours ago. The coroner took her away."

Stella shut her eyes, then walked toward David, whose face looked as if he'd aged overnight. His pants hung loose and low on his hips, and his stomach almost seemed concave. In just a matter of days? Then she realized he'd been caring for Patti for more than year. She was sure it had been an impossibly difficult road to walk and had finally caught up with him.

She wrapped her arms around him and hugged him tightly. "I am so sorry, David. Patti didn't deserve to get this horrible disease. I hate cancer."

"So do I," he whispered.

Stella felt his upper body shake and knew he was silently sobbing. She remained still, hugging him lightly, in case he wanted to pull away.

After a few minutes he leaned back and swiped at his eyes with his fists. "I thought I'd be prepared for this day. But I was only fooling myself. I feel as if my heart died with her. I'm empty. Hollow. A shell. I don't know how to exist without her. We were high school sweethearts. She was my everything."

Stella nodded. "I'm sure it seems impossible the pain will ever go away. But I'm hoping it does. Maybe you'll wake up one of these days and realize you still love Patti and you always will, but she'd want you to be happy. Whenever that happens, it'll happen. And most likely when you least expect it. Patti will always be with you, David. Here." She placed her hand over her heart. "Patti will always be in your heart. That will never change."

He nodded, but words appeared impossible at the moment. He turned and grabbed another tray and walked to the front. Stella followed him with another tray until they were finished. They worked side by side the whole day until four o'clock. When no one had come in for a half-hour, he asked Stella to close the till, and he turned the sign on the front door, notifying anyone who might stop by that the bakery was closed for the day.

He thanked Stella for all her help. "Will you be able to come in tomorrow? It doesn't have to be at five in the morning. If you can make it by nine or ten, that's fine by me."

Stella patted David's arm. "Do you need help at five or six in the morning?"

"I could use it, yes. I can take over the baking for Pascal. He was only doing this as a favor to me. Theoretically, he's retired."

"Then I'll be here at five o'clock sharp. And I don't mean in the afternoon."

He leaned in and hugged her. "Thank you for everything. I'll see you tomorrow."

Stella took the long way home, via the boardwalk. She pulled off her shoes and trudged through the warm sand. The feeling of the sand spilling through her toes made her smile. She ran the last several feet until she reached the water's edge, then dipped her toes in. The water was so much warmer than the ocean off the Oregon coast, like night and day.

She made her way along the edge where the water was only a few inches deep and wished she could go swimming, but she wasn't dressed for that. Just feeling the wind in her hair and on her face, the sun on her arms and scalp, relaxed her to the core. She breathed in the salty air and let it out slowly. Ocean meditation.

And she thought about Patti. Gone forever from David's life. How sad. She couldn't relate. She'd never lost a partner. Not like this. She hoped she'd "lost" Robert, and good riddance to bad rubbish, as her mom used to say. She hoped someday someone treated him the way he'd treated her. Actually she didn't want to feel like a revengeful bitch but… all those years gone to waste.

She shook herself. They weren't totally useless years. She'd given birth to two lovely kids, who made her proud every day of her life. And she had reunited with her sister Kat, had a beautiful home to stay in until she could make it on her own, a fun job at Patti's Pastries, if David needed her for more than a few days. Life was good. And too short to fill with regrets and negativity.

She must have walked about a mile down the beach, almost to Pismo Beach, she guessed, then she sprinted back to Monarch Bay, having found energy somewhere in her bones. When she reached the boardwalk near Kat's home, she walked barefoot the rest of the way.

She found Kat at the kitchen table crying. Remy stood next to her, head draped over her thigh, staring up at Kat with sad-looking eyes.

Oh, my God. What next? Life seemed almost more complicated here in Monarch Bay than in Corvallis. But she knew she would never want to return to her life in Oregon with Robert, no social life, having her kids see the horrible side of their father year after year.

But since she'd arrived in Monarch Bay, Patti had passed away, her daughter's first boyfriend turned out to be much older than she and rode a Harley Davidson motorcycle, and she'd soon be having sex, if she wasn't already. Her son had joined a garage band. Yikes! She guessed this was what it meant to have a full life. She knew, from the mindfulness app on her phone, what caused stress was her reaction to events. She had to learn to watch life flow by like a river and not get pulled in with the undertow.

Stella sat across from her sister and grasped both her hands. "Kat, what's wrong?"

Kat wiped her tears with a balled-up tissue, then drew in a deep breath. "Another negative pregnancy test." She placed her hand on top of Remy's head, rubbing the fur back and forth.

Stella sat next to her sister. "How many years have you been trying?"

"For like, ever… maybe four or five years."

"It probably doesn't help that he's gone for weeks at a time, then he's only home for a week or less. If you're not ovulating during that particular time then it's going to be very difficult."

Kat nodded. "You're right. We talked a tiny bit about him changing jobs. But, Stella, he loves driving a big rig. The freedom. He wouldn't be happy working some desk job, coming home every evening, watching TV, waking up the next morning to do it all over again. He loves the opportunity to see the country in all its seasons.

"And like I told you, when he returns, the romance is almost like it was when we met. We miss each other terribly, which makes for some pretty hot times together when he returns. I'm upset, because I just talked to the doctor. She ran some additional tests. It's all me. I'm the problem."

"What do you mean, you're the problem?"

"At thirty-five I'm already peri-menopausal. That's what the tests show. There's a huge chance if I don't get pregnant, like right now, the statistics are against me for getting pregnant, like ever."

"Oh, Kat. That's so sad. What about a surrogate?"

"Marcus and I haven't talked about it. I don't know."

"There's always adoption."

Kat shook her head. "I really want a baby that's genetically mine and Marcus's."

"Then surrogacy might be the best avenue for you two." Kat nodded. "I wonder if I'd be a viable candidate for surrogacy?"

Kat's eyes widened. "Are you fucking kidding me?"

"I'd do it for you guys. My pregnancy with the twins was a piece of cake." She raised her index finger. "But… and this could be a big but. I'm forty, Kat. I wouldn't be surprised it the doctor told me I'm not a good candidate to be a surrogate for your baby, because I'm peri-menopausal too."

"You'd actually be interested in carrying our baby for nine months, then giving it up?"

Stella nodded. "Yes, I would. And I have absolutely no desire to have another child, Kat, so you don't have to worry about me changing my mind. I'm happy having two kids."

"But it's such a gigantic, unselfish thing to do for… for anyone, Stella. I mean. I can't believe it."

"I love you, Kat. I'd do anything for you. And having children has been the best thing I've ever experienced in my life. Until I held the twins in my arms, I didn't know what falling in love meant. There's nothing quite like it. I want that for you too."

Tears coursed down Kat's cheeks.

Remy lifted a paw onto Kat's thigh and woofed.

Kat held his paw with one hand, swiped at her tears with the other. "That means more to me than I can ever say. Can I talk to Marcus about it? I mean, are you really and truly serious? Don't you think you should think about it for awhile first?"

"No. I don't need to. It's not like I haven't been pregnant before, Kat. I know what I'd be getting myself in for. And I'd love to do that for both of you."

Kat threw her arms around Stella and sobbed.

Remy barked several times.

Stella started to cry as well, and after several minutes they released each other. They both stared at Remy and shared a laugh.

"Thank you, Stella. I love you so much."

"And I love you. And Marcus, of course. And if he agrees to this, you can make the appropriate appointments for me, and we can begin this thing. If they determine I'm a viable candidate, then let's do it."

"I'll call my doctor." Kat stood. "I can't believe this." She clapped her hands. "Wouldn't it be the coolest thing if you're able to do this? I know I shouldn't get my hopes up already, but it's hard not to." She grinned. "You're the best, Big Sis."

"I hope it all works out." Stella stood. "By the way, I accidentally ran into my son a couple of blocks from here. He's in a garage band. Loreen and Harley were there too. I talked to Harley a little and asked him to join us next time we do Taco Night. Is that okay with you?"

"Sounds fun."

"Tonight?"

Kat nodded.

"I'll text Loreen now."

"What do you think of Harley, Stell?"

"You know what? I feel sorry for him. Living with an aunt and uncle who are addicted to drugs and alcohol can't possibly be good for any kid. And Loreen told me he's a straight-A student. He rides the Harley to get to school, because his uncle isn't allowed to drive any more. Too many DUIs."

"What about drug use?"

"According to Harley, he doesn't touch that shit. His words. Then he apologized for swearing in front of me."

Kat gasped. "Seriously? Well, who knew, right?"

Stella raised her eyebrows. "Don't judge a book by its cover, right?"

"Yeah. Just cause he rides a Harley and wears a leather jacket doesn't mean shit."

"I gotta shower first." Stella stopped in her tracks. "Oh, my God. Of course you heard about Patti. David is devastated."

"That's what threw me over the edge today." Kat teared up, and she shook her head. "She's so freaking young. And they were so much in love. Like no couple I've ever met before. Are you going to continue working at the shop?"

"Yeah, I am. It's the only thing I can do for David. He doesn't need any more stress right now. I feel so bad for him. Patti was so young." When Stella reached the stairs she turned around. "And I can work at Patti's Pastries even when I'm pregnant."

Kat swiped at her eyes and chuckled. "I'll think only good thoughts, Stella. It would be the answer to all my prayers. You can't know how much it means to me that you even offered."

"Anything for you, Katrina Dina."

"Been a long time since you called me that, Bella Stella."

"You know what the nickname you gave me means, don't you?"

"Beautiful Stella." Kat chuckled. "But Katrina Dina doesn't have any true significance."

"Just sounds good, is all. What do you expect? You were like five years old when I started calling you that."

"You always took such good care of me after Mom and Dad died."

"I dreamed of having kids since forever. It was my chance to try out my mothering skills. But we both know Fiona did a better job than I ever did."

"Fiona wasn't there when I was bullied in grammar school. You were. She was a loving and gentle person. You were my only living relative."

"We needed each other, Kat. I thought of you almost like my own kid."

"You're right about being related. As much as I loved Fiona and Nason, I was lost after Mom and Dad died. You were like my mini-mom. I was beyond depressed after our parents were killed. I don't know if I ever thanked you for always being there when I needed you. So I'm saying it now."

"Well, you're welcome. That means a lot to me. And thanks for letting me practice my mothering skills. Believe me, when I found out I was having twins, I think I was less freaked out because I'd taken care of you for a few years and knew a little bit about what it was like to take care of a kid."

Kat sighed. "How the years have flown, huh? You better shower. I'll start chopping the lettuce and tomatoes and stuff for Taco Night."

Chapter Eighteen

Taco Night turned out to be a great venue for getting to know Harley better. Kat had seen him around town for years, and since Marcus owned a Harley Davidson motorcycle, too, and Kat and Marcus rode together often, Harley opened up easily. He talked about his love of being on the road, which segued into what he wanted for his future.

Stella was impressed by his intelligence and wit. He blossomed during dinner. Stella thought it had everything to do with being with people who were truly interested in getting to know him. She had the distinct impression his aunt and uncle neglected him, which wasn't hard to imagine. They spent their time loaded and drunk with little time to devote to a young man who'd lost his parents and needed attention and guidance.

David planned on having a memorial service for Patti on October thirty-first. Her favorite day of the year had been Halloween. David told Stella Patti always spent the day decorating their house. She'd dress up as a witch, sit on the porch in a rocking chair next to a cauldron of billowing dry ice, with spiders hung from the porch ceiling. She'd spend hours baking special cupcakes with orange and black frosting, handed out candy for hours, and took pictures of the children and parents who dropped by.

Marcus returned home, and Kat invited Stella to have dinner with them that evening. Stella surmised they'd want to talk about her being the surrogate mother for their baby. Gabriel planned to practice with the band and Loreen hung out with Harley nearly every night studying and listening to music in her bedroom with the door open, per Stella's orders.

Marcus picked up a large vegetarian pizza at their favorite restaurant, and after they each grabbed a piece and had taken a few bites, Marcus took a sip of his beer, then set the bottle on the table and looked across the table at Stella.

Stella looked him in the eyes. "Is this the part where you ask me if I'm serious about volunteering to carry your baby?"

He cleared his throat, and Stella noted his eyes appeared glassy. He looked as if he was going to cry.

Remy appeared by his side and licked his hand then plopped down on the floor with a deep sigh.

Stella held her breath, wondering what he was about to say.

"I never thought we'd be having this discussion, Stella. After not hearing from you for so many years, I didn't even know if we'd see you again."

Stella nodded, letting him have his say. She suspected it might be hard for him to talk about artificial insemination and sperm donation. He and Stella didn't know each other well, hadn't hung out together much. Since she'd arrived, he'd only been home one time, after his last trip.

"It means a great deal to me." He glanced at Kat, "And to your sister that you'd do this for us. We never thought we'd be in this position, but I agree with Kat, I'd love to have a baby who's genetically mine and your sister's. I'm not against adoption at all, which is what I thought would be the next step for us. Your offer is beyond surprising and," he shrugged, "really such a generous, unselfish thing for you to do. I don't know what to say."

"Say yes. Then Kat can set up the doctor's appointments necessary to do this. I want you and my sister to have kids. As I assume she's told you, I love being a mother. It's the one thing in my life that has truly given me joy and filled a need in me like nothing else I've done before or since. I want that for my baby sister." She grinned. "And for my brother-in-law."

Marcus's face flushed, then one lone tear slid down his cheek.

Remy stood and barked once.

Marcus slid his hand up and down Remy's back.

Kat kissed her husband gently on his massive shoulder.

He placed his hand over his heart. "Thank you, Stella. From the bottom of my heart."

Stella pursed her lips, struggling not to cry. She had a hard time not becoming emotionally involved when other people cried. And to see big, burly Marcus with a tear coursing down his face? Stella took in a deep breath and let it out slowly. "I'm happy to do it, Marcus. But you realize I'm forty years old, and if I'm peri-menopausal… I mean, it could be a genetic thing… I may not be a viable candidate. So let's take it one appointment at a time, my favorite brother-in-law."

His lips tipped up at the edges. "Good advice. We don't want to get ahead of ourselves." He turned to Kat. "You, too, babe. Let's not put the cart before the horse, okay?"

Kat bobbed her head up and down. "Got it, honey. No cart before the horse."

Stella grabbed a second piece of pizza and took a bite. After chewing for a few seconds, then swallowing, she picked up her glass of cola. "Did you call your gynecologist, Kat?"

"I'll set up an appointment for the three of us. It's in Morro Bay, not too far from here. Is that all right?"

"Sounds perfect," Stella said. "I can get off a little early so we're not late. We can ask the doctor all the questions you have and I have and then start the process or whatever."

Marcus raised his glass. "To getting the green light in the future for starting the process."

Stella and Kat raised their glasses as well, and the three of them toasted to their future endeavor together.

Stella leaned back and rubbed her stomach. "I think two pieces is my limit. You two have plans for Halloween?"

Kat and Marcus's eyes met. Kat lifted her shoulders. "We always go to Patti and David's place. But because of the memorial—"

Stella nodded. "David and I were talking at work about Halloween. The memorial's in the morning. He asked me if after that I'd help him decorate his house before the treat-or-treaters start coming around. Pascal is going to bake Halloween cupcakes for David to pass out. We'll try to make Patti proud. David wanted to do it in her honor, especially after the service, which'll be sad.

"I think doing the Halloween thing will help David's depression. I don't know him well enough to say what he normally is like, but he's been down since I met him. But we were introduced a day before Patti went to the E.R. and they found out her organs were shutting down. So he's rarely smiled since I met him, poor guy."

Kat took another bite of pizza. "I can't imagine what David's going through."

Marcus grabbed a third slice. "They were always like newlyweds. Pretty amazing."

"Kind of like us, Marcus," Kat added. "I love you as much, if not more, than I did back in the day."

Marcus picked up Kat's hand and kissed her knuckles. "You are the love of my life. I don't know what my life would be like without you, babe."

"Maybe next year there'll be three of us, love."

"I hope so, you two," Stella said.

"How are Loreen and Gabriel getting along at Monarch High?" Marcus said.

Stella gave him the thumbs up sign. "Gabe's in a garage band, which is pretty damn good, Marcus. You should go by his friend's house one afternoon around four and listen. I was impressed."

"And Loreen?"

"Maybe you and Harley can go out together on your bikes sometime in the future. Then you can tell me what you think of his driving skills. I won't let Loreen ride on the back of his motorcycle yet. I'd offer to take a ride, but I'm not much for motorcycles. Even with a helmet, I wouldn't feel safe."

Marcus grabbed another beer from the fridge. "What I've learned through the years is, much of the time it's the people driving cars who cause a lot of the accidents. They just aren't looking for us. They simply don't see us or hear us. Which is why I fooled around with the pipes and shit, so it's really loud. You can't help but hear me comin' about a mile away. There's a reason a lot of us do that. For our own safety.

"Kat said Harley came over for Taco Night. She was impressed. Sounded like he needed someone to just listen to him. Take some interest in his life. Often that's all a kid needs, you know? Best thing for him would be to move out of that house. Aunt and uncle are doing more harm than good."

Stella sighed. "I agree. He's a smart young man."

"What're his future plans?"

"He wants to go to college," Stella said. "He'll probably get his general ed courses out of the way at the junior college in Pismo

Beach, then decide what university to attend. Same goes for Loreen. She doesn't have any idea what she wants to do when she grows up. Maybe they'll go to junior college together. They're both undecided about their majors."

He took a swig of beer. "And Gabriel?"

"Now that one, I'm not too sure about. All he talks about is his band. He's totally focused on, quote unquote, making it big. I mean, more power to him, but I don't want him to be disappointed. However, I've learned you can't hold your kids back from their dreams just because you think you're wiser than they are since you've lived longer. That's horse shit. Oh, and his band will be playing at the Monarch High Halloween dance, if you want to see them."

Kat stood and brought their plates to the sink. "We'd love to. How cool. Both Lo and Gabe are good kids. They've got great personalities and they're looking forward to working on their futures. They're respectful and loving. You did good, Stella."

Stella shook her head. "No thanks to Robert. I hope they're not forever scarred by his abusiveness and emotional ineptitude."

Marcus drew his eyebrows together. "I think kids are resilient, Stella. Kat said they didn't like how Robert treated you. I guess Gabe got into an altercation with Robert right before you left Oregon?"

Stella played with her napkin, folding it into a triangle. "Robert head-butted Gabriel in the stomach. I could have killed him right then and there. Such a bastard. Hurting me is one thing. Being abusive to his son? That's when I decided, it's now or never, and I left with the kids and came here. Thank you both for taking us in."

Marcus lifted his index finger. "Speaking of living here… if it all turns out that you can be our child's surrogate, maybe we can work something out where I build you a house in our backyard. We've got a lot of land and it could easily fit a decent-sized home. Of course, we still want to pay for all your expenses."

Stella looked him in the eyes. "You're not going to pay me anything. We're living here rent-free right now, and I'm not sure how long we're going to be here. Both of you have been very generous about not giving us a date to get out of your hair."

Marcus pursed his lips. "We can work out the details later, Stella. If you're able to be our surrogate and you refuse to accept money, then I think, if you want to live here, I can easily get a friend or two to help me build a house in our backyard, depending on what size you want. I can do it, if the city'll give me the permits."

"Okay, okay," Stella said. "Let's talk about this down the road. I'll think about it. We have a lot to discuss once we talk to the doctor." She stood. "I'm exhausted. Think I'll leave you two lovebirds and go to my room."

Chapter Nineteen

David closed the pastry shop on October 31 for Patti's memorial service, to be held in Monarch Bay Park abutting the beach. Surprisingly, the fog didn't make an appearance that morning, and the sun's rays glistened off the waves. Stella and Kat and Marcus helped set up chairs and tables for the celebration of Patti's life.

By ten-thirty all seats had been taken, and people stood around the back and sides of the area designated for the ceremony. The chairs faced the ocean, and a light breeze blew across the park, the temperature mild at sixty-five degrees. Just the way Patti liked it, David told Stella.

David walked to the podium set up at the front, holding what looked like a statue of a mermaid in his arms. He set it to the side and tapped on the microphone.

He bowed his head, mouthed a few words to himself, then faced what appeared to be a very large contingent of Monarch Bay residents. Stella recognized almost every face from working at the bakery shop—youngsters, oldsters, teenagers, teachers from both the grammar and high schools, the mayor, babies held in their mothers's arms. Patti had obviously made an impact on many people in this small town. Stella realized her impression of Patti was correct. She had been a kind and loving wife and a friend to many.

David cleared his throat, closed his eyes for a few seconds. "I'm not going to make this a depressing event for any of us. Of course I'm devastated to have lost my wife. But she made me promise, when we all got together and she was, in her words, 'sittin' in my urn,' I'd make a few jokes, so people would lighten up. She said, 'David, maybe tell an uplifting story or something, but no tears, okay?' She also said, 'David, I've lived a full life because I had you.' That made me happier than most men who're married, given the divorce statistics in the United States."

He paused, seemed to collect himself for a second, then continued. "I was beyond lucky to have met Patti when I was a freshman in high school. You all know we were high school sweethearts, and, I'll admit, nothing much changed through the years we were together." He touched the side of his head. "Sure, I have a few grey hairs. Nothing Katrina Swanson can't fix." He smiled at Kat and nodded. People chuckled quietly.

"Time just flew by for both of us, what with finishing college, then buying a house, then getting Patti's Pastries going. The bakery shop was Patti's baby. Also, her dream come true. She got her master's degree at culinary school while I was studying drama for awhile at San Luis Obispo College." He shrugged. "Time got away from us, I guess, and our family was you." He perused all the faces of the people surrounding him and smiled. "Patti and I both felt fulfilled. We were happy. We had two chocolate labs over the years, Uje and Splash. They were like kids to us. They both guarded the shop, sitting outside the door on the sidewalk. They ate more croissants and banana bread than I did over the years." Another chuckle erupted, and David's lips curved up a bit.

"Anyway, Patti didn't want you to remember her as someone who died of breast cancer and cry over her leaving us. She did want me to do a public service announcement, urging women to get their yearly mammograms. But overall, she wanted to be remembered with a smile and your mouths stuffed with her legendary butter croissants as well." Another chuckle from the crowd.

"When I think of her greeting the customers at the shop with her big smile and a wave goodbye, that's my Patti. That's the Patti I want to think of when I say her name. 'Don't recall my last day, David,' she told me. 'Remember me at my favorite place in the world—my pastry shop. I was livin' the dream, honey.'

"And so it shall be." David looked up at the very, very blue sky, white clouds scudding toward the ocean, pushed by the offshore winds. "I'll be scattering her ashes way far out from shore." He picked up the mermaid statue. "This isn't your typical urn, but it represents the ocean, which is what Patti loved. She loved living in Monarch Bay. Loved the ocean. Loved this little town. She loved all of you. So, please, think of her with a smile. Do her that favor, will you? And eat all the pastry goods Pascal was kind enough to bake for all of us at four o'clock in the morning today. That's what Patti wanted. And I promised her we'd do that for her." He closed his eyes. "I love you, honeybear. Always and forever."

He picked up the mermaid, and Marcus stood and took it from him. The crowd got up from their chairs and walked toward the tables twenty feet away, covered with bakery goods and urns of coffee and plates and napkins. Everyone hovered around the tables and surrounding areas, some walked toward the water with plates and cups in hand, others returned to their seats in front of the podium.

Stella walked toward David, who was standing far away from the crowd, leaning against a gigantic willow tree. It appeared people were giving him his space and time to reflect. Stella waited to make eye contact before she decided to join him. David glanced up and smiled, hands in his pockets, legs crossed at the ankles. He was a strikingly handsome man. Patti had been a beautiful slender blonde. They had made the perfect couple.

"Hey," Stella said.

"Hey back," David replied.

"I'm not going to say something corny and useless like I'm sorry for your loss. Personally, I don't think it does justice to Patti. I will say that after speaking to a lot of people I served at the shop, I wish to God I'd known her for longer than a day. I think she and I would have been good friends. Kat speaks about her with such love and tender memories. I'm sad about that. And I'm sad you've lost the love of your life." She shrugged. "And with that, I'm gonna go get something to eat. Can I bring you back a pastry?"

David placed a hand on Stella's forearm. "Thank you for saying that. I know people mean well when they say they're sorry for my loss, but hearing your words really means something to me." He placed a hand on his heart. "It means something inside, you know? I don't want to be sad for the rest of my life. Patti would have hated me, if she knew that's what I did. So I'm going to try to always remember the good times and our life together with a smile. And move forward from here. That's what she made me promise her on her last day. She made me swear to move on."

Stella smiled. "Take your time, David. Give yourself the days or weeks or months or years it may take to remember all the good memories. Soak them all up, fill yourself with the positives. You'll know when it's time to move on. Whatever that means. I'm sure she did not want you to be grieving for the rest of your life. So, live up to the promise you made her. Then you'll know that wherever Patti is right now, she'll be proud of you, that you kept your word." Stella leaned in and hugged David, then walked away.

Stella, Marcus, and Kat walked home soon after. Stella didn't have to go in to work, of course, since the shop had closed for the day. She was supposed to meet up with David at three o'clock to decorate his porch. She had to pick up the cupcakes Pascal baked. David needed help setting up the dry ice machine and placing hot cider and candy on the tables.

Stella assumed she'd leave right afterward, unless he needed her to pass out candy to the little ones who were too frightened to climb the steps to the porch, where David planned to set out a skeleton and a few other monsters. It would be dark early, since it was almost November. Plus, Stella promised Gabriel, she and Kat and Marcus would stop by the high school dance to listen to their band. It would be a busy day.

Stella ate lunch, then borrowed Kat's car to pick up the cupcakes from Pascal. When she knocked on David's door at 2:30, there was no answer. She stood on tiptoe and cupped her hand around the small glass window at the top of the door but didn't see him in the front room, so she walked around to the backyard.

She opened the side gate and called out his name but received no answer. Knowing she was a wee bit early, she decided to wait in the backyard for David to arrive home. As she turned the corner, she saw him sitting in a lounge chair on the deck, legs stretched out, staring into space.

"David? It's Stella. I brought the cupcakes."

No answer.

She stepped slowly in his direction, holding the box of cupcakes out in front of her. "Do you want me to put these in the kitchen?"

No answer.

She was beginning to worry there was something wrong, so she set the box on the picnic table next to where David sat and took a seat in front of him.

She leaned forward to place herself in his line of view. "David, it's me, Stella. Are you okay?" Again he didn't answer. She reached out and took hold of his hand, squeezed.

He startled, and his eyes shifted to hers. He glanced down at her hand holding his, then up at her face. He held onto her hand tighter, and tears rolled down his cheeks. "She wanted me to make this a happy day. I have all the decorations ready to hang on the front porch. I bought the candy. I picked up the dry ice machine." He shook his head, side to side. "I can't do it, Stella. I can't do this. I don't know what to do. I don't know how to act. Who am I without her?"

Stella's heart went out to him, and she leaned closer, looked him straight in the eyes. "I can't tell you how to act or how to feel, David. Of course Patti wouldn't want you to be unhappy for the rest of your life, but to be sad is something you need to go through to reach your happy place on the other side of today. Give yourself today and however many more days it requires to mourn, cry, rage, throw something, scream, whatever. You're not a robot, David. And I didn't know Patti, but I am absolutely sure she didn't mean that you should never shed a tear over her death.

"She was a kind and loving person. She'd be the first to hold you while you cried. Think of how it would feel to have her arms wrapped around you right now. Let that vision comfort you. Let yourself live through this time, however you need it to be. When you're ready to recall your time with Patti with a smile on your face and not a tear in your eye, you'll know. You will, I swear. But even then, you can always talk to her, feel her arms around you. That's okay.

"I believe you'll know," she put her hand flat over his heart, "inside your heart, when it's time to be happy again, to reach out to friends again, to laugh, to smile, to love again. Have that faith in yourself… and in Patti's love for you. It still exists—somewhere, I believe—her love for you. It's not gone. Just as your love for her didn't just vanish into the nano-sphere. Feel what you have to feel, David, within your own time frame. No one can tell you what that time frame is, and I'm sure Patti would tell you the same thing, if she were right here in the flesh. If you were to talk to her, even now, I'm positive she'd understand what you're going through, and she'd help you through it. It's hard to understand how to *be* after a loved one passes to the other side. Just let yourself feel what you feel, David. It'll be okay. I promise."

He closed his eyes, then squeezed her hand, lifted it to his lips, and kissed her knuckles. "Thank you."

Stella placed her hand in her lap. "You're welcome."

"How did you get so wise about after-death experiences? Did someone close to you pass away?"

"My parents died unexpectedly in a boating accident when I was fifteen and Kat was ten. Then Kat and I were fostered by two wonderful and loving people, Fiona and Nason Dominguez. They've since both passed on. I've read a lot of books about grief, and I practice mindfulness meditation and yoga. I'm at peace with the deaths of people I've loved in my life who have died. None of them would tell me how I dealt with my grief was wrong."

She shrugged. "It is what it is, David. And each of us will process our grief differently than anyone else. There are no shoulds. Think about it. Would Patti really berate you for grieving her absence from your life? Really? I don't think so. And if or when you find someone else to love, do you truly believe she'd be pissed off? I doubt that. I heard what you said at the memorial service. Patti would want you to be happy for the rest of your life. She would not expect you to be sad until you died. Come on, David. That doesn't sound like the Patti you talk about, that others talk about."

David nodded. "You're right."

"It's not that I want to be right. I'm just trying to help you out during this time. Anything I can do to make things easier for you, so you can be what you need to be and take the time you need to do so, I'm here for you, David."

"Yes, you are. And you've been a big help to me with Patti's service and the shop and Halloween." He looked at the box on the picnic table. "Thank you for picking up the cupcakes." He stood. "Can you stay to help me decorate the porch? Then I can take over."

"Of course I'll stay." He nodded and stared at the ground. "I'll help you set up the dry ice machine, after we decorate. Then I'd love to hand out candy to the kids, too, if that's all right?"

His head popped up. "That would mean a lot to me. I'm not looking forward to doing this by myself. Patti was always by my side."

"I'm hardly a good substitute for her, but I'll give it my best shot."

"Don't say that. You've been great, Stella. Helping me out at the shop and everything else. I can't tell you how much I appreciate all of it. Really. You're awesome."

Stella's face flushed, and she stood. "Kat and Marcus and I are going to Monarch Bay High after I finish up here. My son Gabriel's band is playing at the Halloween dance. If you want to join us, you're more than welcome to come along."

He smiled a teensy-tiny smile. "I may just do that. Can I play it by ear?"

"Of course. Now, come on. Let's get this show on the road. Before we know it, the little monsters will be knocking at your front door with their hands out for some treats."

Chapter Twenty

While Stella handed out candy to the tiniest members of the trick-or-treat group, David poured hot apple cider into miniature paper cups and paired them with a cupcake for those kids brave enough to walk up the stairs to join the monster figures on the porch, while thick smoke-like vapor swirled all around them.

Stella had always taken the twins to certain neighborhoods in Corvallis where decorations were present and candy handed out individually by someone dressed up as a scary movie character. Her own block didn't do much, perhaps because there were fewer kids living there. She was having a great time at David's house, being on the other side of the Halloween picture, giving out treats and watching the smiles on the kids' faces, seeing their crazy costumes. She noticed David smiling as well and knew this had been a good idea, lifting his spirits, if only for a few hours.

Around eight-thirty they waited fifteen more minutes to see if any stragglers dropped by, and when no one showed up, Stella helped David bring the dry ice machine inside along with the tables and the few cupcakes and candy that were left over.

Stella placed the cupcakes back in the box to keep them fresh then washed her hands. "I'm going to take off, David."

He stood with his hands in his pockets, staring at the floor. "Thanks for helping out tonight." He lifted his gaze. "That was the most fun I've had in—," he shrugged, "—over a year. Patti and I didn't do much after her diagnosis. We spent time together at the shop, because that's where her heart always was. Otherwise, we stuck around the house in the evenings. She was just too tired at the end of the day."

"You're welcome to join Kat and Marcus and me. I'm heading to my house to get them, then we're walking to the high school. We won't be there long. Wanna come with us?"

"You know what? I've been thinking about your offer all day. The only thing holding me back is… well… today was Patti's memorial service. Shouldn't I stay here? Won't it look odd for me to be out partying with friends?"

Stella walked over and stood in front of him. "You don't know me that well, so I don't expect you to give credence to anything I say, David. I've never had a spouse who passed away. I can't relate. In my case, if Robert had fallen down dead, I probably would have had a party. I'd have been so overjoyed that I didn't have to suffer any more emotional and physical abuse.

"But you're sad. And yes, you're in mourning. But everyone in this town knows you, David. They know you loved Patti with all your heart. They also know you're close with Kat and Marcus. And I consider you my friend as well. You're allowed to grieve in whatever way works for you. If you want to go with us and remember the times you and Patti danced in high school, then that's your prerogative.

"If anyone wants to gossip about the fact you're getting comfort from your friends instead of sitting at home alone crying… then fuck them. Sorry to be crass, but you're really a nice guy, a good man, an honorable man. No one who knows you thinks otherwise. So if it'll make you smile for a minute to listen to my son and his crazy garage band at the high school for awhile, then I say come on down!"

David laughed and shook his head. "If I ever need someone to stick up for my integrity, I know who to call for a reference. I like you, Stella. You're a good person. Patti would have wanted to be your friend, if she'd had the time." He let out a sigh. "Yes, I'll go with you guys. Sounds fun."

Stella put her arms around him and hugged him. "Good choice."

She grabbed her purse and followed him out the front door to her sister's car. When they reached the house, they met up with Kat and Marcus and walked to the school. Along the way, Stella and Kat walked together and shared about their day, while the guys followed them, talking about Harleys and a possible camping trip in the future.

When they reached the school, they followed the music and entered the auditorium, where a crowd of kids gathered, some dancing, others standing in front of the stage, while others hung around the edge of the room, talking and laughing. The four of them made their way to the front near the stage and watched the guys while they played a popular song even Stella recognized. She caught Gabriel's eye at one point, and he smiled. When they began to play a particularly upbeat song, Stella felt a tap on her shoulder and turned around.

David stood with his hand out. "Would you like to dance?"

Stella laughed out loud. "I feel like I'm back in high school. Yeah, I think I can half-way remember how to boogie."

She followed him to the middle of the crowd, and they both shuffled their feet and turned in circles, clapped their hands together and smiled at each other. When the music segued into a slow song, David grasped Stella's hand in his then wrapped his other hand around her waist. She laid her chin on his shoulder and they swayed side to side with the music.

It had been a very, very long time since Stella had slow-danced with a man, and the warmth of David's body against hers brought back memories of when she was madly in love with Robert back in the day. Her heart thumped beneath her breast bone. David was a strikingly handsome man. Anyone would agree.

But his wife had just died, she told herself. What was she thinking?

David leaned back a few inches and stared in her eyes while they rocked back and forth. He smiled, and she laid her head back on his shoulder while chills trickled up and down her arms.

She felt as if something was happening between them, but told herself she was wrong, that she'd made it up. She was completely aware of David's deep love for his wife. That he'd probably need years to get over her untimely death. So she decided she'd imagined any interest on his part in a "sexual" way and continued to enjoy dancing.

When the song ended, David took hold of her hand and led her back to where Kat and Marcus stood but found them missing. Stella raised on tiptoe to gaze around the room, and David did the same.

"Where'd they go?" he said.

"I haven't a clue. Oh, wait." She pointed to the back of the dance floor. "They're over there next to the refreshment table talking to some people." She turned to David. "Have you had enough for tonight? It's been a long day for you. I can walk you home, if you'd like."

He nodded. "Sure. I had a good time tonight. Thanks for encouraging me to come. Let's say goodbye to Kat and Marcus first."

They spoke to her sister and brother-in-law for a few moments, then headed out the door, both silent for several blocks before David let out a long, slow breath. "What a day it's been. I feel like this morning's service was weeks ago."

"What with setting up for Halloween and decorating and all that, then handing out candy and cider, then coming with us to the dance, it really has been hours and hours since the service. You must be mentally exhausted, David."

"I know this might sound… oh, never mind."

Stella stopped, and he halted next to her. "Say what you were going to say. There's nothing wrong with feeling any way that you're feeling today. You've never experienced a day like this, David. Tell me what's on your mind. I'll listen. No judging."

He started walking again. "There's a part of me that's relieved, you know? And I feel guilty about that. But Patti was suffering so much. Both mentally and physically. Since the day she got her diagnosis and refused treatment, she and I knew she'd be dead soon. For more than a year she's been in the process of dying, and it's been so damn hard. Watching her get more and more tired, losing more and more weight, and yet she tried so hard to not get depressed. She wanted it to be over, but I couldn't agree with her. I couldn't say, 'Yeah, Patti, I wish you'd hurry up and go.' Jesus, Stella.

"But now that she's gone, I'm relieved I don't have to watch my wife slowly but surely descend that horrible slope toward her death. She's finally not physically here anymore, and I feel as if the cloud that's been hovering over my head all this time has finally blown away. It's gone, and there's a freedom for me. It's like the constant looming of her imminent death is gone, and a heavy weight has been lifted off my shoulders and my head and… just everywhere."

They reached David's house, and Stella followed him up the stairs, where he opened the front door and stood aside for her to pass. David closed the door silently, and Stella waited for him to ask her if she wanted a beverage or guide her to the front room, so they could talk a bit more.

Instead he inched slowly toward her, and she backed up against the wall. He cupped her chin in his hands and brought his lips to hers so gently Stella could hardly feel them. But when his tongue touched her bottom lip then circled around the top, all thoughts flew out of her consciousness, and she opened her mouth to let him deepen the kiss.

That slow, sensuous kiss led to another, then another until Stella could hear his labored breath mingle with hers, while she ran her hands along his chest muscles and up his neck. She threaded her fingers through the thick hair above his collar, and their kisses became frantic. It was as if they'd both found water in a desert, so thirsty they couldn't stop themselves from taking huge gulps of each other.

Stella realized how starving she'd been for physical affection, and she surmised Patti's physical weakness had kept David celibate for over a year. He was a tall man, and his erection pressed heavily into her stomach, heightening her arousal. She didn't want what she was feeling to ever stop, but in the back of her mind she didn't want to regret what was happening between them either.

She pulled away slightly, looked him in the eyes. "Are you sure about this, David?"

"Please," he whispered.

He grasped her by the hand and walked down the hall into the bedroom, where he slowly undressed her, then picked her up and placed her on top of the comforter. She watched him take off his clothes in the light shining through the window from the Halloween moon.

Stella's heart beat so fast, she could feel her chest shaking. David knelt on the bed and hovered over her. Their gazes locked, and he lowered himself on top of her as she wrapped her legs around his waist. Their lovemaking was almost manic, starved for what they hadn't had in a long while, both for vastly different reasons. Their bodies collided like two cars crashing into each other, their orgasms exploding at the same time like a volcanic eruption.

Silence fell while their breathing slowly came back to normal.

"What have I done?" David whispered.

"I'm sorry. I should have stopped this," Stella told him. She turned on her side and placed her hand on his chest. "I should go."

Tears dripped from David's cheeks. What a nightmare. She'd taken advantage of him in his time of grief, when he was riddled with sadness and mixed emotions about how to feel after Patti's death. Stella knew that. And yet she'd allowed herself to be an active participant in this inappropriate debacle.

She walked around to the side of the bed, picked up her clothes and silently left the room, dressing in the hallway, then opening the front door and closing it swiftly behind her.

She ran home, tears whisking off her face in the ocean breeze.

Chapter Twenty-One

Stella stepped quietly into Kat's house. Everyone was asleep, lights shut off, heater turned down.

Remy greeted her with a lick on her hand. She gently rubbed his head. He returned to his bed and settled himself with a groan.

She tiptoed up the stairs, not wanting to run into Kat or Marcus and have to explain why she was crying. Granted, she could make up any story she wanted, but she'd always been a terrible liar. Not that she'd made it a point of lying, but when she hadn't told the truth to Robert, he could always sense she wasn't being truthful. And anyway, it was a skill she had no desire to hone. Would she even admit what happened tonight to anyone? She had no intention of doing so.

She jumped into bed and lay on her back, staring at the ceiling. What the hell was wrong with her? If the tables were turned, some would say she'd been taken advantage of, possibly raped, when she was in a vulnerable situation. But because her partner was a male, it would never come to that. What a sexist society existed in America!

And how could she face David at work tomorrow? Her face grew hot and she felt sick to her stomach. Why had she impulsively made love to a man whose wife had just passed away? A woman he'd loved with all his heart and soul. And still loved. Did she think she'd make him feel better somehow, if he had sex with someone who was almost a stranger to him? They'd only known each other a short time, almost two months? Tears burst forth, and she smashed her face into her pillow and cried herself to sleep.

The following day she arrived at the pastry shop at five a.m. and ran into David the moment she entered the back door.

He scurried by her carrying an empty pastry tray. "Morning!"

She stopped, and her mouth fell open. Was she supposed to act as if last night never happened? He hadn't been drunk. He couldn't possibly have forgotten. What should she do? She guessed if he wanted to play "pretend," she could do the same.

"Good morning. Is there anything specific you want me to do?"

"Just start the coffee maybe? That'd be great."

"I'm on it."

Stella spent the day doing her usual duties, and, at the end of the day, they said goodbye to each other as if nothing had ever happened between them.

But something *had* happened. And she wasn't the type of person who liked to gloss over problems. She liked to put things on the table and clear the air, then get on with life. Perhaps this was David's typical M.O. But that didn't make any sense. He'd been devoted to Patti. Kat had been close friends with Patti. Kat would have told Stella if Patti and David's marriage was any different than what everyone thought. Kat spoke of David's devotion to his wife and how in love Patti and David were for most of their lives.

Stella didn't understand what kind of game David was playing. Then again, she doubted he was the type of man who played games. He was probably so traumatized by Patti's death, maybe he had acted totally out of character and was now so humiliated, the only way he could function was to act as if last night had been an aberration. Maybe he'd apologize later. Maybe he'd just erase it from his mind, so he didn't feel guilty over having sex with Stella several hours after Patti's memorial service.

Whatever the case, Stella made up her mind to go along as per usual, do her job with a smile on her face as she always had, and never put herself in a situation like last night ever again. She could act like that, if need be, couldn't she? She recalled her days with Robert. She'd pretended more times than she remembered. Pretend to enjoy having sex with her husband. Pretend she'd given him all the change from shopping, when she'd hidden it in the pocket of her puffy down jacket that hung unused for years in the back of her closet, making it the perfect place for bills as well as spare change. Pretend she meant the words "I love you" after he'd whispered the same words in her ear after raping her. Pretend she liked the sexy lingerie he bought her to wear before they "made love." What a joke! They hadn't "made love" in years. He'd forced her to have sex. But making love? Hardly.

Why was she thinking about Robert anyway? Thank God those days were over.

But now she'd gotten herself into a strange situation with David. She could make it awkward or pretend all was back to normal. That was her choice, since David obviously was acting as if everything was as it had been. So, she decided to do the same.

Stella walked home, making a quick pit stop at Gabriel's friend's house, where their band practiced most days after school. Their playing had definitely gotten better. She easily recognized the cover song they were practicing and tapped her foot, listening to them jam together in perfect harmony. When the song ended, she hugged her son, said hello to the other boys then continued her walk home.

Kat was making dinner when Stella arrived. Stella washed up and helped her sister cut up veggies for a salad. They stood side by side at the sink.

Kat popped a piece of carrot in her mouth and chewed. "Did you have fun last night? I was so happy to see you dancing with David. He needs to get out and have a little fun. He and Patti worked almost every day at the shop, then she was too tired at night to do anything. Seeing him on the dance floor brought a smile to a lot of people's faces. Poor guy. He's had it rough."

Stella focused on cutting up the vegetables. "I know what you mean. I like him. Such a nice guy. He said Patti and I would probably have been friends. I take that as a compliment. The one day I worked with her in the booth at the Faire, she had a certain vibe about her. She emanated kindness and sincerity."

Kat threw a chunk of carrot to Remy who caught it in one quick bite.

Kat rinsed her hands and wiped them with the dish towel. "Okay, salad's done. Casserole's in the oven. Let's sit for a bit. You've been on your feet all day, and so have I. I must have cut seventeen heads today."

"Seventeen heads? What are you? A human guillotine or something?"

Kat let out a huge belly laugh. "Sit. Want a cold drink?"

"Sure." Stella slumped into the nearest kitchen chair and let out a sigh.

Kat reached out and clasped her sister's hand. "Marcus will be home at the end of next week. I set up an appointment to meet with my ob-gyn the week after that. Is that okay with you?"

"Yeah, sure. Do I have to do anything beforehand?"

"I'll give you the name of the lab in Pismo Beach. You're supposed to have the lab work done as close to the appointment as possible. It's a short drive from here. You can take my car, of course. Or I can go with you. Whatever you feel comfortable doing. I want to be with you the whole way on this thing, Stella. I mean, there's a lotta stuff that has to go right before we find out if the IVF is possible. It's pretty involved."

Stella smiled at her sister. "I can go to the lab by myself. You don't need to come with me for that. If it's a go, and the doctor says I'm a viable candidate, then, yes, I'd like you with me, to hold my hand, talk to me whenever they… do whatever they have to do. Inseminate me or whatever the correct term is."

Kat leaned her elbows on the table and cradled her chin in her hands. "Marcus and I are so excited for this to happen, Stell."

"So am I, Kat. I want to do this for you guys. I'm looking forward to the day I can babysit my little nephew or niece."

The bell dinged on the oven, and Kat stood and checked the casserole. "Lookin' good in there. About another twenty minutes or so."

The front door slammed, then Loreen ran through the kitchen. "Gotta go pee. Sorry. Be right back."

Kat and Stella looked at each other and rolled their eyes.

The front door slammed again, and Gabriel sauntered into the room.

"Hi, honey. How was practice?"

"Hey, Mom, Aunt Kat. Practice was good. What's for dinner?"

"Your mom and I made a salad, and we're also having homemade mac and cheese with three kinds of cheeses and olives and all kinds of good stuff."

"Sounds great. I'm starving."

"Go wash up and tell your sister dinner's in fifteen," Stella said.

"What do you think about what Marcus said about building you guys a small house in the back?" Kat said.

"I think that's a huge endeavor. We should wait to see if I get pregnant or not before he builds an entire house for us to live in. Don't you two want your privacy?"

Kat chuckled. "When he's at home, you know if we're not out taking mini-vacations or at a bed and breakfast, we lock ourselves in the bedroom, whether anyone's here or not. That doesn't mean family doesn't mean everything to Marcus and me. We love the old tradition of keeping everyone under one roof, if possible, and you living in the back of our huge yard is the closest thing to that."

"I still say, let's take one thing at a time. See if I get pregnant-"

"You're pregnant, Mom?" Loreen yelled out.

Stella jumped in her seat and slapped a hand over her mouth. "You scared the crap outta me, Lo. It's not polite to eavesdrop on people's conversations."

"I wasn't. I heard you just as I was coming down the stairs."

Gabe clomped down the stairs. "Mom's pregnant?"

"No. I. Am. Not. Pregnant." Stella let out a breath. "Sit down and let Kat and me tell you what's going on."

While explaining Kat and Marcus wanted to have a baby and Kat's difficulty in doing so, then the possibility of Stella becoming a surrogate for her sister, Loreen and Gabriel both nodded. Such twins!

Gabe smiled. "I think that's pretty cool, Mom."

"So do I," Loreen added.

Gabe tilted his head, frowning. "But we're almost eighteen, Mom. Aren't you kinda old to be having babies?"

"Yeah. What if they're like, quintuplets or something? I've read that happens sometimes with in vitro," Loreen said.

Stella breathed in deeply, exhaling slowly, trying to ground herself. "I'm aware of that. Marcus and your aunt and I are going to meet with the doctor after Marcus gets back. I'm going to the lab beforehand to have several tests done that'll tell the doctor if I'm a viable candidate. So we don't have long to wait to see if I can be a surrogate for Kat and Marcus."

Kat's eyes glistened. "I think your mom is the best sister in the world, you two. Not many people would do that for… well, for anyone. It's a lot to go through."

Gabe smirked. "Especially at your age, Mom."

Stella laughed out loud. "Way to make me feel older than dirt, Gabriel."

The buzzer sounded, and dinner ensued. Stella's thoughts weren't on the upcoming appointment with the gynecologist. Instead, pictures of her night with David invaded her mind like a video on replay.

Did she really want to play pretend with him? Act like nothing happened on Halloween night?

She couldn't lie to herself.

She was attracted to him.

<h1 style="text-align:center">Chapter Twenty-Two</h1>

Stella took the short drive to Pismo Beach to have the lab tests done. She enjoyed her time being alone, driving along Highway 1, window down, the scent of the ocean breeze caressing her skin. She couldn't stop smiling, knowing how excited Kat and Marcus would be if all the tests came back positive for surrogacy. Though she knew it was too early to get their hopes up. Stella prayed she wasn't peri-menopausal. She'd hate to disappoint her sister and brother-in-law.

Stella took off early from work after asking David if he could handle the shop for an hour or two while she went to the doctor. Of course, she didn't reveal what her plans were, since they all agreed to keep everything a secret until or if Stella got pregnant. They hadn't even had their first appointment with the doctor yet, which would happen after Marcus returned home.

When Stella entered the house at almost six p.m., Loreen sat at the kitchen table alone, with a spoon in her hand, having soup for dinner.

"Hi, sweetheart. How was your day?"

Loreen shrugged. "Nothing interesting. Gotta study for a test." She stood.

"Where's Harley? You two usually study together in the evenings."

"Dunno." She walked toward the stairs, looking forlorn.

Stella shook her head. This was definitely not normal for her daughter and Harley. They were inseparable, attached at the hip, rarely alone. "Hey, is everything all right with you two?"

Loreen stood stock still for several seconds, then slowly turned to face her mom. "I hate keeping secrets from you, so I'm not gonna start now." She returned to the kitchen table and sat in front of her half-eaten bowl of soup.

Stella sat across the table from her. "I can always count on you being honest with me. Many girls your age hide everything from their parents. They think we're so old we can't relate to the things you do or think or wonder about. It's not like I'm eighty years old. Yet." She reached for her daughter's hand. "What's on your mind, honey? Whatever it is, we can discuss it like adults, right?"

"Well, I don't know about *that*, because after I tell you, you're gonna think I'm about as adult as a two-year old." Loreen covered her face with both hands. Her shoulders shuddered.

Stella moved to her daughter's side and put her arm around Loreen's shoulders. "What's wrong, Lo? You never cry. Did you and Harley break up? Did something happen at school?"

Loreen shook her head, sniffed, then dropped her hands to the table. "I'm pregnant."

Seconds passed, during which time Stella's heartbeat ramped to an uncomfortable pace. Her seventeen-year-old daughter was pregnant? This could not be happening. She took a deep breath. "Wow. This surprises me. You and I talked about birth control."

Loreen turned to face her mother. "I'm on the pill. I've never *not* taken it *exactly* like the directions state. I don't know what happened, Mom." She burst into tears again. "What am I gonna do?"

Stella embraced her daughter and rocked her back and forth. "This obviously is a surprise for both of us. I didn't know you were even having sex."

"We've been having sex since before I introduced him to you. I told you I was the only one of my friends who was a virgin."

"But you implied you were *still* a virgin, Lo."

Loreen shut her eyes for a few seconds. "I know. I was too embarrassed to tell you then. I thought you'd think I was a complete ho-bag."

Stella shook her head. "I do not think you're a ho-bag, Loreen."

"Oh, really, Mom? I had sex with him the day after we met. What would you call that?"

"Oh, honey. It may not have been your wisest moment, but I understand the pressures teenagers have to face from their peers. And I get that kissing can quickly escalate to having sex no matter what age you are. Um… does Harley know yet?"

"That's why he's not here. I told him today, and he jumped on his motorcycle and split, leaving me standing in front of the school by myself. I mean, what a dick, right?"

Stella reached out and swiped the tears lingering on her daughter's cheeks. "To give him the benefit of the doubt, perhaps he was so shocked he did the first thing that came to mind and ran from the problem. Maybe he needs to be alone and think about it."

"It's not just my problem, Mom. It's his too." Loreen focused on her folded hands on the table. "I thought the pill was almost one-hundred percent effective. Why the hell is this happening to me? I did everything right, Mom." She turned her head to Stella. "What am I gonna do?"

Stella covered her daughter's hands with one of her own. "First things first, baby. We get in touch with Harley. Ask him to join us here, and we can talk about it. Unless you don't want me involved directly. Which I totally understand. Then you talk about your options. You can have an abortion if you're not too far along. You can have the baby and put it up for adoption. Or you can keep your baby and either raise it here with your family, or you and Harley can choose to raise the child together and live together. Or you can raise the child here without Harley, and he can still be actively involved in the baby's life. There are a lot of options, Loreen. What are you thinking? Do you have any idea?"

Loreen shook her head, then gazed at the ceiling. "I can't keep this child, Mom. I have plans for my future that don't include a kid or living with my boyfriend or living with my family and raising a child. It takes up a lot of time. I know that. I want to go to college. Travel. Go to Europe with Harley. I don't want to be tied down at eighteen years old." Once again, she burst into tears and laid her head on her folded hands.

Stella rubbed her daughter's back. "Then perhaps adoption is the best option for you, Loreen. But you should still talk to Harley about it."

"He's not answering his cell, and he isn't at home, cause I called and his uncle said he hadn't seen him."

"How far along are you? Do you have any idea?"

"I only missed one period, then I bought a pregnancy test and it was positive, so I bought another brand, and it was positive too." Loreen lifted her head and turned once again to her mom, looking in her eyes.

Stella felt Loreen's laser-like gaze so deeply, it was as if Lo wanted her mother to make the decision for her. "It wouldn't be right for me to make the decision for you, Loreen. You know that. What I suggest is, I'm sure you've already left a message for Harley on his cell, right?"

Loreen nodded.

"Then wait for him to get back to you. It might take awhile, but you're not that far along. You have plenty of time to mull this over together before deciding anything. It's only right that he have a say in this, don't you agree?"

Loreen nodded, then grabbed a napkin off the table and wiped away her tears. "That's the best way to handle this, I know. You're right. I'm just freaking out."

"Of course you are. It's a big decision to make, no matter what you choose to do about the baby. And if you need me to be there when you talk to Harley or after you two have made your decision and you want to run it by me, I'm here, sweetie. And, like I said, if you want to have the baby and not give the child up for adoption, then go to college, I'll help you out in any way I can. Whatever you choose, sweetie."

Loreen picked at her nails, deep in thought. "I can't see giving a baby up for adoption, then wondering if the adoptive parents are treating the child kindly. What if they hit the baby or beat it? People aren't always how they appear to be. The adoptive parents could be totally faking the funk to look all perfect and shit, but they're actually child molesters." She slammed her fist on the table. "Dammit anyway, Mom. Why did this have to happen to me? Why me?"

Stella tucked her finger under Lo's chin and turned her head to face her. "Honey, I don't expect you to buy into any of my personal philosophies on life. However, I believe things happen that lead to other things happening that ultimately lead to how they should happen and not in a negative way. I'm not saying that bad stuff doesn't happen to good people and no matter what, it's bad stuff from the beginning to the end.

"But I also believe there are good lessons to be learned from every bad and good experience. Life hits you in the gut with a hammer and knocks the wind out of you. But once you get your breath back, you straighten up and keep walking or running, and it all means something for your growth, and you learn from it. It gives you experience, which gives you knowledge for your future. It's all part of life—the good and the bad—and you'll get through it no matter what. But you'll gain something from every experience you have, making you the person you're meant to be in the end." She dropped her finger from Lo's chin then kissed her on the cheek. "Am I making any sense?"

Loreen nodded slowly, then encircled her mom in her arms and laid her head on Stella's shoulder. "I love you, Mom. You didn't yell at me once. You are the coolest mom ever."

Stella leaned back and their eyes met. "I've had some bad stuff happen living with your father. And it was awful at the time. But now that I'm out of that situation, I know I've taken a lot away from it that's made me a better person. It's made me strong and resilient, and now I'm happier than I've been in years. I have my two kids. I have my sister and Marcus. I'm making friends. It ultimately led me to where I am today. Granted, I've got some serious personal work to do because of how your father made me feel about myself, but I'll eventually be fine. I know it."

Loreen sighed. "Thanks for talking, Mom. I need to wash my face and try to get in touch with Harley again."

"Good idea. And, Loreen. I'll always be here for you. You know that, right?"

"I know, Mom," she whispered, then ran up the stairs.

Remy jumped up from his bed and followed Loreen.

Stella stared into space for awhile, thinking about her daughter and Harley and their unborn child.

Life was never, ever boring. At times, Stella yearned for a boring life with no drama, trauma, fights, lessons learned, and on and on. But that sure as hell wasn't how her life had been so far. She stood, turned toward the backyard and gazed at the colors of the sunset.

She wondered how this would all turn out in the end. Would she be mothering her grand baby in nine months? If Loreen had an abortion, would she not see a grandchild for years? She couldn't answer those questions right now, but she looked forward to living with whatever decision her daughter and Harley made.

Chapter Twenty-Three

Stella arrived at Patti's Pastries at the usual five a.m., said hello to David, then schlepped pastry trays from the kitchen to the front until the shelves were filled. She was in the middle of measuring coffee grounds when she heard David's footsteps behind her.

"Hey, Stella?"

"Mm-hmm? What's up?"

"Before we officially open I wanted to run something by you."

Stella turned and wiped her hands on a dish cloth. "Sure. I'm all ears."

He smiled—something he rarely did. Since Patti's memorial service and their night together, he'd been morose and uncommunicative.

"I'd like to have more of a life than living at this shop every day, and I can't tell you how much I appreciate you working seven days a week since Patti passed away. But I talked with Pascal last night, and he isn't having the fun he expected in his retirement. He'd like to come back to work. So, I'm thinking I'd like to take off one of the days on the weekend and one day off on a week day, and I'm proposing something similar for you.

"I'm going to hire one of the girls who worked here before, when we'd get super busy. She's looking for a part-time job. So she could work the days I'm not here, and you can take two days off, and she'll work those days as well. That way both of us won't have to be here seven days a week. It's just not healthy. I need to have some free time and really, so should you, Stella."

"Sounds fine with me, David. I'd love to have some free time to explore this area, read, maybe look into getting my teaching credentials. I'll take whatever weekend day you don't want, and I don't much care what week day I have off."

"Super. I'll take Sunday off. You take Saturday. And if you want to take Friday then you'll have two days off back-to-back, and I'll take Monday so I can have two days back-to-back as well."

"Sounds like a plan. Thank you, David. Just tell me when you want to start the new schedule."

"Right away. Julie, the young girl who goes to Monarch High, can start tomorrow."

Stella nodded. "Great."

He returned to the kitchen, and Stella got to thinking. She mulled over the fact it had been awhile since their night together and he'd acted like his usual self since then. They didn't usually spend much time talking while at work anyway. but Stella felt there was a wall between them. They greeted each other in the morning, said goodbye later in the day, and in between they'd pass each other going back and forth to the kitchen, not making eye contact. That was the extent of their relationship. Today was the first actual conversation they'd had.

Yet she couldn't forget the evening they'd spent decorating his house, dancing to Gabriel's band, and finally making love at his house. He didn't seem the type to have sex with random women. He'd been a faithful husband for years. Was Stella just an experiment for his "new" life as a single man? Was he having sex with women all the time, now that he was "free?"

She took a deep breath and stared at the coffee while it dripped into her mug.

And decided to confront him the next evening.

The next day turned out to be the coldest Stella experienced since moving to Monarch Bay, a cool fifty degrees. After dinner, she told Kat she was going for a brisk walk, then she headed to David's place.

She kept her eyes on the stars for most of the walk. When it was clear like tonight, with no clouds or fog, she could see the Big Dipper, if she squinted. She breathed in the awesomeness of the universe, as her meditation video suggested, and calmed her mind for the discussion ahead. Her nerves still jangled inside her head and chest. She had absolutely no idea what to expect from David.

She didn't want to ruin their polite working relationship, but the awkwardness she felt every single day was really getting to her. She needed to know why what happened on Halloween happened at all. Then she could move forward. She'd never had a one-night stand in her life, and for all she knew, David thought she was a slut—a sexist view if she'd ever heard one, since that would make him one as well. But being a male, she was sure he didn't think of himself that way. But she wasn't a slut either. Granted, she was still married, but her situation was complicated.

She walked up the stairs to his front door and knocked lightly. Footsteps scuffled on the hardwood floor, and the door opened.

"Stella! Hello. What are you doing here?"

Stella stared at her feet and tried to calm her mind, then cleared her throat. "David, I've been thinking about this every day since Halloween. What went on between the two of us… it meant something to me. But I've felt guilty since that evening because maybe it happened because you were vulnerable and I took advantage of the situation. I wanted to apologize. I—"

David opened the door wide. "Please come in, Stella."

Stella walked inside, followed him into the front room, where he took a seat in an arm chair, and she sat across from him on the couch. She unwrapped the scarf from around her neck and leaned back, trying to seem at ease, though she was anything but. Her nerves zinged inside her veins and she took long, slow breaths, waiting for him to speak.

He leaned his elbows on his knees, hands dangling between his legs, and looked up at her. "You did not take advantage of me, Stella, so don't feel guilty." His Adam's apple bobbed up and down as he swallowed. "Patti was the only woman I'd ever made love to in my life. One part of me feels as if I betrayed her by making love to you, but another part of me knows she would understand. So the only thing I feel guilty about, really, is the fact that I should have at least waited a small amount of time before allowing my attraction to you to blossom into having sex."

He shook his head. "After you ran out of the house I thought you felt *I'd* taken advantage of *you* because I was lonely without Patti and I needed some sort of sexual release after what she and I had been through for over a year. I'm sure you guessed we weren't having sex. She came home after work exhausted. I was lucky if she made it through dinner before going to bed alone, without me. She said she needed her rest in order to work the next day.

"But in truth, Stella, I wanted to make love to you because I really like you. I think you're an extraordinary individual. Since you come from an abusive relationship, I wasn't sure if we'd make it to the bedroom, because you'd have flashbacks of what Robert did to you, that the last thing you'd want to do is have sex with me or anyone, for that matter. So when you flew out of here, I thought, dammit, that's what happened. You freaked out and regretted our evening together. I shouldn't have allowed anything to happen between us. I was a complete idiot for kissing you, for putting you in a situation where you might have felt if you didn't have sex with me, I'd abuse you in some way, just like Robert."

By that time he was wringing his hands, frowning. "I didn't know how to bring up the subject. I wanted to run after you, say I was sorry. But then I thought, I bet that's exactly what Robert used to say to you. He'd force himself on you, then apologize afterward… for essentially raping you because you didn't want to have sex with him any longer because he beat you all the time." He ran his hands through his hair, eyebrows furrowed. "I wasn't thinking straight, and I feel so bad about that, Stella. I—"

Stella stood and knelt in front of him, grasping his hands in hers. "That's not what was going on that night, David. Not at all. I wasn't having flashbacks about Robert. I didn't feel I had to go along with having sex with you because I was afraid of what you'd do if I said no, that you'd hurt me if I pushed you away." She shivered and closed her eyes. "That's not what was going on at all. At all." She opened her eyes, stared at him. "I'm attracted to you. But I shouldn't have acted on that on the same day as Patti's memorial service. Afterward I was like, 'What the hell were you thinking, Stella?' Maybe I took advantage of your grief, David. Your grief and your sadness. And I'm so sorry I did that. I'm an awful person. I—"

David reached out and grasped Stella by the shoulders, pulling her slowly toward his chest. He kissed her gently on the lips, then circled her lips with his tongue until she opened her mouth. He explored the warmth of her tongue as he pulled her onto his lap, their bodies meshed together as he held her tightly in his arms.

Stella pressed nearer to David, needing to feel him close. She gasped as his arousal grew more obvious between them.

Then he abruptly stopped and pulled back, looked into her eyes. "Do you want me as much as I want you?"

"I do," she whispered. "I've wanted this since that… night."

"But I thought—"

She placed her finger to his lips. "We both thought wrong." She took hold of his hand and walked to his bedroom, then undressed before him while he watched her take off each piece of clothing until she stood naked.

"You're so beautiful."

She pulled his T-shirt over his head, threw it to the floor, unzipped his pants then shoved his briefs and boxers to the ground, and he kicked them away.

As if in slow motion, they lay on the bed and made love quietly, touching each other as if each were made of glass, until their orgasms shattered them, and they fell asleep wrapped in each other's arms.

They awoke together in the middle of the night and made love again. Stella fell into a dreamless sleep until she awoke and glanced at the clock. It flashed four a.m.

"David. Don't you have to be at the bakery?"

He grumbled something she couldn't make out, then his eyes switched to the table next to the bed. He reached out and pressed a button. "It must be broken. It's supposed to flash and play music at the same time." He coughed once, then turned toward her, encircling her in his arms and pulling her close.

"Are you okay?" he whispered.

"I am, if you are."

"I'm okay. More than okay." He slid his fingers through her hair and kissed her. "I try not to care too much about what others think of me. What about you?"

"David, I'm not from here. You're a big part of this community. It was obvious at the memorial service how many people cared about Patti… and you. In this situation perhaps you *do* want to care what people think. And if you want to keep us a secret I'm okay with it." She paused. "If any of this means there's such a thing as an 'us'."

"I will always be honest with you, Stella. I'm surprised as hell this is happening. I have no words to explain it. It's bizarre. There's something happening between us that I never thought would happen to me… ever again. It's like I've been hit by an avalanche. The connection I feel between us… I can't explain it."

Stella kissed him once, then again, then again, until they made love for the third time, and she lay on top of him with her head on his chest while she listened to the rapid beat of his heart.

"I'd say something trite like 'I feel like that, too, David,' but that would diminish what I'm feeling right now." She lifted up and focused on his eyes. "I haven't had feelings for a man in years. The only feeling I had for Robert was hatred… for all the cruel things he did to me and said to me during our marriage. So, for me, the emotions going through me right now are so new and so vivid. It's almost as if I'm already in love with you. But I don't want you to take that the wrong way. I don't expect anything from you. Your wife just died. But I want to be honest. And if you need to back off from me until you feel more comfortable, I'll totally understand."

He ran his hand up and down her side with his eyes closed, then he took a deep breath and opened them. "I don't know what I'd call my feelings right now, Stella. I've only been in love once, and I still love Patti. But there's something going on inside me, and… I want to be with you. Not just for the sex. Honestly, it isn't. I wouldn't use you that way. But there *is* something between us, unnameable perhaps. But it will all become known in its time. It's all good. And I want to see where we go with this. But the one think I *do* know is, it's a positive thing. I'm not scared of it. I'm looking forward to it even. You know what I mean?"

Stella nodded. "I think I do." She sat up. "I should go. Before I get fired from my job."

David took a quick look at the clock again. "I'll drop you off at your house. Don't worry too much about being late. I'll cover for you."

Chapter Twenty-Four

Working with David was still awkward but in an entirely different way than previously. Now they shared short glances, eyes meeting with a quick smile when they passed each other in the pastry shop. It was as if they had an unspoken agreement to keep their nascent relationship solely to themselves. Stella was the interloper in Monarch Bay, and she respected the fact David, an integral member of the small community of Monarch Bay, might want to be a little discreet about their relationship.

He had suffered enough during the last year while Patti lived with a death sentence. He didn't deserve nor need any more grief, on the off-chance customers and friends might talk or wonder or gossip about whether anything had been going on between Stella and David while Patti was still alive.

Marcus was scheduled to return from his latest haul that day, and the three of them had an appointment to see Kat's gynecologist the following day. When Stella arrived home from work, Marcus's truck was parked on the side of the house. Stella hadn't felt this happy in years after having cleared the air with David and spending quality time with him the night before. It had been such a long time since she'd enjoyed sex and the company of a man. It all felt new and different and exciting. She had to suppress a smile throughout the day.

Now she had another event to look forward to - finding out the results of her tests and whether she'd be a viable candidate to carry Kat and Marcus's child. On the one hand, her heart swelled at the thought she could give her sister and brother-in-law something they'd longed for for years. On the other hand, she hoped to have a relationship with David and didn't have a clue how he'd feel about dating a pregnant woman, carrying a baby that wasn't his.

If Stella had to guess, based on her short time knowing David, he'd be all for it and happy for Stella, that she was able to carry the baby to term and give his friends, Kat and Marcus, what they'd been dreaming and wishing for.

Stella entered the kitchen and found Kat and Marcus having a glass of wine. An array of crackers and cheese lay on a plate on the table.

"Hi, Marcus! How was your trip?"

Marcus raised his glass in a salute. "I can't wait for tomorrow. I'm like a kid in a toy store."

Stella smiled and took a seat across from them. "I'm eager to know the results too." Kat motioned toward the plate, and Stella picked up a cracker and took a bite.

"Glass of wine?" Kat said.

Stella stood. "Thanks." She took a wine glass from the cupboard and sat back down, then Marcus poured her a glass. She took a sip. "I can't imagine how nervous you two must be."

Kat grasped Marcus's hand. "I want this so badly, Stell. I can't describe how much. But Marcus and I have talked about what to do if you're not a viable candidate, and we're totally cool with adoption."

Stella sighed. "That's fantastic. The two of you will make great parents to any baby, whether I give birth to him or her or it's a child from someone else. Your dream's going to come true. You *will* have a child. I know it."

Marcus nodded. "That's what I was telling your sister. Sure, I'll be disappointed if we can't be the biological parents. But that's not what's the most important factor in this equation. We want to raise a child and love him or her. And we will find a way to make that happen." He turned to Kat. "I promise you that, babe."

Kat smiled and gave Marcus a quick kiss. She patted Stella's hand. "I forgot to ask you. Where's Harley been these days? I haven't seen him."

Stella instinctively knew Loreen's pregnancy would remain a secret until Loreen felt ready to tell someone besides her mother about the situation. "I don't know. I hadn't thought about it. Maybe they gave him more hours at his job at that guitar place? I've been so busy lately with work, I haven't had a chance to talk to her much. I think she goes to Gabriel's friend's house most days after school to listen to them practice. Maybe she and Harley are studying there now. I don't know."

"Speaking of work," Kat said. "Where were you last night?"

Stella's stomach twisted into a knot. She'd been so quiet, entering the house from the sliding glass door off the back deck, often left unlocked. That door represented the exit to "potty time" for Remy, and in the middle of the night all of them had forgotten to lock it at least a time or two. Stella had taken off her shoes and tiptoed up the stairs, didn't use the restroom, walked straight into her bedroom, and pulled the door closed. No creaking stairs, no slammed doors. She hadn't made a sound. If she was caught sneaking in, what the heck was she going to say?

A hot flash burned through her neck and face. She took a sip of wine, then reached for a cracker and cheese, biding time, thinking of what to say without telling the whole truth. "I stopped by David's place to see how he was doing. He seemed down yesterday. We ended up watching a movie, and I fell asleep on his couch in front of the fireplace. I tried not to make too much noise when I came home. I'm sorry if I woke you."

Kat shook her head. "No worries. I was already up. I've been so anxious about tomorrow. I can't sleep." She grabbed another cracker. "Are you two becoming friends? You work together, so I would expect you're getting to know him pretty well by now."

Stella bit into her cracker, chewed, swallowed, hoping to end this conversation quickly, uncomfortable lying to her sister, yet not sure what Kat and Marcus would say if she actually told them the full truth. Stella was still a married woman. David was a newly grieving widower. If they knew what had happened, they might think Stella had seduced David during his time of sorrow, that until Stella officially divorced Robert, she should remain celibate. She had no idea what either of them would think and was scared to find out.

"David's a good man. He's had a rough year. All of this is so fresh right now, I think he's just trying to make it through each day. He and Patti, as you told me once, had been together since high school. That's a lot of years. They were truly unique."

Kat nodded. "Marcus has known David since forever. Right, babe?"

Marcus poured himself another glass of wine. "There's a story you probably didn't tell your sister, Kat." He glanced at his wife. Kat smirked. "I dated Patti for a couple of months and introduced her to

David. Way back in the day." He laughed. "I kissed her once. God! We were like, thirteen years old. But once the two of *them* set eyes on each other, she dumped me like a hot potato."

Kat chuckled. "Good thing, though, right? Otherwise, maybe we wouldn't have met."

Marcus tucked his finger under Kat's chin and turned her head toward him. "We were meant to be together. I'd never have stayed with Patti. I've told you that before, babe. It was destiny that brought us together."

They kissed, and Stella's heart melted, watching them. Her sister and Marcus were still very much in love.

"I'm jealous, you two. But tell me, Marcus. What was it about Patti that makes you say you'd never have stayed with her?"

Marcus swirled the wine in his glass. "This is gonna sound weird, but Patti was almost too sweet. Your sister, on the other hand—"

"You!" Kat slapped him on the forearm. "I can be sweet."

Marcus laughed. "Sure you can. But I need someone with fire in their eyes, someone who speaks their mind." He fisted his hand. "Someone who'll stand up to me in a fight." He kissed Kat again. "And that's you, babe. I can be difficult to live with. Moody. I need someone who won't take my shit lying down."

Kat stared into his eyes. "Frankly, I like taking your shit lying down."

Stella burst out laughing at their banter. "You guys are too much." She stood. "Go into the bedroom, will you?"

The three of them shared a good laugh, and Stella walked upstairs. After taking a shower, she heard Loreen in her bedroom and knocked on the door. "Lo? You in there?"

"Yeah," Loreen mumbled.

Stella opened the door. Loreen lay on the bed in a fetal position with a pillow tucked under her head, her face blotchy and wet. Stella gently sat on the bed next to her daughter and tucked an errant lock of hair behind Loreen's ear. "You feeling okay?"

Loreen sat up and leaned into her mother's side, their shoulders touching. "Harley's been MIA since I told him I was pregnant."

"Really? I figured you two had spoken, and when you were ready, you'd share with me what you decided."

"Nope." Loreen sniffled, staring at her feet. She rested her head on Stella's shoulder. "I don't know what to do. One of my friends drove by his house for me and said his Harley wasn't in the garage. I don't know why he's doing this, Mom. It's his baby too. I shouldn't have to make this decision all on my own."

Stella took Loreen's hand in hers. "Lo, it's his child. He definitely has a say in this, both legally and emotionally, because he's the father and your boyfriend. I mean, if you decide to keep the child, he'll have visitation rights, if you two break up. You know what I mean?"

Loreen nodded.

"So the best case scenario is, he returns from wherever he's hiding out, and you discuss this like adults. If you're going to be parents, there are a lot of issues you have to take care of. Or if you decide to have an abortion, it would be great if he went with you to the doctor to support you. If you put the baby up for adoption, you'll both have to sign legal documents. He can't just take off and ignore this."

"That's exactly what he's doing though, Mom. He's left me to figure this out all on my own. I just don't know what to do."

"So has he been at school at all?"

"No. And that's so totally not like him. Thanksgiving vacation's coming up, too, and I was looking forward to inviting him over, if that's okay with you and Aunt Kat and Uncle Marcus. Then it'll be Christmas. and I wanted to buy him …," she paused, stood. "What the hell am I thinking? He's not fucking coming back to *me*, that's for sure. He obviously doesn't want anything to do with me. And, geez, it's so goddam easy for him to dump my ass and take off on his Harley, leaving me to figure it all out. He's so fucking irresponsible."

Stella stood and wrapped her arms around her daughter, while Loreen cried. Stella rubbed her back until the sobbing subsided. then she leaned back and looked in her daughter's eyes. "I'm going to play devil's advocate here, Lo. It could be he's taking time to make some serious decisions about his life now that this has happened. Maybe he's weighing the pros and cons. Maybe he's remembering how his parents died and he was shuffled off to his aunt and uncle, who turned out to be a terrible combination of irresponsible people for a young boy. And maybe he doesn't want to put his child up for adoption because of that experience, doesn't want to take the chance of that happening to anyone else. Maybe he suffers from abandonment issues after his parents abandoned *him* and he doesn't want his child to feel the same way he does. Maybe he doesn't believe in abortion." Stella paused. "See what I mean, Lo? It could be any of those reasons or something we don't even know about."

"But we could talk about all this stuff *together*. He doesn't have to do it all alone, Mom."

"Maybe he's used to making life decisions alone. God knows, his aunt and uncle aren't helping him out much. Otherwise they'd clean up their acts and support him emotionally. They probably don't even know you're pregnant."

Loreen rolled her eyes. "They don't even know he has a girlfriend."

"Really? How do you know that?"

"Cause he told me. He doesn't talk to them the way I talk to you. He says every time he comes home they're passed out in the front room on the couch. Bottles of whiskey tipped over on the tables. A syringe on the rug in front of the couch. One time he found his aunt lying in her own vomit in bed. Because her head was turned sideways, she didn't suffocate and kill herself. Though I think he wishes she had. He hates them both. They've never done anything for him but given him a place to sleep. There's never any food in the house. It's totally fucked up, Mom."

"It sure sounds like it. That's awful. And he's so young to have to deal with that. Maybe he's thinking about the difficulties he'd encounter if he wanted to keep the child. How would he support the baby, if he has no money. You know. That kind of stuff."

Loreen slumped onto the floor and crossed her legs, looked up at her mom. "It's important to him to go to college and get a degree and then a good-paying job. It means everything to him and his future."

Stella sat on the side of the bed. "If he doesn't want to have a child right now because he can't support it and he wants you to have an abortion, maybe he's feeling bad about that because he doesn't want to pressure you into making a decision you don't agree with. I personally think he's taking this time away to think about all the ways this could go down. I don't think he's run away forever, Loreen. I feel it in my gut. He's going to come back."

Loreen pulled her knees up under her chin and wrapped her arms around her legs. "I hadn't thought of all the stuff he could be thinking. I guess I'm taking it really personally, because it seems like he dumped me. He could just drive off and get a job somewhere, and I'd never hear from him again."

Stella shook her head. "I don't think that's what's going on here, Lo." She shrugged. "I could be wrong. But I'm hoping I'm right this time." She leaned forward toward her daughter. "Let's give him a little more time to do what he has to do. Set up a time frame, if you want to. Say… in two weeks if you still haven't heard from him, then you make the decision yourself. I'll be with you the whole way, Lo. And I'll support you no matter what you decide. Okay?"

"Yeah. I can do that." Loreen stood. "I've got homework to do."

"I'll get out of your hair." Stella walked to the door and paused. "I love you, honey. And I'm sorry this has happened with Harley. But let's have a bit of faith in the guy. I think he's going to come through for you in the end. And if not, you're strong enough to do whatever you need to do… with a little help from me and your brother and Aunt Kat and Uncle Marcus. You're not alone, baby."

Loreen smiled and swiped her tears with both hands. "Thanks, Mom."

Chapter Twenty-Five

The following day Stella told David she had a dentist appointment and left work early to return to the house and meet up with her sister and Marcus to make the drive to Pismo Beach.

It was a crisp and sunshiny November day. As Marcus drove down Highway 1, Stella sat in the back seat staring at the waves barreling toward the shore, breaking apart at the sandy shoreline, then pulling away and returning, over and over. She never tired of seeing the infinite tide flow in and out.

Marcus kept his eyes glued to the road, didn't say a word. Kat turned the radio to a classical station, folded her hands in her lap, clenching and unclenching them. Usually they'd be talking and joking with each other. Stella didn't feel anxious at all. She was more worried than anything. Though she'd volunteered to be a surrogate mother for their child, she guessed there was a high likelihood her eggs were too "old" and she wouldn't be a viable candidate. She didn't want to see her sister and Marcus's faces if the doctor gave them bad news.

Stella's mind wandered all over the place about the baby growing in her daughter's womb. Stella felt sick at the thought her daughter was going through this without Harley's support. Loreen must be feeling lonely and abandoned at a time when she and Harley should be coming together and talking about their future—if there was going to be one.

The car suddenly stopped, knocking Stella from her reverie. She looked around and realized Marcus had flicked his blinker on, about to make a left turn into a parking lot with a guard station at its entrance. He slowed down, gave the name of their doctor, then drove through. He found a spot near the front of a very modern-looking building with smoked-glass windows covering every inch of the five-story structure. A valet stood in front and opened the door for them.

The three of them took the elevator to the top floor. The elevator doors opened onto a large area with a half-circle reception desk at the front. A young woman immediately took their information and asked them to be seated.

Stella glanced at her sister sitting next to her, and their gazes met. Marcus sat on the other side of Kat and grasped his wife's hand. His knee bounced up and down and Kat placed her hand on his thigh. Stella took her sister's other hand and squeezed.

Only a few minutes passed before a nurse entered the room and called out, "Mr. and Mrs. Swanson? And Mrs. Jensen?" The three of them stood. "I'm Dr. Campbell's nurse. You can follow me to his office."

They walked behind her down the hall, where she stopped in front of a doorway and gestured for them to pass. "He'll be right with you."

They took seats in front of a huge mahogany desk, Marcus on the left, Kat in the middle, and Stella on the right side. Within seconds they heard a deep voice say hello.

The doctor passed behind them, then sat in the rolling chair at his desk. "I'm Dr. Campbell."

It surprised Stella the doctor looked so young—tall, about forty years old, with a full head of dark brown hair and a clean-shaven face, one tiny diamond earring in the lobe of his left ear. He settled himself in the chair and glanced at Marcus. "You must be Kat's husband, Marcus."

Marcus stretched out his hand. "Nice to meet you, Dr. Campbell."

The doctor then turned his attention to Stella. "And you're Kat's sister, Stella Jensen?"

Stella nodded and shook the doctor's hand as well.

"And hello to you, Kat."

Kat smiled and said hello.

Dr. Campbell opened the file his nurse placed in the center of his desk, scanned it for several seconds, then leaned forward in his chair, set his elbows on the desktop and steepled his fingers.

He took a deep breath and stared at Stella for what seemed like an eternity. Stella glanced at Kat next to her. Marcus switched his eyes to Kat then Stella, frowning.

Marcus placed his hand on the edge of the desk. "What is it, Dr. Campbell?"

Stella's stomach fisted. Did the tests show she had cancer? An STD? Some other disease? "What's wrong with me, Dr. Campbell?"

The doctor leaned back in his chair, eyes fixed on Stella. "This will probably come as a surprise Mrs. Jensen, but… around eight days after ovulation, trace levels of hCG can be detected in a woman's blood from an early pregnancy. And that's what your lab results indicate." He hesitated for a few seconds. "You're pregnant."

Stella covered her mouth with trembling fingers, then slowly let her hand fall into her lap. "Wh-what? I—"

Kat twisted in Stella's direction. "How—"

At the same time, Marcus stood. "What the hell is going on?"

Stella shook her head, her mind hopping with thought after thought, ecstatic she didn't have cancer or an STD, happy there wasn't something wrong with her, gobsmacked she was obviously carrying David's child. Horrified she was still fertile and it wasn't her sister and Marcus's baby, embarrassed she was sitting in a doctor's office looking like a liar and a fool after talking about becoming a surrogate mother and willing to undergo numerous tests, only to discover her lovemaking with David had produced a child.

Her birth control prescription ran out shortly after moving in with Kat and Marcus, and she'd never thought for a second to refill it. She totally forgot about birth control, what with all that had gone on before escaping from Robert. The fear of being caught before they could get on the road with Tom and making it out of Corvallis safely. The newness of living in Monarch Bay and finding a job, overwhelmed with life since arriving in town. Now she felt like a silly teenager, having sex without the use of birth control—something she'd have lectured any woman about who was conscious and had a brain in her head.

"I… don't… I'm sorry. I don't know what to say." She stood, looked the doctor in the eye, then Kat then Marcus. She turned and ran out of the room.

She stood outside the office doors, feeling like a complete fool. The elevator doors remained shut, and she turned left then right. A sign for the stairway caught her eye, and she hurried past the elevator, wrenched the door open and scrambled down five flights of stairs to the first floor. She flew through the lobby, yanked open the entrance doors, and stood stock still on the walkway in front of the parking lot, breathing as if she'd run a marathon, dizzy, weak, nauseated.

She felt a hand wrap around her upper arm and jumped.

"Stella, how did this happen?" Kat said, tears coursing down her face.

Stella turned and faced her sister, shaking her head side to side. "I… we… David and I made love. The night of Patti's memorial service. I didn't think about using protection… I… I'm so sorry, Kat. I—"

Kat held her hand up, palm facing outward, like a stop sign. "Don't. Just don't, Stella. How could you be so… you knew how much this meant to Marcus and me. You—"

"Stop it, Kat," Marcus said, his voice deep, stern. He put his arm around Kat's shoulders, and they walked ahead of Stella to the car.

Stella followed, feeling like a teenager in trouble. What the hell was going on? Would life ever cut her a freaking break? First a wonderful husband turns into a wife-beater, who won't allow her to work. So she wasted years of her life inside the house, almost a prisoner, only to manage to escape to a safe place, where her seventeen-year old daughter gets pregnant. And the cherry on top of the sundae? She has sex at forty freaking years old and gets pregnant, like an air-headed fifteen year old.

She realized all this amounted to a whole lot of pity talking and shook herself, then opened the door to the car and climbed in the back seat.

Silence reigned during the entire car ride home. No one talked. Kat didn't turn on the radio. The rumble of the car's engine, along with the whoosh of the air through the windows, rang through the inside of the car. When they arrived home, Kat and Marcus walked into the house, then trudged upstairs.

Stella walked at a snail's pace through the front door, feeling as if she was carrying a load of bricks on her chest, she was so exhausted. Sitting at the picnic table on the deck, she rested her elbows on the table top and covered her forehead and eyes with her hands. What was she going to do? What could she say to make this situation better? How could she get her sister and Marcus to forgive her?

She hadn't done this on purpose. They had to understand that. They were probably thinking her cruel to have taken advantage of poor

David as well as stupid for not using birth control. Negligent for having unprotected sex and an idiot for then going through with lab tests to determine the viability of her eggs for surrogacy. Irresponsible. A fool.

She stood, made her way up the stairs to her bedroom with Remy following close behind her. It was only six o'clock, but she wasn't hungry for dinner. She threw herself on top of the bed next to Remy and draped her arm over his back. When would she tell David? Should she tell David? She cuddled up next to Remy, shut her eyes and instantly fell asleep, woke up the next morning, and went to work early at four a.m.

Chapter Twenty-Six

David scurried around the kitchen baking pastries. Stella's mouth watered at the sight and scent of freshly-baked croissants, especially since she hadn't had dinner.

He glanced at the clock on the wall. "Morning, Stella." He squinted. "Or is it?"

Stella tried to keep her emotions from showing on her face but her lower lip trembled when she smiled. "I couldn't sleep so I thought 'why not go to work'? At least here I can accomplish something. I can help you with the cookie dough when you're ready."

David laid the pastry tray on the sideboard, took her hands in his. "It doesn't take a genius to see you're upset, Stella. You look sadder than I've ever seen you. What is it? Or if you don't want to tell me now, what about later? You could come over for dinner at my place. We could talk then."

Stella nodded. "You're right. It's more than just exhaustion from losing sleep. I accept your dinner invitation. Thank you."

"Seven o'clock?"

She nodded again and gathered the supplies she needed to make a fresh batch of coffee. The day flew by. Customers lined up for most of the morning, then it slowed around lunchtime, only to pick up again around two o'clock until closing. At five, Stella told David goodbye and went home to shower and change clothes.

When she arrived home, Kat and Marcus sat at the kitchen table. Kat stood, walked toward Stella and wrapped her arms around her, hugging her tightly.

"I'm sorry," Kat whispered.

Marcus joined Kat and placed his arm around Stella's waist and kissed the top of her head. "Kat and I are both sorry."

Tears trickled down Stella's cheeks, and she sobbed.

Remy barked once and nudged the back of Stella's leg.

"I'm okay, Remdog," Stella said.

Kat led her to the table, and Stella sat. Marcus and Kat took seats across the table from her. Remy dropped to the floor next to Stella.

Stella grabbed a napkin and dabbed her cheeks. "You two have no reason to apologize. I'm the one who's sorry. About all of this." Stella took a deep breath. "I screwed up, but I didn't mean to." She looked from Kat to Marcus. "I would never want to hurt either of your feelings and that's exactly what I did. But it wasn't on purpose. I—"

"Stop," Marcus interrupted. "We should never have taken our anger out on you. It was just sheer disappointment over something that you, obviously, had no idea happened. You would never have gone to see Dr. Campbell with us had you known you were pregnant. Our anger was totally misplaced. We had no idea you and David were involved. But that's none of our business. Until you feel comfortable telling us about your relationship, it's not our right, if you want to call it that, to know anything about your love life."

"He's right, Stella." Kat grabbed Stella's hand, squeezed. "I acted like a spoiled brat yesterday. Sure, I was bummed out you were carrying someone's baby that wasn't ours." She chuckled. "It's not funny but when I look back at my response, it was completely out-of-pocket. I mean, totally inappropriate, given the situation. It was obvious, you were as surprised as the two of us. But as Marcus said, we had no clue you and David had… you know, been sexually active. And that's okay with us. Shit! You two are both adults… and great people. We love you both. We feel like complete assholes, Stella."

Stella sniffed then smiled. "You're both being way more understanding than you should be. I, at forty years old, didn't use any protection when David and I had sex. But that's not what's important. What's important is that I never thought about contraception. At forty years old? What was I thinking?"

She shook her head back and forth. "I was an idiot. I hadn't renewed my birth control after I arrived in Monarch Bay, because I was no longer with Robert, who insisted I use it, so I wouldn't get pregnant when he… raped me repeatedly." She began to cry. "Then when David and I were at his house after the memorial service, he was just so kind and we talked about all kinds of things and were getting to know each other. Then there was this… this, I don't know what you'd call it. A pull between us."

She paused and glanced over their shoulders, as if reliving Halloween night with David. "Something was happening between the two of us, beyond just horniness. It's like we… we connected." She shrugged and wiped her cheeks again. "I don't want to sound all 'woo-woo,' but he and I were pulled together like two magnets. I wasn't thinking straight. And neither was he. And—"

"Does he know?" Kat said. "About the baby?"

Stella glanced at the two people she so dearly loved, her only relatives besides her two children, and her heart hurt. "Not yet. I'm telling him tonight. We're having dinner together. But, you guys, I'm so sorry this has happened. And I have absolutely no idea what I'm going to do."

"Do you want to keep the baby?" Marcus said.

"I don't know, Marcus. But I can't picture destroying it. Having an abortion, I mean. It would be cruel. This child wasn't conceived out of rape as it would have been if it were Robert's. David and I care for each other. But I can't speak for him. His and my relationship is brand new. We're not ready to get married. We just met. I don't know how he'll react."

Marcus tilted his head and looked Stella in the eyes. "What I do know, because David and I have been close for a long time, is… um, he was disappointed Patti was so involved in the pastry shop, she had no interest in having kids right away. But right away turned into forever. When she got sick David knew their chances had come to an end, and he'd never have kids. It just added more sorrow to the whole situation. He was losing his wife as well as any opportunity for them to have a kid. Underneath it all, I think he blames her for that missed opportunity. But he loved her to death and would never actually have said that to her."

Stella stared at her hands folded on the table. "I had no idea. I know the pastry shop was Patti's 'baby'. I guess in the literal sense, it truly was."

Kat nodded. "You could say that, yeah. So, I predict David's reaction won't be negative at all, Stella. And Marcus knows him better than I do."

Marcus folded his arms over his chest. "I agree with Kat. But don't let what I just told you sway your decision. In fact, I'd appreciate you not telling him I told you in the first place. Maybe I shouldn't have. But I think if he keeps that from you, that wouldn't be honest. He might not say anything, because he wouldn't want to sway your decision. Personally, I think you ought to know. He's my best friend, Stella. And if you want this child, I know for a fact he'd be over the moon to have a baby."

"I appreciate you telling me. But you know what? This conversation has totally veered from what's most important right now. I can't be your surrogate. At least not at the moment. Are you okay with waiting? Perhaps in a year or two?"

Kat and Marcus smiled, shaking their heads.

"If you keep this child, my sweet older sister, you will not want to go through IVF and be pregnant when you have a toddler running around, then hand the child over to us. It's too much."

Stella frowned. "Well, it could be an option."

Marcus put his arm around Kat's shoulders. "Kat and I talked about it. We want to adopt. There are so many children in this world who need parents who will love them and take care of them. We've changed our minds about the whole surrogacy thing. We're going to adopt."

"Oh, you two," Stella whispered. "You're the most understanding and special people I think I've ever known. And it's not just because we're related. You are really cool. I mean it."

"We're looking forward to this new decision of ours," Kat said with a grin. "Maybe this was meant to be, you know?"

"Yeah," Marcus added. "Fate. Or whatever you wanna call it. I'm psyched."

Kat stood. "Now, you go upstairs and get ready for your date with David." She glanced at Marcus, then back at Stella. "We wish you happiness, Stella. And if you and David decide to keep this baby, Marcus and I will love him or her so much. You just tell us if congratulations are in order after your talk."

Stella pushed herself to a standing position and took in a deep breath. "Thank you. Both of you. I love you so much."

Marcus grinned. "We love you, Stella."

Chapter Twenty-Seven

Stella felt as if she were walking through quicksand on her way over to David's house. She didn't know what to expect. What Marcus revealed about David's desire for children, and his disappointment that Patti didn't want kids, impacted Stella greatly.

Climbing the steps to his front door felt like making her way up Mt. Everest. She knocked and waited, holding her breath for what she surmised would not be an easy discussion.

David opened the door with a smile that quickly disappeared. "You don't look much better than you did last time I saw you."

Stella stepped through the doorway, and David put his arm around her shoulders. "You wanna talk now or wait until after we eat?"

She made her way into the front room and slumped down on the couch. David sat across from her, hands dangling between his knees.

She cleared her throat, looked him in the eye. "I've been mulling this over all day long, and honestly, there's no easy way to say this, so I'll just blurt it out." She paused. "I'm pregnant, David. With your child."

His face looked as if she'd just told him he was headed for the electric chair at midnight. His smile fell. He stared at her like he had no idea who she was.

Her eyes began to water, and she tried to hold back the tears. She didn't want to play on his emotions. "I'm sorry, David. I have no excuse other than I forgot about contraception. My birth control ran out, I didn't renew it, since the only reason I was taking the pill was because Robert didn't want any more children, and neither did I. Especially not from rape. And that's what he did to me all… the… time. I didn't want a child that way. I forgot I wasn't taking them any longer. I'd been on them for so many years, I just didn't… didn't think. It was stupid of me, and all this is my fault. And I—"

David stuck out his hand, palm facing her. "Please stop, Stella. Don't say any more."

Stella pursed her lips, let the tears flow down her cheeks and off her chin. She would let him have his say. She could tell he wasn't happy. She'd handle this on her own, as soon as he finished yelling at her or speaking his mind or whatever he was going to do. His face spoke more than words could ever say. He was ticked off and not happily surprised.

"I told you before how Patti's baby was the pastry shop. She put her heart and soul into that business, and it seemed to make her happier than anything else in the world. I went along with putting off having a family until it became obvious she had no intention of ever taking any time off."

David looked down at his hands. "Right before… I mean, literally the day before she got the cancer diagnosis I brought up the subject of having a baby. She hadn't been feeling well even then, but she always pushed herself when it came to working in the shop. She became a whirling dervish when she was baking and serving customers.

"But at home… god, she was exhausted. More exhausted than was normal. Which is what prompted her to go to the doctor for a complete physical." He shrugged. "Anyway, when I asked her if she could picture having a child in the near future, she exploded. She yelled at me about how insensitive I was, I didn't understand, she couldn't do everything.

"Couldn't I see it would be impossible for her to run the shop and have a kid at the same time? Was I going to take over the shop while she stayed at home feeding the baby, changing diapers, doing dirty laundry? She went over the edge. I think the exhaustion and waiting for the results of all the tests was having an impact on her. She'd never acted that way before.

"But it was really—" He glanced up at Stella. "—I don't know… pretty clear to me. Having children was once again going to take a back seat to the pastry shop. It had become her living, breathing child. It was her reason for getting up every day, seeing people's smiles, hearing their compliments, chatting with all those who had become family to her. That was the only family she really wanted or needed, I guess. I know she loved me with all her heart, but it was as if she had no more room inside her heart for a baby."

His eyes teared up. "I don't know how you feel about this child in your womb, Stella. But my heart is in my throat right now. Please don't tell me you want an abortion." He jumped off the couch, startling her, then knelt in front of her, took hold of her hands. "I want you to give birth to our baby. Please don't take this from me."

Stella cupped his face in her hands. "Oh, David. You don't know how much this means to me. I don't want an abortion. I'm worried you may think I want you to marry me or have a dedicated relationship. I do not want you to feel obligated to do anything. We just met. I like you a lot. But we, you and I, are brand new. I don't even know if I'd call us a couple. Yet. But I want to try. With you. To be a couple. You're a good man. I'm attracted to you." She smoothed her thumbs along his jawline. "But what do you want? Besides having this baby, what do you want? From me? Do you want to try or… ?"

David got off his knees and sat next to Stella on the couch, took hold of her shoulders and turned her towards him. "Yes, I want to have a relationship with you, Stella. And I want this baby too." He placed a hand on her abdomen. "It's all I've wanted for years. To have a child to love and protect and nurture. I want it so much, it hurts." He placed a hand on the side of her face. "And I'm falling for you already, Stella. There's something about you. I don't know what it is. It's a feeling I have when we're together. That together we… we're strong. That we can do anything we put our minds to. You're a formidable woman, Stella. You escaped an abusive husband who held you captive for years. A weak woman wouldn't have been able to pull that off. They'd have succumbed forever.

"But here you are. Taking responsibility for two teenagers. And you did it all on your own. When I'm with you, I don't feel weak. And I felt so weak for so many years with Patti. As much as I loved her deeply, I couldn't tell her how I really felt about having a child. She was so adamantly against it for so many years… I finally just acquiesced. I let her take control of that part of our lives. I wanted her to be happy. But I sacrificed too much, I think, because I began to resent her for that decision. And then when she got sick, I couldn't help her. So I felt even weaker."

He paused and gave his head a little shake. "I know that doesn't make sense. The cancer was much stronger than the both of us. So I couldn't fight for her against the cancer. And I couldn't fight for myself against her decision not to have kids. So ultimately I was weak. Which made me feel bad about myself. So I want to have a say in this decision about the baby, Stella, and I want this child growing inside you."

Stella kissed him gently on the lips, and he answered the kiss with an urgency even greater than before. They never made it to the bedroom but made love on the Persian carpet in front of the blazing fire warming their naked bodies. And when they were sated, they fell asleep in each other's arms.

David woke up automatically at four a.m. and left the room. Stella felt his departure and after seeing the time, knew he had to get ready to go to the shop. During the night she guessed he must have covered them both with a soft blanket. The fire had gone out, and there was a chill to the room. She picked up her clothes, dressed, then went to the kitchen and splashed cold water on her face. She searched the counter, found fresh coffee grounds, and made a pot of coffee.

When David rounded the corner and caught sight of her, he joined her while they waited for the coffee to finish brewing.

He slid his arm around her waist, and she turned, facing him. After tucking a stray lock of hair behind her ear, he kissed her. "Last night was very special."

She smiled. "I was about to say the same thing."

"I think we have the foundation for a solid beginning of a really good relationship."

"I have no doubts about that, David. In fact, I have no doubts about us at all."

He nodded, slowly. "You still want to keep the baby, right? No second thoughts?"

She shook her head. "With you as the father, I think she has a fantastic chance for a happy life."

"She? You've seen the doctor already? You know that for sure?"

"No, silly. It's too early for that. It's just my guess, is all."

David placed a palm on her abdomen and rubbed round and round. "I don't know about that. I detect some strong masculine vibes." He nodded. "No doubt about it. It's a boy."

She chuckled and playfully pushed him away. "I'm starving. We had no dinner last night. Can I make some toast or something?"

"I brought some croissants I baked yesterday. Will that do?"

"Oh, you betcha. I can pop them in the microwave for a few seconds."

"After we eat, I can drop you off at home, if you'd like, or are you going to come into the shop too?"

"Yes, I'll go in with you. I was thinking, would it be okay if I left a little early today? I have to talk to Loreen after she gets out of school."

"Of course. I can get one of the girls to cover for you at the register for a couple of hours. Is that enough time?"

"It's perfect."

David grabbed the croissants, and Stella placed them in the microwave for a few seconds, then brought them to the table.

He poured two cups of coffee, set one mug in front of Stella, and sipped at his before sitting next to her. "Is Loreen okay?"

Stella took a bite of her croissant. "Mmm. You are such a great baker. Thank you." She dabbed at her lips with a napkin. "This is supposed to be top secret but I need to share this with someone I trust. And that's you." His eyebrows lifted. "Loreen has a boyfriend, Harley. You know that, right?" He nodded. "Well, she's pregnant."

His eyes widened. "Are you kidding me? You're both pregnant?"

She closed her eyes for a second and sighed. "It gets even more involved. I was planning on becoming a surrogate for Kat and Marcus, but when we went to see the doctor the other day, that's when the doctor informed me… no, he informed the three of us, I was pregnant. I was so surprised then humiliated and guilty, I can't tell you."

"How'd they take it?"

"At first they were really pissed off, but yesterday they apologized for taking their disappointment out on me. I told them how sorry I was. Had I known I was pregnant, of course I wouldn't have gone to the doctor with them. I had to admit how I got pregnant, so …"

"That's okay. Marcus and Kat would understand, I'm sure. I've known them for years. They're good people."

"They *do* understand. And they *are* really special people. I love them to death, and I'd never do anything to hurt them on purpose. But I sure accidentally made them very sad. They were counting on me. And I let them down. Totally."

David draped his hand on her forearm. "They could adopt."

"They told me that's exactly what they want to do. I'm excited for them. And they're excited too."

"So what's Loreen going to do about her and Harley's baby? Kat and Marcus could adopt the child."

Stella's mouth dropped open, and she gasped.

"I'm sorry, Stella. I didn't mean anything bad by saying that. I—"

She shook her head. "No. No. That's a fantastic idea. I mean, if Loreen decides to carry the baby to term, that is. But what if at the end she changed her mind, you know? I mean, if she bonds with her child. Then Kat and Marcus would be devastated… again."

"You're right. Maybe you should all talk about it, if it's something your daughter wants to do."

"I'll talk to her today. Then I'll have to tell both Loreen and Gabe, I'm pregnant too."

He let out a breath. "You've got a lot on your plate, Stella. If I can help in any way, just let me know."

She leaned in, kissed him on the lips. "Just being able to talk about it is a huge help. And your idea about Lo's baby is genius. If she agrees to it."

They finished eating, then David drove to the shop to start the day.

Stella spent the entire morning mulling over how she was going to bring up the subject of Kat and Marcus adopting Loreen's baby. Then she'd have to sit down with her two kids and inform them she was carrying David's child. They'd be so surprised. Perhaps mad, since they had no idea she was even interested in David romantically.

This evening would be one she'd remember forever.

Could life get any more complicated?

Chapter Twenty-Eight

At three o'clock it quieted down considerably. After thirty minutes with no customers Stella decided to count the till. The keys to the cash register hung on an elastic bracelet she kept around her wrist. She slid it off her hand and it dropped to the floor. She bent down, grabbed it, then stood up. As her head popped above the glass shelf she noticed a man's legs through the glass, then his chest, and when she straightened, her breath caught in her throat. She stumbled backwards, heart pounding in her ears.

"Hello, Stella," Robert said.

Stella shook her head, and her arms shot out in front of her like two stop signs. "No, no, no, no, no. What are you doing here?" She swallowed. "How'd you find me?"

He smirked. "You mean, how did I find not just you but my two kids?"

"I want you to leave."

"I'm not going anywhere without you and the twins," he snarled.

"That'll never happen."

"That's what you might want, Stella. But that's exactly how it's going to go down. Right now. Today."

She shook her head. "You can't do this. They'll be eighteen next month. You can't keep them against their will, Robert. That would be kidnapping. And I'm not going anywhere with you. Ever."

He walked slowly to the end of the glass counter where a four-foot high wooden door led to the back area. He pushed it with his knees and came around, as Stella backed away from him in the other direction.

He pushed her into the far corner until his body smashed against hers then he pressed her further into the wall. "You're coming with me," he whispered. "You're my wife, and as far as the children are concerned, I have rights. *You're* the one who kidnapped them. *You* took my children from me. That's a crime, Stella." He grinned, looking like Jack Nicholson playing the Joker. "But I found you. And I'm going to make it right," he growled.

Stella shut her eyes. She smelled alcohol on his breath, and his body against hers repulsed her, made her feel like vomiting on his crisp white shirt and maroon tie. "Help!" she screamed, turning her head to the side so as not to have to look him in the face.

He covered her mouth with his hand, and she struggled to move, but he outweighed her, she couldn't escape.

"What the hell is going on here?" David yelled.

Robert dropped his hand from Stella's mouth and turned to face David.

David moved swiftly, grasped Robert's arm, twisted it behind his back. Stella wriggled out from under Robert and skirted to the doorway leading to the kitchen. David shoved Robert's face into the wall, hard.

Robert grunted. "What the hell do you think you're doing? She's my wife."

"That doesn't mean you can hurt her." David pulled Robert's arm up higher.

"Goddammit!" Robert cried out. "Let go of me or I'll—"

David pulled Robert away from the wall, then slammed him back into it. "What're you gonna do, big man? Do you get off by hurting women? Huh? Cause it sure seems like it to me. How many more years is she supposed to let you treat her like this?"

Robert let out a whoosh of air. "Oh, right." He laughed out loud. "What kind of lies is she telling you? I never laid a hand on her."

Stella stood transfixed, watching this unexpected scenario play out in front of her eyes. "Please, Robert. Stop this. Just leave. Or I'm calling the police. They'll be here in a matter of seconds. Please, just leave."

Robert twisted his head in her direction. "I'm not leaving this backwards-ass place without you and my two kids."

David shoved Robert into the wall again, pulling his arm up even further. "Never gonna happen, Robert. Either leave now on your own, or Stella calls 9-1-1. Your choice, man."

Robert screamed out in pain. "All right. All right."

David abruptly let go of him and backed up several feet and

pointed toward the door. "Get the hell out of here. And if I see you around here again, I'm calling the cops."

Robert stumbled toward the front of the counter, then seemed to find his balance and made it out the front door. "I'll be back, asshole." He stopped, turned and stared at Stella. "You're coming with me, and so are the kids. Maybe not today, but watch your back." He exited and stumbled down the street, weaving back and forth until he was out of sight.

Stella ran toward David. He opened his arms, and she fell into his embrace. He hugged her as she wept.

"I'm so sorry, David. I never wanted you to be part of this."

David stroked her hair. "Shhh. I'm not surprised he found you. He probably hired a detective. Everyone leaves a footprint of some sort. And a good detective, given enough time, will be able to find most anyone." He leaned back, looked into her eyes. "What do you want to do? Call the police? File a complaint? You could talk to an attorney. Get a restraining order."

Stella took a deep breath and held onto David's waist. "I don't know what to do, to make him go away. That's all I want. He can't take my two kids, David. What if he kidnaps them? I don't know what I'd do if—"

"Shhh. Don't go there, Stella. I'll close up the shop. We'll find the kids and take them to Kat's house. Marcus is still on leave, right? He'll be able to protect you, until we come up with a plan of action."

Stella nodded, took a deep breath. "Okay. Okay. That sounds good."

They closed the shop, got into David's van, and drove to Gabriel's friend's house. The sound of guitars and drums echoed through the neighborhood.

Stella jumped out of the van, gestured to Gabriel to come talk to her.

He set down his guitar and sauntered over. "'Sup, Mom?"

Stella grasped his forearm. "Please don't ask a lot of questions, Gabriel. Just get into the van with David and me and, I'll explain when we get to Kat's. Okay? Can you please just do that for me? Trust me. I'll wait for you to get your guitar." Gabriel opened his mouth, and Stella got into his face. "Please. Just. Do. It. Do you know where your sister is?"

Gabriel sighed. "She's at home." He turned, packed up his things, and got into the back seat of the van. He remained silent for the short ride home, where the three of them got out of the van and entered the house.

Kat, Marcus. and Loreen were busy rolling out the dough for pizza night. They turned their heads when David, Stella, and Gabriel entered the kitchen.

"What're you guys doing?" Loreen said. "I mean, all together?"

Stella gestured to the kitchen chair. "I have something to talk to you about. In fact, Marcus and Kat? Could you join us? It involves everyone in this household."

Kat and Marcus and Loreen rinsed off their hands, dried them, then sat down at the table across from David, Stella, and Gabriel.

Stella clasped her hands in front of her on the table and drew in a deep breath. "Robert showed up at the pastry shop today and accosted me." She glanced at David.

"He attacked Stella," David explained. "He pushed her into the wall and was yelling at her that she and the kids had to go with him." He looked at Marcus. "Of course, he had no idea I used to get into fights in high school and," he shrugged, "I guess I haven't lost my ability to overpower pretty much anyone. Let's just say he left with his tail between his legs."

Marcus leaned forward. "Do you think he'll come back?"

David glanced at Stella.

"I know he will," Stella said. "And if he knows where I work then I'm sure he knows where we live. David thought it would be safer if we came here right away, being that you're here, Marcus. And given your size, you can be pretty intimidating."

Marcus shook his head. "From what Stella's told us, Robert isn't exactly the fighting type. He only likes to beat up women. Man, what an asshole."

He reached out and patted Stella's hand. "Don't worry about anything. I can handle him. Plus," he glanced at David, "my friend and I know the guys on the police force here in Monarch Bay pretty well. We've partied with them throughout the years. I'll alert them to the situation. They'll send a cruiser by the house, look out for him in Monarch Bay. When Robert shows up, believe me, they'll arrest him."

Stella's brows scrunched together. "But don't they have to see him actually *do* something illegal in order to pick him up?"

Kat put her arm around Loreen sitting next to her. "Things work a little different in small towns. At least they do here. I don't want you," she glanced at Loreen, "or you, Gabriel, to worry about this. Marcus and David will handle it."

"What if he has a gun?" Gabriel said.

Stella pulled back her head. "Why would you say that, Gabe?"

"Cause I saw one. In his tool box in the garage. Not a very good hiding spot. I think he wanted easy access, in case he needed to pull it out and threaten any of us."

Stella shook her head. "Your father is violent but not that kind of violent."

Loreen sighed. "Mom, you're still sticking up for him? I mean, really? Gabe and I aren't stupid. We know what he did to you. We heard the threats. Maybe you didn't actually see the gun, but Gabe did and he told me about it. And that's scary. He never pulled it out and shoved it in your face, but he has it for a reason, and it's not to scare off squirrels in the backyard."

Kat nodded. "Stella, it's typical for abused women to suffer from denial. Sometimes the way you talk, you sound like it's your fault he slapped you around because dinner wasn't ready or he saw you talking to a male neighbor or whatever. Or you make it sound as if his constant physical abuse wasn't as bad as it is for *other* women, as if your situation was somehow not as dangerous. That's called minimizing.

"You underplay the importance or the significance of what he did to you and the kids. He was emotionally and physically abusive, Stella. And whether he actually shot you with a gun or kicked you in the stomach, that's called abuse. What? You need him to shoot you before you file charges against him? What more proof do you need? One of these days, and maybe it'll be today even, he's going to hurt you or the kids. Then what're you gonna do? Still stick up for him because he didn't actually *kill* you, he just shot you in the arm or the leg? Jesus Christ, Stella—"

"Kat, stop," Marcus said.

The look on Stella's face said it all. Tears coursed down her cheeks, and she folded her arms over her chest. "I'm sorry," she sobbed. "I'm not sticking up for him. He's a horrible person." She looked at Kat. "I never wanted the kids to hate him. I tried to hide the bruises and the split lips and keep my voice down when he was raping me. He's their father. He never touched *them*."

Gabriel laughed out loud. "And somehow that makes it okay, Mom? Like the fact he didn't touch us makes him less *bad*? Fuck!"

Loreen glanced at her brother. "He's right, Mom. We've known for years what was going on, but we were too young and scared to say or do anything about it." She shrugged. "There was a time when I was really young that I thought that's just what moms and dads did. They yelled at each other, or at least Dad yelled at you, and then he'd hit you because you did something wrong. Some of our friends' fathers used to use a belt on them, and I'd see the welts on their legs and the bruises on their arms and legs. So I just guessed that you'd been a 'bad girl,' you know? Then when I got older I knew exactly what was going on." Loreen covered her trembling lips with her hand. "He's a fucking monster, and I hope the cops shoot him and he dies."

"Oh, Loreen, no," Stella whispered.

"There you go again, Mom," Gabriel said. "He deserves to suffer for everything he did to you. And Lo and I were scared he was gonna turn his anger on us next. But we didn't tell you because we didn't want you to worry about us. It was enough that you were afraid of your own husband, our father, without being even more afraid that he'd beat us too."

"Oh my God, Gabriel… Loreen. I—" Stella turned to Kat. "And after listening to what you said, Kat. Talking to a therapist might help. Maybe I diminish what Robert did to me to make myself feel less like an idiot for staying with him for so many years. I talked myself into believing I could take whatever he threw at me. And I lived with it until the kids were old enough to understand that we had to get out of there. That I had to take them away from their father for their own good. To keep them safe.

"For years, we had nowhere to go. I had no money, no job. All those years he wouldn't let me contact you, Kat. He monitored my phone calls. You got married, and I didn't know your last name. I couldn't find you. It took me years to save up enough money to hire a private investigator to search for you. Did I stay all those years because I felt I deserved his abuse? I hope that's not the case.

"But he made me believe I'd done something wrong every single time he hit me or kicked me or ..." She paused, took a shuddering breath. "I'm sorry. I wasn't strong enough, I guess. I was weak." Stella shook her head as she cried. "None of you should have to deal with this… this whole Robert thing. It's *my* mess, and I need to take responsibility for getting Loreen and Gabe and me out of it."

Kat stood, came around the table, and hugged her sister from behind, kissing the top of her head. "You are not doing this alone, Stella. You have me and Marcus and David now."

Stella had almost forgotten David was there. She glanced at him, then covered her face with both hands. "I am so sorry, David. This is humiliating. You shouldn't have to listen to this family drama."

Remy clawed at the sliding glass door and Marcus let him in. He ran to Stella's side and snuffled against her leg. Stella stroked his head and let out a sigh.

David curled his hands into fists. "You're wrong, Stella. I'm glad I'm here. Marcus and I will get in touch with our friends in the police department. We'll take care of that for you."

Kat knelt down next to her sister. "And you and I are going to find an attorney who specializes in this type of harassment and abuse. Yesterday a client of mine told me about the problems she's having with her husband. Sounded very similar to you, Stella. She's going to give me the number for her therapist, and you can set up an appointment. My therapist Roslyn? This isn't her specialty. But this other therapist would be perfect for you. You need to get a handle on this, Stella. You need to understand abusive men."

Kat grasped Stella by the shoulders, turning her so their faces were inches apart. "Someone will be with you at all times. From now on, if you leave this house, you will not go alone. Marcus or David or I will accompany you. At least until we know Robert's either locked up or your attorney tells you what to do. You hear me?"

Stella swiped at her tears and nodded.

Loreen and Gabe pulled their mom to a standing position and enveloped her in a group hug.

"We love you, Mom," Gabe said.

"Yeah, Mom, we love you so much," Loreen added. "We don't want anything to happen to you. I don't know what I'd do without you."

"Me neither," Gabe added.

Stella looked from Gabe to Loreen with a half-smile. "I don't know what I'd do if anything happened to either of you. That's my greatest fear. I'm not worried about myself."

"Well, you should be. *We* all are," Loreen said.

Gabe kissed Stella on the cheek. "You're our mom. We don't want to lose you. Don't you get it?"

Stella stared at the floor, shaking her head. "Maybe I don't get it. I don't know. Maybe I feel like I don't deserve anything good that happens to me. Robert beat me down for years. I don't feel good about myself." She shrugged. "I need help."

"I'll call my friend right now," Kat said, standing. "I'll get the name and number of her therapist. You could call and leave a message."

Stella took a deep breath. "First, let's make pizza, guys. That should make us all feel better."

Remy barked twice, making them all chuckle.

"I'll give you one small piece," Stella said, patting him on the head. "But no pepperoni."

Gabe laughed out loud. "We all know what happens after he eats that!"

Stella shook her head and smiled.

Chapter Twenty-Nine

While waiting for the pizza to bake, Stella excused herself and flew up the stairs to Loreen's bedroom. She knocked on the door.

"Come in, Mom," Loreen yelled.

Stella opened the door and smiled. "How'd you know it was me?"

"We both knew it was you," Gabe said. "We recognize the sound of your footsteps up the stairs, and your knock is always four thumps."

Loreen laughed. "Not two, not three, always four."

Stella shut the door behind her. "I hate being so predictable."

"Wassup?" Loreen said.

Stella sat in the desk chair and turned toward the two of them lounging on the bed. "What I have to say is going to come as a complete surprise to both of you. I wanted to tell you immediately."

"Sounds scary, Mom," Gabe said, chuckling.

"I assure you, it's not scary. Surprising, yes." She fiddled with her hands in her lap, looked up at the ceiling, took a long breath, then faced them head on. "Okay. You know I had tests done to see if I'm a viable candidate to be a surrogate for Kat and Marcus, right?" They both nodded. "Well, we went to the doctor's office the other day, and he told us some surprising news." She cleared her throat a couple of times, not wanting to blow this one opportunity to explain why she was no longer a surrogacy candidate for their aunt and uncle.

"Okay. Ummm ..."

"Come on, Mom," Loreen said. "Get on with it."

"Yeah," Gabe added. "The pizza's gonna come out of the oven soon, and I'm starving."

Stella looked at each of them in turn. "The doctor informed me I'm already pregnant and—"

"What the hell?" Gabe said.

"Who's the baby daddy?" Loreen said, bouncing on her butte on the side of the bed.

"You know my boss, David, of course. Well…"

Loreen covered her mouth with her hand. "You mean, David David? Who was married to Patti who just died? That David?"

Stella nodded. "Yes."

"He's already messing around with another woman?" Gabe asked.

Stella shut her eyes momentarily, knowing how indiscreet this looked. Mom screws around with the grieving widower moments after his dead wife's memorial service. Yeah, right, Stella. Way to go! "I don't know how to say this without sounding like I'm trying to justify my behavior, but the two of us just connected, pretty instantly. He's a really nice man, kind, understanding, and not a player. I really like him."

"So are you going to keep the baby?" Loreen said.

Stella nodded. "Yes, we are."

Gabe's eyes widened. "You're gonna marry him?"

"No. At least not now. We don't have any plans… about anything. But I don't want to abort this child, and he's always wanted to have a baby, but it never happened with him and Patti, so …"

Loreen stared at her mom. "This is totally bizarro. You realize that, right?"

Gabe shook his head. "Yeah. Now you and Lo are both pregnant at the same time. What a trip!"

Stella frowned. "Gabriel knows?"

"I told him the other day," Loreen said. "I needed to talk to a guy about this whole thing. I still haven't heard from Harley." She lifted her shoulders then dropped them. "Maybe I never will."

"What an asshole," Gabe muttered.

Loreen slapped him on the knee. "Is not. Wait until he gets in touch with me before you label him, 'kay?"

Gabe scrunched up his lips. "And if he never gets in touch with you, like, ever?"

"I'm giving him another month, then I'm moving on," Loreen stated.

Gab smirked. "Yeah, right. Like you're gonna have a ton of guys knocking at your door wanting to play who-da-baby-daddy with you!"

"Stop it, you two," Stella announced, standing. "Wait." She sat back down. "I have something I want to put out there on the table for you to think about, Lo." She crossed and uncrossed her legs. "You mentioned adoption once when we were talking. How would you feel about allowing Kat and Marcus to adopt your child? They're talking about adoption now, since this surrogacy thing with me fell through."

Loreen's face was blank for a few seconds. Then she broke into a smile. "I hope to talk to Harley one of these days, but that sounds like an awesome idea." She turned to Gabe. "What do you think?"

He tilted his head. "I think it solves several problems. You don't have to become a teenage mom, for one, and our aunt and uncle get the child they've wanted for a long time. Everybody wins."

"Ideally you'll want to talk to Harley, as you said," Stella interjected.

"For sure," Loreen said. "He'd have to sign off on all that shit, if I put this child up for adoption, right?"

"Yes, he would," Stella answered. "So, hopefully he'll show up one of these days, and you two can talk. In the meantime, don't mention it—either of you—to your aunt and uncle. It would break their hearts... again... if you changed your mind after talking to Harley, Lo."

Loreen stood. "Sure, no problem. Of course."

"Don't you say anything either, Gabriel," Stella said.

He zipped his finger across his lips, then stood.

The three of them clunked down the stairs to join Kat and Marcus and David for pizza.

While Loreen and Gabriel set the table, they heard a knock at the door.

"I know who it is," Loreen said and ran out of the kitchen.

Seconds later, Harley shuffled into the room behind Loreen, looking like a guilty prisoner, his head angled toward the floor.

"We're just gonna go upstairs for a minute to talk," Loreen said. "We'll be right back. Save us some pizza." Stella grabbed Harley's hand and dragged him up the stairs.

Stella glanced at Kat and Marcus, then David and her son. She shrugged. "Guess they'll figure out what's going on in their relationship."

"Hope so," Kat said. "I remember being that young. Oh, the heartbreak!"

Marcus slapped Kat gently on the rear end, then kissed her on the neck.

"No PDA, you two," Gabriel shouted, then laughed out loud.

"Sorry," Marcus said with a smile.

"I'm gonna go home now," David said.

"No pizza?" Stella asked him.

"I'll be back after I shower and change. I can sleep in the front room on the couch, make sure Robert doesn't sneak in somehow."

Stella hugged him. 'You don't have to do that."

David lifted Stella's chin with his finger. "I don't *have* to do anything. I want to." He glanced for a second at Marcus. "Between the two of us here under one roof, you ought to feel safe, get some sleep, be ready to greet tomorrow with a calm mind."

Stella nodded. "Thank you, David. And Marcus."

"Then I'm off." He kissed her on the lips, waved goodbye to everyone and slipped out the front door.

The four of them sat down and devoured one entire pizza and a small portion of the second one before they heard the sound of Loreen and Harley coming down the stairs.

Loreen smiled. "Did you leave any for me and Harley?"

Harley glanced up, face flushed. "I don't have to stay."

Kat grabbed his wrist and pulled him toward the kitchen table. "Of course you're going to stay. We have a third pizza that isn't even cooked yet."

"That's right," Marcus added. "Enough for an army, man."

Harley's lips curved up at the sides. "Thank you. That's very generous of you."

For several minutes it was quiet at the table until Loreen swallowed the last of her first piece of pizza and wiped her mouth with a napkin. She faced Kat and Marcus, across the table from her and Harley. "Harley and I have something we'd like to talk to you about."

Kat sat back. "Us? Well, sure. What is it?"

Marcus put his napkin on top of his plate and leaned back in his chair, arms folded across his chest.

Loreen nudged Harley in the side.

Harley's head popped up. "Oh. Yeah. I don't know if you guys know, but Loreen's gonna have our baby."

Kat stared at Loreen, mouth agape. "We had no idea."

"Whoa," Marcus said. "This comes as a surprise."

"To me too," Harley said.

Loreen nudged Harley again.

Harley ran his hand through his hair, fidgeted in his seat. "So… Lo and I have talked about it, and if you two are interested, well, um—"

Loreen let out a whoosh of air. "Oh, for fuck's sake, Harley." She faced her aunt and uncle. "We'd like you to adopt our baby, if you want to."

Kat gasped, covered her lips with the tips of her fingers. "Oh, my Jesus."

"Are you kidding me?" Marcus whispered.

Loreen smiled. "We're totally serious." She and Harley glanced at each other for a second. "And there's no way we're changing our minds, just for your peace of mind. Harley and I both want to go to college, get good jobs, travel through Europe and shit. I know all about bonding with your baby, and I'm supposed to feel different after I hold it in my arms after giving birth and all that crap. But the baby'll be like my cousin or something. So I'll be able to babysit sometimes or at least see him or her. It's not like I'll be totally out of its life." She paused. "So?"

Marcus put his arm around Kat's shoulders, turned his head, looked in her eyes. They smiled at each other, then Marcus faced Harley and Loreen. "We'd love to adopt your child. And I know Kat would agree when I say this is one of the kindest and most unselfish things anyone's ever done for either of us."

Tears trickled down Kat's cheeks. She reached out and grasped one of Loreen's hands and one of Harley's, held them tightly. "Thank you, thank you, thank you."

Remy appeared at Kat's side and she rubbed his back. "This is a dream come true."

Marcus sat up straight, hands folded on the table. "So, you've both discussed this, thoroughly and it's all good? Neither of you feels pressured to do this? You don't need more time to think about it?"

Loreen cleared her throat. "I am so relieved, Uncle Marcus. Really, I am. I thought Harley was gonna leave all this up to me." She turned to him. "But I was wrong. He freaked out when I told him I was pregnant, took off on his Harley and went all the way to the Oregon border."

A red blush covered Harley's face. "I wasn't gonna leave you to figure this out all alone, Lo. You know me. I just needed time to think."

Loreen huffed. "How the hell was I supposed to know that, Har?"

Harley kissed Loreen on the cheek. "Have a little faith, babe. It's my kid inside there." He glanced down at Loreen's stomach. "Even though I'm not responsible enough… yet… to have a kid, I wouldn't want you to have a frickin' abortion. Especially when we've got two cool people here who wanna give the baby everything it needs. Like love and a good home and a dog and relatives and shit." He glanced from Kat to Marcus. "You're good people."

"Thank you," Marcus and Kat said at the same time.

"This means so much to both of us," Kat added. "Whenever you two want to make this legal, we'll pay for the attorney fees and also for any medical expenses. So, don't worry about any of that."

Loreen and Harley nodded, together.

Stella stood. "Shall we celebrate then?"

"You mean like, have a glass of champagne or something, Mom?" Loreen said.

Stella gave her "the look." "You're underage, Loreen."

"I'm not," Harley said, smiling.

"Ah, Mom, come on. One little glass of champagne. It's not gonna make me drunk," Loreen insisted.

"I have a bottle of the bubbly a buddy of mine gave me for my last birthday," Marcus said.

Stella twisted her mouth side to side. "All right. But just a teensy bit for me and Loreen." She raised her eyebrows at Loreen. "Remember, no alcohol for pregnant women."

Loreen slapped the table. "Shit, man! I totally forgot about that."

"What about me, Mom?" Gabe said with a grin. "I'm not pregnant."

Stella rolled her eyes. "We wouldn't want to leave you out, of course. But just one small glass."

Gabe rolled his eyes. "All right!"

Loreen kissed her mom on the cheek, then grabbed Harley's hand. "I'm so happy this is gonna happen. Thanks so much, Aunt Kat and Uncle Marcus."

Harley reached out toward Marcus, and they shook hands. "Thanks, Marcus." He put his arms around Kat, and they hugged.

Kat leaned back, tears in her eyes. "This means the world to me. To us, Harley." She turned and wrapped her arms around Loreen. "I love you, honey. Thank you so very much."

"You're welcome, Aunt Kat. I can't wait to see Uncle Marcus holding this teeny tiny baby. That'll be funny."

Marcus's dark eyebrows drew together. "What's so funny about that?"

"Cause you're so big, Uncle Marcus. I'd hate to be a teenager and have you as my dad."

"Explain, young lady." Marcus folded his beefy arms across his chest.

"You can look scary sometimes," Loreen answered.

"You've got a bike, Marcus," Harley said. "Maybe you and Kat and Loreen and I can ride sometime."

"Enough about riding motorcycles, guys," Stella interjected. "I don't want Loreen to get into an accident." Her eyes met Harley's. "I want my daughter around to give birth, so we can all enjoy the little one who's already on her way."

"Her way? Her?" Marcus laughed. "We'll see about that. When can you have an ultrasound, Loreen?"

"The earliest would be fourteen weeks, depending on what the doctor wants," Loreen answered. "Wanna be there when we find out?"

Marcus grabbed Kat's hand. "We'd love to."

"Okay," Stella said. "I'd like to as well. So, there'll be Loreen and Harley and Kat and Marcus and I in the room?"

"What about me?" Gabe said.

"I don't think you can all be there, but if it's possible, it's okay with me," Loreen said.

Marcus turned and walked toward the basement door. "I'm getting that bottle of champagne. Be right back."

"Then it's lights out," Stella said. "Everyone's gotta go to work or school."

"It's *almost* Thanksgiving break, Mom. We're celebrating early," Gabe said.

Stella thumped her forehead with her hand. "Oh my God, I forgot. With everything that's been going on, it completely escaped my mind."

The thudding of Marcus's feet echoed up the basement stairs. He entered the kitchen carrying a bottle of champagne.

Marcus pried the bottle open, and the cork flew across the room. The bubbling liquid fizzed out the top and drizzled down the side, covering his hands, dripping onto the kitchen floor.

They all burst out laughing. Kat grabbed six glasses, handed them out, and Marcus poured the champagne.

Marcus raised his glass and smiled. "To Loreen and Harley's upcoming baby."

Loreen lifted hers a little higher. "To the newest addition to Kat and Marcus's house."

Harley chuckled. "Yeah, that sounds good to me."

They clinked glasses.

"This doesn't mean I have to babysit, does it?" Gabe asked.

Marcus put his arm around Gabe's shoulders. "Of course it does, Gabe. What are relatives for?"

A cell phone chimed, and Marcus patted the pocket of his jeans, pulled out his phone, checked it. "Gotta get this. Work." He stepped out of the room. Within seconds he returned, shaking his head.

Kat frowned. "What is it, babe?"

"They need me to do a short haul at 2 a.m. Fill in for a guy whose wife just went into labor. Only down to San Diego. Be back tomorrow night." He glanced around. "Shit. I forgot David left."

"Call him, Marcus," Kat said.

He phoned David while he walked in circles in the kitchen. "Hey! Gotta go to work at 2 a.m. Think you can handle things alone while I'm gone, bro?" He nodded, listening. "Gotcha. Thanks, dude." He stuffed the phone back in his pocket. "He'll be over in a bit."

Chapter Thirty

Harley left, and Loreen and Gabriel went to bed. Kat and Marcus retired to their room, since Marcus would have to wake up around one in the morning. After the day she had, Stella felt amped and decided to wait for David to return.

She texted him to knock softly at the door, then lit a fire in the fireplace and sat on a pillow on the floor, watching the crackling flames. If not for Robert's sudden appearance in Monarch Bay, things were looking up. Kat and Marcus would be adopting Loreen and Harley's baby. Gabriel's garage band had another engagement at a high school in Morro Bay around Christmas time. Her relationship with David seemed like it had the potential to blossom into something permanent. They both wanted to keep the baby Stella was carrying. The most surprising events were turning out to be positive outcomes for the future of her entire family.

She heard a car idling nearby, snuck a peek out the curtains in the front room window. David. She knocked on the window pane, and he waved. Stella opened the door and he slipped inside.

"Everyone's gone to bed," she whispered.

"What are you doing awake?"

"I feel as if I've drunk ten espressos. I'm so nervous after seeing Robert."

He took hold of her hand and brought her to the couch. They sat next to each other facing the blazing fire. David wrapped his arm around Stella's shoulders and brought her closer to his side.

Stella turned her head toward him. "This is nice. I need some peace and quiet after a day like today."

He leaned in and kissed her none too chastely, then wiggled his eyebrows up and down.

"If you think we're going to do anything more than make-out on this couch, you're crazy."

"Of course I don't. I just like kissing you. I'm not trying to seduce you in my friends' front room."

She chuckled. "Glad to hear it." She snuggled even closer to him. "I feel safe right now."

"And tomorrow Marcus and I will go… oh, wait, he's leaving in a few hours. Doesn't matter. I'll go to the police station myself, talk to our buddies about your ex. They'll keep an eye out for him, send a squad car by the house, maybe drive by the bakery and the kids' school too. You and I will be together most of the day at the bakery."

She nodded as she listened to his voice, soft and low in the quietude of the house. "And I'll tell the kids to wait for me to come get them after classes are over."

"No. You and I will close the shop early, and we'll pick them up in the van… together. I'm going to keep you safe."

She smiled. "That would be really kind of you. I'd appreciate it. I don't want them walking home, in case Robert lures them into his car and takes them to Oregon." She shivered. "That's the one thing that totally scares the crap out of me. What if he retaliates and kidnaps them, since he feels that's what I did. That I started this whole mess, and he'll one-up me and turn the tables. It would be just like him to do something retaliatory. He's ticked off and he wants revenge."

"I get it. I get it. However, if it comes to fist-fighting, we already know he'll lose. And Gabe and Loreen are smart enough to know not to get in a car with him, aren't they?"

"I would hope so. I'll leave them a note before I leave in the morning so there's no misunderstanding. Kat can drop them off at school. But Robert can be quite charming and seductive in the way he talks. I fell for it numerous times." She paused, took a deep breath. "He'd suck me right in with his words, then turn right around and cut me to pieces in the next sentence. Then, of course, he'd follow that by shoving me to the floor and kicking me in the ribs." She could feel tears coming and took another cleansing breath. "I refuse to go there tonight. Not with you sitting next to me."

David kissed her cheek. "I want to hear about your life with Robert. Don't keep things from me."

She stared at the flames.

"Was it like that from the beginning, Stella? Did you live like that since you had the twins? For seventeen years?"

She inhaled through her nose, let it out through her mouth. "No. Not from the beginning." She smiled. "I remember when we met. We were both going to the university in Monterey. We had a class together. Um, Philosophy? Yeah, that was it. It was in an auditorium with about four hundred upper classmen. Huge. You could hardly see the professor. He was way down at the bottom at the podium, and he had to use a mic in order to be heard.

"Anyway, I was later than usual, so I had to sit in the nosebleed section. And there were a couple of empty seats, but they were in the middle of this long row. I had to squish past about fifteen people in order to find a seat. Right next to Robert, as it turned out." She shook her head. "Man, was he a charmer. I remember my gramma used to say something about men who could charm an Alaskan into buying ice cubes." She laughed under her breath. "Of course, I fell for him hook, line, and sinker, as my gramma also used to say. He was very good looking, very sweet, solicitous, smart.

"So after dating him for about, oh, I'd say a year or so, we knew we were in love. We both graduated in March instead of the usual June, because we were high achievers. We both had enough units to receive our degrees. His in Spanish. Mine in English."

Stella leaned her head back and stared at the ancient chandelier hanging from the ceiling. "I found out I was pregnant, and Robert got a job offer at Oregon State University, so we moved to Corvallis. We planned to marry in September. His parents both passed away when he was a freshman in college, before I met him. Some sort of car accident. My mom and dad, as I told you, died in a boating accident. So he and I had that in common. But, unlike him, I—Kat and I—had Fiona and Nason, our foster parents. But he wanted to get married in a private ceremony, just the two of us, no guests.

"When I picture myself back then, what the hell was I thinking? Granted, Fiona and Nason were getting up there in years and didn't travel anywhere, but they really wanted to be at my wedding. They said they'd fly up to Corvallis. But Robert insisted it be just the two of us. More intimate, he said. He wanted to start our life together without the distractions of other people. But they were like parents to me. And I let him talk me into phoning them and explaining we'd already eloped. I'd never lied to them in my life. And then they passed away after Robert and I had been married for a couple of months. I never got a chance to see them again.

"But the whole elopement lie… that should have been a huge red flag." She didn't take her eyes off the flames flickering in the fireplace, mesmerized by their colors. "Soon after I had the twins and was fully healed, little things started to happen. He wouldn't let me join a book club. I wanted to make friends, but he said the twins needed me full time, that I was the one who got pregnant and had the responsibility of raising them… while he was the breadwinner. Obviously he wasn't about to let me get a job and have a babysitter. I didn't even ask to do that.

"It became so damn obvious, he wanted me all to himself. But the weirdest thing is, I acquiesced. I let him tell me what to do. I let him be the man of the house, while I played the role of the perfect wife, perfect lover, perfect housekeeper. That's not what I ever wanted to do with my degree. That's not why I went to college. But little by little I gave him more and more rope, until he finally hung me with it. I dangled there underneath his ultimate authority like a kidnap victim.

"Then, I'll never forget. It was Valentine's Day. The twins were five years old. I'd given them each a heart-shaped box of chocolates from Barron's Candy Shop. Handmade. The minute after they opened their gifts Robert just went off, yelling about how expensive Barron's chocolates were, that I should have asked him first before spending all that money.

"He'd bought me a card and one red rose. And I had to make a special dinner for him. I'd knitted a beautiful beanie for him to use during the cold winters in Oregon, and I didn't even give it to him. I spent the evening slaving over a hot stove, making him his favorite pot roast with potatoes and carrots and celery. I distinctly recall wanting to pour the stew over his head. I had visions of him screaming while the hot stew burned his face off. I was so sick of looking at him, sick of being controlled.

"But that was nothing… nothing compared to what was ahead of me." She shook her head, then turned to David. "Are you sure you want to hear this?"

He nodded. "Yes. I want to know everything about you."

She rubbed her hands up and down her denim-covered thighs. "I swear, it was like the most cliche'd thing you could imagine. He always wanted me to put the twins to sleep so we could eat dinner together. Alone. No family dinners for him. At least not when they were so young and needed their meat cut for them, stuff like that. Oh, no. It had to be just the two of us. So I made something… oh, yes, I made one of his favorite meals—lasagne. From scratch too. I sit down, and I dish out the salad and the lasagna, and I look at him and smile and I was about to take a bite when he gets this look on his face. As if something horrible had happened. For a minute I thought he was having a heart attack or something."

She laughed. "I wish." She sighed. "He sat there, not eating. Didn't even pick up his fork. He said something like, 'Aren't you forgetting something, Stella?' And I looked around and was about to say I thought everything he liked was right there on the table, when he stood up and backhanded me across the face. My chair tipped over, and I flew onto the kitchen floor on my back. When I looked up. he was walking really slowly toward me and brought his foot back and kicked me in the side with his shoe as hard as he could. He knocked the breath out of me." Tears dripped down her cheeks.

David reached out and brought her onto his lap, cradling her like a child. "I can't believe this. I mean, I don't want to believe someone could do that to you." He ran his fingers through her hair, kissed her forehead. "It makes me sick to hear this."

She swiped the tears from her chin and cheeks. "I don't need to tell you any more, David."

He looked her straight in the eyes. "I want to know. The good and the bad. You are who you are today because of everything that happened to you in the past, so I want to hear it. But if it's too much for you, then please stop. I don't want to cause you any more pain than you've already been through."

She gave him a half-smile. "No, I want to tell you. It's cathartic for me. It's like I can vomit all of this out, and maybe it'll help me forget it ever happened."

"That's why Kat wants you to see a therapist. That's what they're for. It might help you."

She nodded. "I'm going to call soon." She slid off his lap, lay on her side and put her head on his thigh, facing the crackling fire. "I'd forgotten he liked garlic bread with his lasagne. That's what made him so mad."

"Oh, my God," David whispered.

Stella stared at the flames, remembering those days.

Remy padded into the room and lay down on the floor beside the couch.

Stella stroked Remy's head. "I have many stories just like this. Different reasons for his anger and why he always lashed out at me for the smallest thing. I tried so hard to be perfect. No wrinkles in his shirts. Packed a lunch for him every day with everything he liked. A hot meal every night after he arrived home, promptly at the time he wanted it.

"It was a double-edged sword, though. If I did everything right, unfortunately having sex with him would follow." She shivered.

David leaned to the side and grabbed a blanket and covered her gently.

"Thanks." She took a deep breath. "Sex with Robert was always rough and …" She hiccuped and tried to stop crying.

Remy stood and licked her face.

Stella kissed Remy on the cheek and he settled back down on the floor. "Robert liked to slap me. Everywhere. Until I had bruises on my breasts and buttocks. He'd make me do whatever he wanted me to do, even though he repulsed me. I can't even tell you. I won't tell you what he made me do. It was disgusting.

"Anyway, if I messed up during the day, and he hit me and got angry, then I wouldn't have to have sex with him that evening. I knew if I did everything right, he'd rape me over and over and over that same night. So sometimes I messed up on purpose, telling myself it was worth getting punched, since then I wouldn't have to go through the abusive sex later on." She stopped and turned onto her back, looked up at David.

"If that's all you want to tell me, Stella, that's okay. You're really upset."

More tears rolled down the sides of her cheeks. "That pretty much is what my life was like, until I got into that big rig with a man named Tom who brought us here to Monarch Bay. For the last year I could see I'd have enough money to escape by August. I'd legally changed our names—the twins' and mine. I hired a PI who found Kat.

I made connections with the waitresses at the truck stop. They're the ones who hooked me up with Tom. So I got the kids and ran." She stared at David. "And here I am."

David gathered her into his arms, rocked her softly back and forth. "You're an amazingly strong woman, Stella. I'd think you'd be so jaded by now you wouldn't want to try another relationship. I feel blessed that you're sharing your past with me." He leaned back, looked into her eyes. "I have no words to tell you how much it means to me that you've chosen to have our child. That you didn't run off and abort it without telling me. That you're allowing me into your life."

"I think you're amazing too, David. The love of your life just passed away, and you've had a horrible year with everything she had to go through, knowing she was dying a little day by day, and you had to watch it happening. That takes a very special, caring individual. I'd think that *you* wouldn't want to get involved with anyone for a long time, if ever."

He smiled. "Then I guess we have a mutual admiration society going on between the two of us. We're just so totally amazing." He laughed. "I'm betting we're going to be totally amazing… together." He slowly brought his lips to hers and kissed her, then continued to hold her close until she fell asleep in his arms.

They both awoke when they heard Marcus and Kat in the kitchen at one in the morning. Stella stood and walked into the kitchen.

"Whoa!" Marcus said. "Where'd you come from?"

"David and I must have fallen asleep on the couch. I'm going to bed now. I guess we'll see you soon, Marcus?"

"Late tonight, I'm thinking. Only going to San Diego."

"Have a good one. Oh, and Kat, I'll be going into work early with David. Can you drive the kids to school for me?"

"Of course. Don't worry. I'll take care of it. Night, Stell."

Chapter Thirty-One

Within a few hours Stella's alarm buzzed. Four a.m. She had to shower and wake up David, so they could go to the shop. She left a note on the kitchen table for Loreen and Gabriel, explaining their Aunt Kat would take them to school, and they shouldn't leave the school grounds for any reason whatsoever. She and David would pick them up after school, and they'd all have dinner at the house.

Stella shook David's shoulder. The poor guy hadn't gotten much sleep. Neither had she. But she figured they'd go to sleep early that night, and she'd let David have Gabriel's bed, since there was a pull-out couch in the family room where Gabriel spent most evenings anyway, watching TV or playing video games. David took a quick shower, then they drove to Patti's Pastries, arriving at almost five a.m.

David parked in the lot behind the shop, and they entered through the rear door. "I better start baking, since I usually arrive at four. Had a rough time waking up this morning."

"I'm sorry I kept you up so late with the long story of my life with Robert. It's so pitiful, really. So many years spent allowing myself to be manipulated like that." She took off her jacket and hung it in the small lunch room located at the back of the bakery. "I should have fought back. I shouldn't have exposed the kids to a situation like that."

David met her as she exited the lunch room and held onto her shoulders with both hands, looked her in the eyes. "You did everything you could, Stella. You know as well as I do, you're among thousands of women who endure abusive husbands for years, imprisoned both physically and emotionally by men who know instinctively how to manipulate them to do exactly what they want them to do and think and feel. That's what abusive men do, Stella. If you ever read a book about it or see a movie, you'll know you're not alone."

Stella hung her head and stared at the floor.

"Stella, look at me, please." Stella brought her head up to meet his gaze. "You tried hard to be what he wanted, so he'd stop hitting you. But no matter what you did, it was a toss-up between being beaten up and left alone at night or acting like his slave, only to be raped later on. He was an abusive bastard." He squeezed her shoulders gently. "You did all you could do. And he never touched the kids, right?" She nodded. "And that's because of you. You saved your two kids from that bullying asshole. So you did good. And emotional abuse is insidious, Stella. I don't know enough about it to counsel you. That's why you've got to get into therapy. It'll do you a world of good."

Stella nodded and gave him a watery smile. "I plan to do that. I promise. I'm going to call Kat a bit later to ask how the kids seemed today when she dropped them off at school. I'll get the phone number of that therapist she told me about."

He kissed her forehead. "You have to try your best to stop blaming yourself for everything that happened in the past, Stella. Your life is on the upswing. Now, let's get to work. Can you start on the croissants? I'll do the scones."

They worked together, side by side, until it was time to open. Stella turned the sign hanging in the window of the front door, then unlocked it. She and David schlepped the trays from the kitchen to the front cases, then Stella prepared the coffee.

The morning crowd lasted for the first two hours, then the typical lull ensued. David took over the register in the front, while Stella worked in the back, frosting the small number of donuts they made each day for those people who enjoyed more traditional pastries.

She entered the small refrigerated area to get a tub of prepared frosting when someone grabbed her from behind, stuffed a piece of cloth over her mouth, and dragged her backward. When she opened her mouth to scream she breathed in a disgustingly sweet scent, and her vision went black.

She heard someone singing along with a tune from the radio, felt the hum of tires along the road, and opened her eyes. Realizing her hands were tied behind her back, she struggled to sit up. She was in the back seat of a car that wasn't Robert's, but he was driving on a freeway, and the ocean sparkled on the left side of the car. She guessed they were heading north and recognized a particular sign on the side of the freeway stating how far they were from San Francisco. Instinctively she knew he was headed for Oregon.

"Good morning, sunshine," Robert said.

In the rear-view mirror she saw his smile. and her stomach lurched. She could not let him get away with kidnapping her, but she didn't know how she'd ever exit the back of a two-door car. She'd never be able to climb between the two front seats and grab the door handle with her hands tied behind her back while he was going more than sixty miles per hour.

"Robert, please. What do you think you're doing?"

"Robert, please," he mimicked in a high-pitched voice. "Give me a break, Stella. You kidnapped my kids. Took them away from their father." He laughed hysterically. "Now I'm taking their mother away from them. How does that make *you* feel, Stella?"

"You won't get away with this. Someone will have seen you leave Monarch Bay. It's a small town. Plus the owner of Patti's Pastries will notify the police. They'll be looking for you."

She wasn't quick enough to see the back of his hand before it met with the side of her face, knocking her against the back seat. She'd felt much harder slaps and punches from him in the past and sat up, leaning forward between the seats.

"Robert, please. Just let me go. I won't press charges. I just want to get back to Loreen and Gabriel. They'll be sick with worry about me, when they find out I'm gone."

"You won't press charges? What they hell are you thinking, Stella. You're as stupid as the day is long, woman. You kidnapped my children. And until they're eighteen years old they don't get a say in where they live, and they live with me. I'm their father. You can't bring charges against me. I can bring charges against you, you idiot." He poked his index finger against his temple several times. "Think, Stella. Use that pea brain of yours to get it through your empty head. You started this. You're the one who took my children away from me."

"David will call the police, Robert. You'll be caught in no time."

"David will call the police," he mimicked again in a high-pitched voice. "You're screwing him, aren't you? You're a married woman."

"Robert, listen to reason, will you? You know you've been abusing me for years. I had to leave you. One of these days you would have killed me. Then where would you be? You can't take care of your two kids if you're in prison."

"Don't try to make this all about me, Stella. You're the one who deserted your husband and kidnapped two innocent kids. You're the one who's going to face charges. Not me. But, hey, think what you want with what little you have inside that thick skull of yours."

She caught a whiff of alcohol and realized he was, once again, drunk. She glanced at the speedometer. Ninety miles an hour! She wanted desperately with every cell in her body to kill him with her bare hands. She was so sick of being manipulated and physically hurt by him. She wanted him to get a taste of that. If only she wasn't in the car. She wished he'd get into a bad accident and die a fiery death.

She closed her eyes, knowing these horrible thoughts were unkind and not like her at all. She tried to think how she could get out of this situation and came up with nothing. She was in the back of a car going ninety miles an hour on the freeway. Looking around, there were very few cars on Highway One at the moment, so she couldn't flag down any passing vehicles.

Robert kept scanning the side mirrors, looking behind the car instead of paying attention to driving. Suddenly he swung the steering wheel to the left, then to the right, trying to straighten out the car and keep it from hitting the guard rail.

"Some crackhead's driving on my tail. Who do you know who owns a black Dodge Charger? Another of your boyfriends, Stella?"

Stella huddled in the back seat with her knees tucked under her chin. "I don't have a boyfriend, Robert, and I don't know anyone with a Dodge Charger. Why don't you just pull over into another lane? You've been drinking, and you're swerving all over the place."

He reached into the glove box, pulled out a bottle of whiskey, unscrewed the cap, and guzzled what was left, which amounted to half the bottle. This situation would only get worse once the liquor hit him. Stella's whole body shook. Her teeth chattered. Her wrists ached from the zip ties. She wrested her hands back and forth to loosen them, but it was obvious that would never happen without something sharp to cut the ties. There was nothing she could do. She was, once again, helpless against this monster she'd been married to for most of her life.

Robert sped up, moved over two lanes, and exited the freeway at the next turnoff. He turned right at the first street, zoomed down the block and pulled over on a dead-end street and cut the engine. "Gotta take a leak." He fumbled for the door handle, trying over and over to grab hold of it, missing each time. He was plastered. Stella's stomach cramped, knowing when he got back on the freeway they would surely have a bad accident and both be killed.

She turned around and looked out the back window. The Charger had followed them. Gravel spit out from all sides as it came to an abrupt halt behind them. Gabriel jumped out of the Charger at the same time as Robert pushed his door open, swung his feet to the ground, and stood up. Gabriel grabbed hold of the door and smashed it, hard, against Robert's body, opened the door again and smashed it against Robert again. Then grasped him by the front of his shirt and pulled him away from the car. Gabriel punched his father in the stomach, then kneed him in the crotch.

Robert crumpled to the ground, groaning.

Gabriel jerked the driver's seat forward, leaned in, and reached his hand toward his mom. "Come on, Mom. Let's get you outta here. You all right?"

"Oh, Gabriel. Thank God you found us." She turned half-way around. "Cut these off, please, if you can."

Gabe took a knife out of his pocket and sliced the zip ties around his mother's wrists, then pulled her out of the back seat and encircled her in his arms.

Robert lay writhing back and forth on the ground next to them.

Gabriel kept one arm curled around Stella's shoulders while he called 9-1-1, explained the situation then stuffed the phone back in his pocket.

"Get inside my car, Mom. I'll take care of him. There's probably something in the trunk of the car I can use to tie him up. The Highway Patrol will be here in a minute."

Stella opened the passenger side door of the Charger. "Whose car is this?"

"Harley's uncles. The band was practicing when we saw some car swerving down the street. Harley noticed you in the back seat. When I recognized Dad driving, I knew he'd kidnapped you. Harley threw me the keys to his car, and I took off. He said he'd phone the police, but the Highway Patrol might arrive sooner."

Stella snuggled into the front seat of the Charger and watched her son tie his father's hands behind his back with a rope he'd found in the trunk. Then he picked Robert off the ground and shoved him in the trunk of the other vehicle and left the hood open. Gabriel stood nearby, arms folded over his chest, waiting for help to arrive.

The next hour passed in a haze of cop cars and Highway Patrol vehicles. Everyone hammered her and Gabriel with questions, until they let Gabriel and Stella leave the scene. Gabe drove back to Monarch Bay, while Stella stared out the front window, weak and traumatized.

"You saved me, Gabriel." She wrapped her hand around his forearm. "Thank you, honey. I owe you."

"You owe me nothing, Mom. You've been the best mom any guy could ever want. I love you. Don't you know that? I'd do anything for you."

"You just did." Tears ran down the sides of her face. She'd done a lot of crying lately. But she acknowledged that these tears… these were happy tears. Tears of thanks and relief. She was safe again and away from Robert's maniacal hands.

Chapter Thirty-Two

Gabriel drove home, and Kat, Marcus, Loreen, and Harley were there to greet them. Stella hugged each of them, one by one, as her tears continued to flow.

"Thank you, Harley, for letting Gabriel use your car. He saved my life."

Harley blushed. "I like to listen to Gabe and his friends play while I watch the cars go by on that little street. It was so weird to see someone swerving down the road, and when I noticed you in the back seat, I was sure something was wrong." He shrugged. "After I told Gabe, he fucking freaked out… sorry. 'Language alert,' as Loreen tells me."

Stella smiled. "No need to apologize. Your Spidey sense was totally correct. There was something very wrong. Robert was so angry that I'd kidnapped his two kids, he retaliated by doing the same to me."

She turned to Gabriel. "Thank you, honey. Your father was so drunk. It was pretty inevitable he'd get into a terrible accident and we'd both be dead."

Gabe nodded. "I know. I clocked him going almost ninety miles an hour. I could hardly keep up with him. I knew you wouldn't have gotten in the car with him voluntarily."

"Yeah, what happened, Stella?" Kat said.

"I've got to sit down," Stella said. She slumped into a kitchen chair.

Everyone sat around the kitchen table, and Kat brought out colas and chips, setting them down in the middle.

Stella inhaled deeply and let her breath out slowly. "He grabbed me in the kitchen at the pastry shop, covered my mouth with something that put me to sleep instantly. I woke up in the back of his car with zip ties around my wrists. I could smell he was already drunk, and he continued to drink whiskey while he was going ninety down

Highway One. Luckily, Gabriel followed us, and after Robert pulled over to go pee, Gabriel was able to pin him down and tie him up while we waited for the police to arrive."

"Oh, Mom," Loreen said. "You must have been so scared."

"And your face looks swollen," Marcus added. "Robert hit you?"

Stella wiped the tears from her cheek and winced. "Nothing I haven't felt a hundred times before. It would have been worse if he'd taken the kids, better he got me instead. You both are my life. I don't know what I would do without you."

"The guy's a fuckin' bastard, Stella," Marcus said. "You're very lucky Harley noticed you and Gabe came to your rescue."

Stella's eyes widened. "Hey, what're you doing home, Marcus? I thought you were on the way to San Diego."

Marcus shook his head. "My damn truck broke down half-way there. I hitched a ride home with a buddy of mine who was coming back this way. I'll be home for awhile until they get me another truck or fix that one." He reached into his pocket, pulled out his phone, and scanned it, then shoved it back in his pocket. "David's on his way. He just finished talking to the cops. He didn't know what the hell happened to you when you disappeared from the shop. He got in touch with me just as I got home. At the time I didn't know what the hell was going on either."

"So, now what, Mom?" Gabe said.

Stella shrugged. "I would assume they put your father in jail for kidnapping and whatever other charges they can hit him with."

Kat took out a piece of paper from the pocket of her jeans. "I got the name of an attorney *and* a therapist for you, Stell. You can call them tomorrow maybe?"

There was a knock at the front door, and Marcus left to answer it. They could hear him explain to David what happened to Stella, then they both walked into the kitchen.

David leaned over and kissed Stella on the forehead. Gabriel moved over so David could sit beside her. David curled his arm around Stella's shoulders, bringing her toward him. "How're you holding up?"

She sighed. "Better now that I'm surrounded by everyone who's important to me."

David cleared his throat. "You know, we ought to think about getting you in to see the doctor. Make sure everything's okay. Maybe get an expected date for having the baby too."

"Yeah, Mom," Loreen said. "Gabe and I wanna know when to expect our new baby brother or sister."

"Brother," Gabe teased. "Gotta be a boy. There's too many females in this house."

"Amen to that," Marcus said, chuckling. "Need more testosterone in this place."

Kat laughed out loud. "You guys are a bunch of sexist pig-dogs."

"I have to set up an appointment too, Mom," Loreen added.

"I'll go with you," Harley said.

Stella sighed. "Man, we'll be the talk of the town after today."

"What do you think they'll do to Dad?" Gabe asked.

"Honey, I told you, I don't know," Stella reminded him.

Gabe leaned forward, elbows on the table. "Well, can he make us move back with him, since you supposedly kidnapped us and took us away from him?"

Marcus knocked on the table. "That's not gonna happen, Gabe. You all can testify about his abusiveness to your mom when you were in Oregon. Your mom was trying to save your asses from him, which is the only reason she took you away. I don't think they'll look at that as kidnapping. She's done nothing wrong. Now, what Robert did is kidnapping, which is a very serious charge. He'll probably do time. They might force him to go to rehab for his drinking problem too. By then you and Lo will be eighteen and free as birds."

Stella chewed at her bottom lip. "I hope you're right, Marcus. I pray the judge will be lenient in my case, given the verbal evidence from me and the kids about Robert's behavior. It was a terrible environment to raise kids. I hope the judge will understand that."

David grasped Stella's hand. "Don't forget about his job at the university. He may get fired."

Stella sighed. "I didn't even think about that. But you're totally right. I'm sure he'll lose tenure. But still…"

David lifted Stella's hand, kissed her knuckles. "Don't worry about all that right now. Everything will turn out okay. You've got witnesses, and you have no record."

"Hey, Mom. I forgot to tell you," Gabe interrupted. "When the cops were calling it in, I overheard one of them say it would be Dad's third DUI. Don't they have a three strikes, you're out clause or something like that?"

"I think so," David said. "That would mean he'd go away for a significant amount of time."

"He deserves it," Loreen said.

"Okay. Okay," Stella said, wringing her hands. "Let's hope for the best and in the meantime, I'd like to have dinner."

Kat reached for her phone. "Let's order in. Anyone for pizza or Chinese?"

Stella leaned back into David's arms. "Anything sounds good to me right now. I'm just happy I'm alive, and my kids are safe."

"And Robert's in jail right now," David said.

Stella turned toward David. "Maybe I watch too much TV, but I don't think he'll be in jail for that long. He's a university professor, and the cops were never called to our house in Corvallis. Yes, he's got three DUIs now, but he has enough money to hire a good attorney and fight it. He'll get years shaved off his sentence because he has no prior record, except for the DUIs of course. But he's never been in jail. I'll bet he gets years off for good behavior too, if he does go to jail.

"He'll be back on the streets in no time. Maybe walking, because he won't be allowed to drive a car, but he'll get out. And then what? Even if he gets clean and sober, he's messed up in the head. He'll come after me, I know he will. Especially when he finds out I'm pregnant with another man's child, and he and I aren't even divorced." Stella's heart beat so hard, she could feel it below her sternum.

David rubbed her arms, which were covered in goosebumps. "You're forgetting something, Stella." He pulled away and gestured to everyone in the room. "You have all of us. You're surrounded by people who love you and want to take care of you. He'd be completely stupid to think he could return to Monarch Bay."

Stella screwed up her lips. "You may be right. I just don't feel comfortable. I don't. I'm sorry. For the moment, yes, I feel safe. But in the long run, no. He'll be back. Like Arnold Schwarzenegger."

Harley coughed. "Can I interject here?"

Stella turned toward him when she heard his voice. "Sure, honey. What is it?"

"Obviously it depends on the courts since his first two DUIs I'm assuming were in Oregon. But in California, a third-offense DUI is typically a misdemeanor. Even though he can expect to serve a minimum of 120 days in jail, the court can order up to one year imprisonment, but his attorney may be able to negotiate alternative sentences like community service or house arrest."

Stella's eyebrows dipped. "How the heck do you know all this, Harley?"

"My uncle. He had three DUIs. And he's got an awesome attorney. You may want to contact the guy and ask him some questions since it's stressing you out, not knowing what could happen or what might happen. It's a little weird, since it involves two different states, you know?"

Loreen leaned over and kissed Harley on the cheek. "You're awesome, you know that?"

Harley's face turned a medium shade of red, and he coughed into his fist. "Stop, will ya?"

"Hey!" Gabe yelled out.

Everyone turned in his direction.

Gabe fiddled with his cell phone and looked up. "I Googled what happens if you have three DUIs in Oregon. It says they don't care whether any of the DUIs is out of state or not and—" He picked up his phone and read out loud, "A third DUI conviction within ten years is now a class C felony in Oregon. This could result in actual prison time. There's a mandatory minimum jail sentence of 90 days and a minimum $2,000 fine for a 3rd DUI, and the DMV will revoke your driving privileges for life."

The doorbell rang.

"I'll get it," Kat said.

As she walked by, Stella put a hand on her sister's arm. "You and I both know the law isn't exact. Kinda like Forrest Gump. 'Life is like a box of chocolates. You never know what you're gonna get.'"

Stella's smile looked rather sickly, and Marcus walked over to her and hugged her, then stepped back. "Robert will be counseled extensively by any attorney he hires about his future behavior. He'll be told he can't get off scott free, then come back here and assault you or the kids or whatever you're thinking, because then he'll go straight to prison. He's not that stupid. Not from everything you told Kat about him."

Kat came around the corner holding three huge flat boxes in her arms. "Pizza time!" She placed the boxes on the kitchen table and glanced at her sister. "Take the night off, Stella. Eat too much pizza, drink too much cola or something and fuhgetaboutit, as Tony Soprano would say."

Stella gave her a watery smile and swiped under her eyes. "That's exactly what I'm going to do." She glanced around at each one of them. "And thank you all for being so supportive. I love all of you."

David pulled her in for another hug and whispered something in her ear.

She leaned in closer to him and kissed him thoroughly.

"Hey," Loreen called out. "No PDA, all right?"

"Yeah, gross me out," Gabe added.

They all laughed out loud and took seats at the table.

Stella patted her abdomen. "I'll find out later if this little one likes pizza or not. I had major heartburn after eating pizza when I was carrying the twins."

Remy walked over to Stella's side and nudged her leg. She snuck a piece of pepperoni off the pizza and let him take it from her fingers.

"I guess I'm gonna find out the same thing about pepperoni," Loreen added, rubbing her stomach.

Harley grinned and took a huge bite of pepperoni pizza. "Mmm."

Gabe nudged him in the side, and they both laughed.

"One big, happy family," Marcus muttered with a sly grin.

"And it's getting bigger every day," Kat added.

David nodded and put his arm around Stella's shoulders. "Sure is."

One Year Later

Stella grabbed a pot holder, opened the oven, and pulled out the bottom shelf. "Ooh, lookin' good, Mr. Turkey."

David leaned over and waved his hand over the bird, wafting the scent toward his face. "Mmm. Smells delicious."

She smiled. "I think we can pull this guy out now, let it sit awhile. Everyone should be here any minute."

David grabbed two pot holders, lifted the turkey out of the oven, and set it on the sideboard.

The doorbell rang, and they glanced at each other.

"Here we go," David sang.

Stella gave David a quick peck on the cheek. "Will you answer it, honey? I'll get Charlie." She headed to Charlie's bedroom at the back of the house. By the time she returned to the foyer, Charlie on her hip, David was greeting Kat, Marcus, baby Peter—and Remy.

"Happy Thanksgiving, everybody!" Stella said, her heart soaring with the joy of hosting their first Thanksgiving since she and David tied the knot.

Remy ran to her, his tongue hanging out of the side of his mouth. Charlie reached down to pet the big boy, and Remy gave his hand a big, juicy lick.

"Hey, Rem!" Stella called out, laughing. She wrapped her arm around her sister's waist. "I'm so glad you brought Remy."

Kat jostled Peter on her hip. "If we didn't, we would have been in the dog house."

David groaned at Kat's pun, then bent down and gave Remy's ears a good rub. "One of these days we're going to get a lab of our own, and you two can play in the backyard, just like these two kids are going to do."

Kat turned to Marcus. "Will you put Remy out back while David takes this casserole? Someone requested yams covered in marsh-mallows. They just need a bit of heat to melt into a tasty, gooey mess."

Stella winked at Marcus. "I bet I know who put in that order."

Marcus clucked his tongue. "Come on, boy. Let's put you outside."

The two women followed David, Marcus, and Remy through the front room into the kitchen. David set the yams on a butcher block beside the oven, while Marcus let Remy outside.

Kat draped her shawl over a kitchen chair, then scurried over to Stella. "Lemme get a closer look at Charlie. Oh, he's gotten bigger since we saw him a couple of days ago, I swear." She waved Peter's tiny hand. "Say hello to your cousin Charlie."

Stella jiggled Charlie on her hip.

The babies stared at each other, eyes wide, then broke into drooly grins.

Stella gestured toward the adjoining family room to the left of the kitchen. "I put two reclining bouncy seats on the coffee table right there. We can sit them next to each other. That way they'll be close to us where they can see everything that's going on at the kitchen table."

"The boys' first recliners." Kat winked. "Sounds perfect."

The doorbell rang again. "I'll get it," David said.

Seconds later, Loreen, Harley, and Gabriel entered the kitchen.

"Welcome, welcome," Stella said, hugging each of them in turn. "Come on in and have a seat."

David took everyone's coats. "I'll put these in our bedroom."

"The table's all set in the dining room," Stella announced. "Let's sit in the kitchen until everything's ready." She turned to her sister. "Let's put the boys in their recliners."

After buckling Charlie and Peter in their bouncy seats in the family room, Stella returned to the kitchen and placed a platter of sliced veggies and ranch dressing in the center of the table.

Loreen turned around and waved at the two babies. "Charlie and Peter are going to be best friends one day."

"Definitely," Harley said.

Kat smiled. "It's inevitable."

"Totally," Gabriel agreed.

"How're classes going, Harley, Loreen?" Marcus asked.

Loreen grabbed a cracker and popped it into her mouth. "We both have all As so far."

Harley grinned. "I got a few A-pluses."

Loreen nudged him in the side. "Braggart."

"I'm on the wait list for U.C. San Luis Obispo," Gabe said, smiling.

David patted Gabe on the back. "Congratulations!"

Out back Remy suddenly let out a barrage of furious barks, pawing at the glass door, nails scraping up and down the panes.

Stella stood, sliding the glass door open. "What's wrong, Rem?"

Remy scrambled past her, growling and baring his teeth while he ran toward the front room.

Stella frowned. "What's up with him?"

Kat shook her head. "I've never seen him act like that before."

David glanced at Marcus.

Marcus shrugged. "That dog never growls."

The doorbell rang.

Stella looked around the table. "Everyone's here."

"We missing somebody?" Marcus said.

David stood. "Whoever it is, Remy's not too happy he's here."

Marcus glanced at David. "Want me to grab him?"

David patted Marcus on the shoulder. "Relax. I'll take care of it. Probably just a neighbor wanting to borrow a cup of something." He walked into the front room.

"Thanks, babe," Stella called after him, wiping perspiration from her forehead. "The oven's been on all morning, or I'm having hot flashes." She chuckled. "I can't believe we all managed to be together today—especially you, Marcus."

"Luckily, I've got seniority with the company and—"

"What're you doing here?"

Stella froze in her seat.

Kat and Marcus turned toward her. Kat raised her eyebrows. "Who's that, Stell?"

Please no. It couldn't be. Stella glanced quickly at Gabriel.

"Oh, my God, Mom. It's Dad."

Loreen grabbed Harley's hand, her face pure terror.

Kat and Marcus rose from their seats. "We'll hang out in the family room with the babies while you and David deal with this."

Stella girded herself for the confrontation with Robert. She glanced from Loreen to Harley to Gabriel. "I'll handle this, kids. You stay here." She stood slowly and walked through the front room to the foyer.

Remy stood a few feet from Robert, growling, mouth open, teeth bared.

Stella glared at her ex. "Robert, what're you doing here?" She reached down to grab hold of Remy's collar but instantly lost her grip, hands slippery with sweat.

Robert took one look at her, his face red, eyes narrowed into hateful slits. He nodded at David. "So this is the guy you've been fucking since you left me?"

Beside her, David bristled. "Hey, man—"

"Robert, keep your voice down," Stella said.

Robert let out a loud laugh. "Keep my voice down? Keep my voice down? You don't tell me what to do, woman." He reached his arm around to the back of his waist and pulled out a gun.

Stella sucked in a breath. "Robert. Please. You don't have to do this. If you want to talk, let's sit down. There's no need to get violent. Take a breath and calm down."

Robert pointed the gun straight at David, sneered. "And you." He waved the gun left to right, hand shaking. "I don't want to hear a word out of your fucking mouth. Your baby's in this house somewhere, isn't he? I wanna see him."

Robert shifted his gaze to Stella. "I'm gonna kill everyone in this entire place. All of you testified against me. Even my own kids." He reached out his arm, aiming the gun directly at Stella. "Lying to the judge. Lies about me hurting you. You never had to work a day in your life. I treated you like a queen."

David inched toward Robert, hands held out like two stop signs. "Robert, give me the gun. You don't want to do this. Stella's the mother of your two kids. Don't do this, buddy."

Robert whipped his head in David's direction. "Don't call me buddy, you asshole. Don't talk to me. Ever. Again."

Robert slipped his finger through the trigger hole.

Remy lunged, grasping Robert's forearm in his teeth, wrenching it left and right, snarling, spittle dripping from his jaw.

A shot rang out.

David grasped his shoulder, fell backwards onto the floor.

Stella's gaze flew to the living room. To the babies.

Someone screamed, and the babies' cries pierced the air.

Loreen, Harley, and Gabe ran into the front room.

Marcus followed, punching numbers into his phone.

"Mom!" Gabriel shouted.

"Jesus Christ," Loreen croaked.

"Oh, my God," Harley muttered.

The gun fell out of Robert's hands. Remy jumped on Robert's chest, knocked him down, stood over him, growling and snapping at his face.

Robert struggled to get up, but Remy had the full force of his ninety pounds on Robert's chest and refused to back off.

Stella knelt next to David on the floor, tears streaming down her face. David lay there, clutching his shoulder. Blood stained his shirt, spilling over his fingers. "Stella, get the gun," he choked out.

The gun, the gun. Of course, the gun. Stella twisted her body toward Robert. He lay on the floor, struggling. Remy refused to let go of him, Robert's arm trapped in his teeth in a vise-like grip.

The gun lay near Robert's feet. She crawled over and grabbed it. Holding it with both hands, she slowly stood, hovering over Robert, gun pointed directly at his chest. "Don't you move, you piece of shit."

Marcus reached Stella's side and slid his hand down her forearm. "Give me the gun, Stella. You take care of David. The cops and EMTs are on their way."

Stella slowly released her grip, all the while wishing she could shoot the bastard.

Marcus yanked his shirt off and passed it to her. "Press this down firmly on David's wound." He took a step closer to Robert, gun directed at Robert's mid-section. "Remy! Off! Remy! Leave it!"

Remy backed up, never letting his eyes waver from David.

Loreen, Harley, and Gabe stood in a group behind Marcus, mouths agape.

Stella held the shirt on David's shoulder, pressing down with both hands.

David moaned, eyes shut.

"You took my kids, Stella. You made me go to jail. I lost my job at the university. You gave birth to this guy's baby. I told you, I'd never give you up. You're my wife."

Stella turned her head to where Robert lay on the floor, blood dripping from his forearm, shirt shredded to pieces.

"If only you knew how much I hate you, Robert. I wish you were dead." Tears flowed down Stella's cheeks. "You've made my life and my kids' lives miserable, you son of a bitch. I hope you rot in hell."

Sirens blasted through the silence.

Kat inched her head around the corner and slowly made her way to stand behind the kids. Both babies stared up at her, sucking on pacifiers while she cradled one in each arm. "My God," she whispered.

Three police officers ran into the house, weapons drawn.

Marcus placed Robert's gun on the floor and backed away. The female police officer bent over and picked it up with gloved hands.

The second officer spread his arms wide. "Could the rest of you please be seated, so we can figure out what's going on here?" He turned, nodded at the third officer, who then gestured for the EMTs to enter.

Four EMTs rushed in and knelt beside David.

Stella kissed David on the forehead, stood, and shuffled backward.

The female officer touched Stella's forearm. "Did you call nine-one-one?"

"I did," Marcus piped up. "I didn't actually see what happened, but Stella did." He nodded in Stella's direction.

Two more EMTs entered the house with a gurney, which they set down next to David, then unfolded the legs.

"I want to go with him," Stella cried. "He's my husband."

One of the EMTs walked over to her. "He's going to be all right. The bullet went straight through. A clean shot. We already recovered the bullet." The EMT handed a plastic bag to the officer in charge.

The female officer took a quick look at one of the other officers, who nodded. "I'll ride in the back of the ambulance with you," she said to Stella. "You can talk to me on the way to the hospital."

"I'll need statements from the rest of you," another officer said.

Everyone made their way to the couch and lounge chairs.

Remy sat in front of Kat, head held high, glancing from the babies to the officers, who were reading the Miranda rights to Robert while cuffing his wrists behind his back.

Tears rolled down Loreen's face.

Kat lifted Charlie and handed him to Loreen. "Take care of your little brother, Lo."

Gabe walked over to his mother and put his arm around her shoulders. "He's going to be okay, Mom."

"Thanks to Remy," she whispered, tears coursing down her cheeks.

Gabe kissed his mom's forehead. "I'll come to the hospital as soon as I finish talking to the police."

Stella nodded. "Okay, honey."

"I'll be there soon too, Mom," Loreen said.

Stella smiled at both of her kids. "Thank you."

Marcus knelt down in front of Remy, taking his muzzle in his beefy hands. "Good boy, Remdog."

"He saved the day," Kat added.

Harley leaned over and patted Remy's head, glanced up at Stella. "I think you and David should get a lab too."

Stella managed a smile through her tears. "I think you're right."

"Maybe tomorrow or the next day we can go to the shelter," Kat said. "If David's up to it."

Stella gave Charlie a kiss on his check, mouthed "thank you" to Kat, and walked with the officer toward the front door. The EMTs were rolling the gurney down the driveway. She stopped at the threshold, turned to her family. "I'll be back as soon as I can, but if David has to stay the night at the hospital…"

"We'll do Thanksgiving whenever you both return," Kat piped up.

"Thank you," Stella said, grateful beyond words for her family.

Remy barked.

"Thank you, Remy," Stella said. "Our hero. You saved David's life." She glanced around the room, then out the door to where David— her dear husband David—was being loaded into the ambulance. "But maybe now we can have a little peace here in Monarch Bay. It's about time."

Behind her, Gabe said, "You think?"

TO BE CONTINUED IN BOOK TWO -
SUNRISE ON MONARCH BAY

BOOKS BY PATRICIA YAGER DELAGRANGE

A Heart Life
Mending Fences
Moon Over Alcatraz
Maddy's Phoenix
Taken Away
Passing Through Brandiss

ABOUT THE AUTHOR

Born and raised in the San Francisco Bay Area, Patricia attended St. Mary's College, studied her junior year at the University of Madrid, received a B.A. in Spanish at UC Santa Barbara then went on to get a Master's degree in Education at Oregon State University. She lives with her husband and two children in Alameda, across the bay from San Francisco, along with two chocolate labs, UJE and Remy. Her Friesian horse Maximus lives in the Oakland hills in a stall with a million dollar view.